Of Light and Sounding Brass

A novel

in two parts, by

V.S. Yanovsky

Author of "No Man's Time"

Translated from the Russian

by Isabella Levitin

in collaboration with

the author

The Vanguard Press, Inc.

New York

Of Light and Sounding Brass

Published simultaneously in Canada by the
Copp Clark Publishing Company, Ltd., Toronto

Manufactured in the United States of America by
H. Wolff Book Manufacturing Company, New York

Library of Congress Catalogue Card Number: 72–83353
SBN 8149–0719–9

Designer: Ernst Reichl

"I learned not long ago that Pechorin had died on his way back from Persia. I was glad to get this news for it gave me the right to publish these notes, and I took the liberty of signing another man's writings with my own name."

M. Lermontov

Part One (or Two)

Rehearsal for a Confession

"Photons and waves also go astray."

Xavier de Przeszczynski

1

Morning, as usual, had replaced night. Kassianov awoke: yellow spots reflected from windows across the way beat upon his eyes. Only after waking up had he noticed those pale yet piercing tiny pools of ricocheted light, but someone in Kassianov easily arrived at the slavish conclusion: it was the rising sun that had awakened him.

The sight of the brilliant slanting rays made him think about freedom. Light consists of photons: as they strike a pane of glass some pass through, some are absorbed, and some bounce off at an angle. Impossible, however, to predict which will penetrate and which will be deflected. A single photon can be isolated and thrown onto a screen—but the course it will elect can never be foretold! These microscopic particles are free in their choice, and their life or path is in no manner predetermined.

This is why yellow pools of reflected light—on the sea, on the plains, or in the city—always set Kassianov to thinking about free will, reminding him that we too are endowed with the characteristics of photons, electrons, neutrons, if only because we consist of these infinitely small corpuscles.

Excited by his thoughts, he trotted off to the bathroom in high spirits and started on his morning toilet. He had to perform those tedious, even repulsive maneuvers that allow a man to leave the house clean, decently dressed, and, by bus, subway, or car, proceed to his place of work. (Kassianov, for one, would tear frantically toward the thirty-seventh floor of a skyscraper where he lectured five days a week in sociology, thereby securing a comfortable living for himself and his wife.)

While rinsing his mouth, he suddenly remembered that it was now more than twenty years since he had last gone to confession. There was no connection between this thought and the preceding ones, and this too gave him pleasure, since it was proof of a complete break in the chain of causality.

At any recollection of the sacraments, Kassianov usually burst into tirades of self-justification that always followed the same lines: "For almost a quarter of a century I have not participated in the life of the Church. During these years my paths of spiritual communication have been overgrown by weeds. And now to tell a priest in the course of ten minutes all that I have done in times of war, revolution, emigration, pointing out quickly and accurately the most blatant trespasses—this seems to me a shameless trick, a fraud. It can't be done, I know, I tried it once. . . ."

As a matter of fact, only those who exercise their memory unceasingly and who have undergone extensive trials are able to recall from their past that which is genuinely important and in true proportion to everything else. Long ago Kassianov had kept a diary; now, as a sort of experiment, he decided to record on the blank pages of an old notebook (not chronologically, but rather according to an intrinsic relationship) his participation, voluntary and involuntary, in the deadly sins. . . . After all, our life can be compared to a railroad trip with repeated stops at seven major stations; if every passenger could manage to reproduce his itinerary on this earth, with all the changes between trains, it would only increase his chances for a well-deserved last rest.

"Imagine Kassianov languishing on a desert island" (I often find it easier to speak of myself in the third person, as if I were already in the past). "Bored, dejected, in despair, he begins to write his confessions on the bark of a sandalwood tree. The manuscript is addressed to a spiritual father whom he can at any moment, miraculously, summon up again. And remission of sins, even if only granted post mortem, is perhaps not completely devoid of its sacramental character."

It seemed simplest to start with gluttony as his station of departure, both because it is the first sin and because it looks so innocent, not mortal at all, unlikely, so it seemed to Kassianov, to cost anyone the loss of his right to everlasting bliss.

2

Gluttony occupied a special place in the Middle Ages: monks and ascetics were tortured primarily by this temptation. In those days life seemed to goad the fallen Adam toward gluttony while paralyzing his other vices. Thus he perfected himself in the culinary arts, submitting fully to the power of that hollow sin which gradually assumed mythical proportions.

It is only fair to note, spiritual Father, that some of the greatest discoveries of the Renaissance came about under the influence of gastronomical yearnings (truly, it is an ill wind that blows nobody good). In those centuries trade with the East developed to a great measure thanks to spices! The Spice Islands attracted pirates, merchants, and adventurous youths. Vasco da Gama rounded South Africa in order to shorten the distance to pepper, vanilla, and cinnamon. Columbus sailed west in the hope of finding a direct route to saffron. The same goes for Magellan and many other daring seafarers.

The habit of using aromatic plants was historically justified: in the absence of refrigeration, meat spoiled fast in the southern countries. (Tainted meat plus spices—that is civilization! The northern peoples, saintly Father, do not have so varied and complex a kitchen.)

Continuous abuse of tropical condiments became a passion: people grew addicted to cloves and nutmeg as they would later to hashish and tobacco. Even the nineteenth century still knew a kind of overindulgence in food that would seem unthinkable today.

To Kassianov's surprise, Father Nectarius, I do not detect this sin in my past: with me gastronomy never reached the proportions of a vice, although I confess that at times we all ate to excess, glutted ourselves.

To begin with, Kassianov always considered eating without drinking an unnatural, repulsive process. But with a jug of wine or some brew on the table, simple, gross gluttony is out of the question: everything is suddenly illuminated by the light of ancient, awesome Dionysus.

As a child I would sometimes relish (yes, that's exactly the word!) food as such. This usually happened after some grueling sickness and was accompanied by such an intense feeling of general well-being that it could hardly be counted a sin. However, it is true, sweets, nuts, raisins had a hypnotizing effect: having taken the first, one was unable to stop. The only possibility: finish the lot at once, and the faster the better. Here there was no "relishing." This probably is the sin: to devour—without pleasure, yet unable to stop! But rather than its being simple gluttony, is this not an over-all paralysis of the will? So one smokes without need, or downs vodka, sniffs cocaine, grovels at the feet of a worthless woman.

Later, a grown man in international emigré Paris, Kassianov could not get enough of feasting in the company of friends. . . . Those were full-fledged agapes, where homemade cabbage soup and modest libations mingled with Russian talk about "ultimate matters."

Yes, there was indeed something dissolute, something spiritually sloppy and treacherous in our discussions. And yet, how many inspired thoughts, religious longings, intellectual revelations were born at those gatherings around the table!

However, Father Nectarius, gluttony as such there was not: the grapes of the vine and the proud intoxication of our minds altered the character of this rudimentary sin.

3

We assembled on holidays or after work on Saturdays, sitting at the feast for five or six hours—and neither stew nor wine ever interfered with inspired debates. If sin there was, it lay in the complete abandon of our talk. Of course, intoxication played its part, but anyway Father Nectarius, most of us believed that we were born with wine in our blood (in those days this was considered flattering).

Everything firmly established through time, custom, common sense, was subjected to criticism and re-evaluation, so that in the heat of the verbal barrage we would, like vipers, end up biting our own tails, denying what at the outset we had defended with such valor.

What we indulged in was the feeling of complete freedom —no authorities whatever! Nothing but our reason and our conscience—or some other sacred quality of the soul. (As in chess, to which we also gave ourselves inordinately: within the framework of the game, fantasize freely! But for every mistake, for any exposed piece, you are personally and fully responsible.) As for the rest—husks, old skins that the upcoming generation sheds to array itself in new vestments.

It was justice we were after; prudence and temperance only made us laugh. And also, Father Nectarius, there was faith: the faith that God had given to each of us "something special." Though we be unrecognized, stripped of all rights, exiles from different, even opposed regimes, yet we belong to one brotherhood, a brotherhood that includes many great companions from the past. (As for the others, the gray folk, we need not worry: they too are happy in their own way.) And hovering above all this—the triumphant feeling of freedom: huge, like the Victory of Samothrace, like the Grace of God. (For still, drunk as we were from the consciousness of our creative achievements, we could not ascribe these metaphysical miracles solely to ourselves.)

The last samples and orders were being finished when Ter appeared in the atelier, freshly shaven and festive with his trimmed goatee. Laden with packages, bundles of greens, and, above all, with bottles, he courteously greeted each of us separately. Kassianov, the student dyeing ties between two exams, was favored with a special hearty handshake.

Ter looked like a graying buffalo. He was the best and purest of souls and had preserved his inner riches even after losing all his material goods—and this in spite of being a convinced atheist in the spirit of eighteenth-century enlightenment.

He took no active part in our intellectual battles, except to inquire from time to time: "Why do you think that? I'd be very interested to know your reasons!" Still, to us he was extremely useful, for besides wine and cheese Ter also brought with him an atmosphere of old-time etiquette, of order, and conventional reasoning.

In spite of his kindness and integrity, Ter, in some part of his soul, belonged to those demonic people who darken ominously at the very mention of the Holy Ghost. In the course of his life Kassianov was to come across many such strange creatures dwelling under the shadow of dark forces from which only fervent prayer might, perhaps, save them. Pray, however, Ter, citing the latest advancements in science, could not or would not do.

"Why do you think so?" he would ask, cupping his hand behind his right ear (he was somewhat deaf). "Why do you say that? I'd be very interested to know. Your health!" and he would refill our glasses. We had just been speaking about the resurrection of Lazarus, about the thief on his cross, about Christ asking His executioners for water. . . . What was there to explain, spiritual Father? To be polite we would mumble something and raise our glasses.

Now, having wiped his spoon with the flap of his coat, Ter

gets ready to ladle out the steaming chowder he has prepared from the enormous, doglike head of a sturgeon. The sight of the monster's jaws in the pot embarrassed, appalled us young ones.

The different stages of exile had carried Ter from Constantinople to Tunisia. He had wandered from hovel to hovel, sheltering where primeval filth, abuse, and darkness, both literal and figurative, reigned. There, in the East, his way of wiping the communal spoon with the border of his coat had stood for solid bourgeois upbringing. As for us, we found his manners strange but delighted in them, although some of the ladies would make wry faces. (Thus what is exemplary, *comme il faut,* in one milieu becomes gross, even offensive, in another.)

Freshly arrived in Paris, young Kassianov had met Ter and grown to love him like a father.

4

"Your health!" Ter again clinks glasses with each of us. "Please, don't mention it: the food is yours, the wine's on me. I beg you not to mention it!"

Our friend Valerik approves of such lavishness and, having drained the first liter of Red Bordeaux, is bound to intone Rubinstein's *Demon:* he knows the opera by heart and can sing it straight through, only now and then throwing in some prosaic remark concerning the libretto or scenery. *The Demon* brings tears of rapture and sadness to his eyes. He thinks of Russia, of Moscow, of his youth—and he cries.

"In cosmic space," Kassianov says, "it is as difficult to determine time as the directions to which we are accustomed. Who, traveling from the moon to Mars, can decide where east is and where west, where the poles of the earth are situated and where its equator? The same happens with time. . . . The only guideline is entropy. If, after two successive measurings, entropy has increased, it means time has moved forward. In a world where entropy decreases, time goes backward. This is an absolute fact as long as the Second Law of Thermodynamics holds true."

Skovoroda, the owner of the workshop, is the only one able to follow the meaning of his words; but, being of a Socratic turn of mind, he attempts with a sequence of questions to uncover the error in the budding philosopher's elaborations.

"It happened in the Crimea . . ." Valerik begins his epic narration. After a pleasant evening at the house of mutual friends, he would escort his lady to her doorstep, then she would accompany him to his hotel, where they would again turn round toward her cottage. And so back and forth: but to get her into his room or enter her house—impossible. It dragged on like that for a whole month!

"Finally it became clear that this was what she liked: to tease, promise, but not give in," explains Valerik with a sly, yet guileless, smile. "Sometimes I would actually be lying next to her and there she was, pressing her knees together. It turned out that that was what she wanted."

Skovoroda, by now amply fortified, is upbraiding his wife, who thinks talk of this kind not suitable in the presence of women. "Otherwise there would be no need to get together. One cannot say the whole truth in front of children and ladies even about religion. . . . You are my dearest friends," he addresses us. He rises and bows deeply. "You are as close to me as she!" with a nod in the direction of his now silent wife.

Ainer explains how it is possible to develop astral sight so as to distinguish the aura of a flower or tree.

"A coin that has been dropped can rise again," Kassianov stubbornly continues to weave his web, "the dead will be resurrected like Lazarus, and the old will grow young again. Our determinism is based on statistics and percentages: nobody cares about the individual case. We must always bear in mind that the improbable is, still and all, possible."

"Your health," Ter declares with a bow and continues didactically: "I should like very much to know how you arrived at these conclusions."

"A universe where the process of entropy decreases and where time is reversed must be magnificent. There is cause to believe that such worlds, such islands in the cosmos, exist. Instead of the Laws of Thermodynamics, of Freud, Darwin, and Marx, there reign the reality of the 'other cheek,' of love, self-sacrifice, resurrection, and eternal bliss."

5

The ladies, who work long strenuous hours during the week, are by now drowsing peacefully on the hard sofas around the cumbersome table that resembles a carpenter's bench. Half-bald Ter, with his short Mephistophelian beard, is paternally stroking the plump knee of Raissova, the aging actress.

"Let's finish the bottle," Valerik shouts, and shakes himself like a bewildered wet poodle. (He trembles at the thought that the fire of our talk may ever be extinguished.)

"Finish the bottle? We can hardly stand up straight as it is," Ainer protests.

"Don't worry, we'll manage!" and, turning to Kassianov: "I'm drinking to your saint!" Valerik feels an obligation to further the development of this callow youth who has never seen Russia and yet is attached with all his fibers to her language and her past. Clearing his throat like a true basso, Valerik intones:

> That which is According to the Image
> was really saved in you, O Father:
> For you accepted the Cross and Followed Christ.

"Cassian taught that, in the natural state, any person, though sick, is spiritually alive and therefore can recover completely," Kassianov explains, stressing his words. Then he adds quietly: "I love Saint Cassian."

Valerik, by tradition closely bound to Orthodoxy, is moved; he gazes at the young man as if he were a living miracle.

During the summer months Valerik performs in a little cabaret in Montmartre. Then he dons a secondhand tuxedo, puts on rouge and mascara. When a prostitute accosts him in some dark street, he tells her, not without humor: *"Faîtes voir, faîtes voir d'abord."* (Why, saintly Father, do people with the best of Moscow accents express themselves all their lives in such tasteless, dull French?)

"Saint Augustine teaches that we cannot achieve salvation by our own means, that the Grace of God is needed for it. But at the same time we are quite able to ruin ourselves on our own, since God certainly does not assist in our destruction. . . . There is something wrong with this reasoning."

Skovoroda cannot accept such cavalier dismissal of predestination and sweetly questions Kassianov: "In other words, you are convinced that God would under no circumstances desire a man's ruin?"

"Your health!" declares Ter through a fog. "I would very much like to know the reasons for your statement."

Ainer, somewhat revived after a rest, becomes overanimated: "I have been looking at you people while you blabber on. What beautiful faces you all have, what expressive foreheads, what shining auras! Each of you wants to find the truth in his own way, even at the cost of suffering. Yes, a holy shadow falls on God's creatures and inspires them."

"Is a holy shadow the shadow of holiness?" inquires Skovoroda. "Does this mean that holiness too has its dark side?"

In the meantime Valerik again has the younger ones hypnotized with his romantic adventures. Last year, at the Riviera . . . what fastidiousness! After a whole day's bathing in the sea, she still had to have her shower in the evening. "Very well," she said, "let's imagine I stay with you; what then? How are we going to live?"

"How right she was!" Valerik laughed heartily. "Smart girl!" After this followed the story of how the clean beauty became pregnant, how Valerik, penniless, had rushed about Nice in search of a Russian doctor, and how God had come to his rescue.

He told his sorry tale without a trace of bitterness, dear Father!

6

Tired of sitting in the same place, we moved to the café next door. The ladies played *belote;* the men, pool. And above it all, like the Victory of Samothrace, hovered freedom, faith in human justice, in the greatness of our thoughts (and lives). Of course, tomorrow there would be again the humiliating treadmill, but that could not be helped. . . .

We ordered brandy, coffee, rum; munched nuts, divided oranges. If there was mortal sin in all this, it was not gluttony. (In any case, Kassianov was not guilty of it, dearest Father.) Throughout my life, like an archipelago, stretch the islands of such meetings: at a table—with wine, meat, fruit, but rather sagging under the weight of intellectual revelations. It seemed to Kassianov (and so it still seems) that those were agapes, brotherly communions, mysteries, probably not quite orthodox but yet not counterfeit, and all in all of a lofty nature. During a meal, with a glass of wine and friendly arguments, we sometimes experienced spiritual raptures that cannot possibly deserve blame. . . . And it is fitting to emphasize this here, saintly Father.

Of the non-Russian feasts, Kassianov enjoyed most of all those with Ott (twenty-five years later—in the New World). As if Ott belonged to those to whom Belinsky, in the nineteenth century, had called out: "You mean to say you're going home when we haven't yet solved the question of immortality?" We ate more, now the dishes were elaborate, and we sipped vintage wines, but we got drunk only on talk.

Yes, it was different from the past: toward morning, Kassianov would return home to his ailing wife and an established routine. (At the banquets of our youth we knew no schedule, no regularity, no obligations; eventually we dispersed, but we could have continued our dialogues for another day or a century—at least, so it seemed.)

As for the feasts in the village—on the piazza or at the castle, when he first visited Zora's family—they certainly were no temptation to Kassianov.

In summing up Kassianov's personal experience with gluttony, Father, I honestly declare that this apparently is the only sin in which he has never participated. I don't quite understand its nature and herein probably lies the error. Is the sin perhaps the dumb, blind devouring of everything in sight, even if it is completely tasteless or harmful? But how far removed is such perversion from simple gastronomical temptation?

"I, mine, for me . . ."—everything flits around these syntactical monsters that destroy the living tissue of our soul. Pride, ambition, jealousy, envy, wrath, greed, indifference, lust, sloth, this whole poisonous nosegay is kept in bloom by our manic instinct of self-preservation. If man could think without the aid of the first person singular, the mortal sins would vanish from this earth. Blessed the people whose language does not know the words "I, mine, for me, myself." But alas, such tribes cannot be found any longer, Father Nectarius.

In early childhood the concept of "I" is lacking or blunted, so that the infant dwells in an impersonal and sinless Eden; the same applies to all parts of our body and to its different members and cells. But as soon as a boy's small penis begins autonomously to stick out of his pants, this organ of his proclaims to all: me, here, give, more!

(A knock on the wall from Zora's quarters tells me it is time to feed my wife. I do not consider her supper metaphysically more important than this confession; nevertheless, it would somehow not be right if she remained hungry on account of my writing exercises.)

7

Kassianov must have been four years old when he first became aware of a strange itch in the region of his penis, and of the fact that this small organ had suddenly assumed a horizontal position.

Like a kitten or a growing puppy, I would rub my belly against any available surface; for convenience's sake I pushed two chairs together and lay down on them so that my little member fitted exactly into the crevice between them . . . and this, Father Nectarius, in broad daylight, in the living room where my mother was bustling about.

It was in the era when psychoanalysis and complexes were not yet cultivated in France; people lived more roughly, more courageously. To my surprise, my mother—I called her Anyuta—unaccountably angry and excited, yelled at me and threatened to throw me out of the house and keep me in the stable where boys like me belonged. (These were not her exact words, but I can vouch for the meaning.)

She was obviously upset and also embarrassed; she suffered for me (I sensed it) as if in anticipation of a new, pitiless cycle, such as first vaccinations, and at a loss as to how best defend her child.

Kassianov understood that he was being desperately protected from something and, at the same time, pilloried. As a result, he took to hiding, concealed himself from everyone, until he found his first natural accomplice who shared the responsibility with him.

At that time, dear Father, Kassianov did not yet have ejaculations; those came later and scared the stripling no end. He was surprised and distressed, too, when suddenly, at thirteen, rough, sparse hair began to crop up, accompanied by unbearable irritation around his private parts. . . . (Some years later Olivia told him about the experience of her first menstruation: she went back to bed in the morning, and her mother, sitting down beside her, explained in honeyed tones that this was a perfectly "normal" phenomenon that would now repeat itself throughout much of her long life.)

Originally, at the dawn of his progress in sin, Kassianov nurtured no fantasies and had no lustful yearnings; the thoughts whirling about in his mind were vague and disconnected and in no way linked to that carnal burning in his loins. Later on I got into the habit of conjuring up, while falling asleep, the vision of the cobbler's wife who lived in a basement on the outskirts of our small Alsatian town. Strong, with large breasts, a white throat, naked arms, bare feet and glistening calves, she was probably an ideal image of voluptuousness.

Kassianov of course did not know this, but some cells in me must already have guessed everything, for at night I stubbornly imagined her. In a seductive pose: standing, with her knees slightly bent and her skirt gathered up in one hand, making water at the fence (as did the peasant girls who brought the milk down from the mountains). Precisely in this position Kassianov's imagination pictured the full-breasted cobbler's wife—and she allowed him to put his hand under the refreshing stream. . . . This seemed desirable to him, pure and beautiful, and inspiring to great and virtuous deeds.

Once her son hit me; I complained to my father (the second or third—I had several) and together we went to the cobbler's basement. This father of mine, a former Russian officer, was remarkable for his height and had to bend his head cautiously at the threshold.

There, in the depth of the room, next to a high bed, she stood, casting a bewildered (Lermontov would have said "wondrous") glance at us. They began to argue; before long the cobbler's wife, with a howl, dug her fleshy hands into my father's ashen cheeks. A short, fierce struggle . . . and suddenly, simultaneously, they both raised themselves softly onto the bedstead with its mountains of down-filled comforters.

My enemy and I stood dismally together, far below them; we could see four heavy, jerking, trembling legs that seemed to live their own autonomous lives and, finally exhausted, came to rest.

My father slowly got down from the feather bed, in soldierlike fashion straightened his shirt and belt, and, stepping up to the white-lashed cobbler's boy who was still completely stupefied by what he had just seen, administered two resounding blows. After which he again took me by the hand and, stooping as before at the threshold, walked up into the street. (In the fall of 1939, at Aachen, he was hit by a stray German bullet and killed outright.)

8

Across the hall from us, in the other half of the house, lived a young couple with two children my own age. About this woman, Father Nectarius, there must also have been something grossly attractive, for she too began to appear to Kassianov in the dark, competing with the ample-breasted cobbler's wife.

Even her name was alluring: Isolde. She was red-cheeked, juicy (like a pear), with dark hair and glittering black eyes. Her husband, who was no less ruddy, with curly hair and beetle brows, looked puny and insignificant next to her.

Their family life was one boisterous frenzy. Often, late at night, singing and yelling came from their apartment, then a man's howling and his uncontrolled, helpless sobs. For a time the southern beauty vanished completely, leaving the children to their fate. I can still faintly see, Heavenly Father, a bronzed Swiss with a most elaborate arrangement of curls piled high on his head, who regularly turned up at their place in the daytime during working hours. (On such occasions the grownups around me would whisper angrily.) But all these details, far from stopping short his fantasies, only stimulated Kassianov. And once I told my little neighbor, a girl two years my senior, that one did not necessarily have to kiss a lady's hand, one could also kiss her foot: pick it up by the toes and kiss first one side and then the other. The foot I was picturing was that of the torrid, unfaithful wife.

The girl, deep in *Don Quixote*, gave Kassianov a surprised look and said soberly, "It wouldn't be hygienic." (Many years later, and under circumstances by no means particularly hygienic, she was shot by a German firing squad.)

Until then, spiritual Father, it had not yet come to a complete triumph of the flesh. For better or worse, Kassianov was not able to divert himself properly with his hand. So that this entire period of childhood remained for him bleary and incomplete; which, however, in no way lightened the heavy burden of carnal desire. He bore his yoke with indifference, a lamb (albeit a not quite pure one) led to the slaughter.

As a matter of fact I now see that even at the very dawn (that is, before the age of three and the enticing fantasies) woman had already entered into Kassianov's life, presaging vaguely the reality of love, beauty, and happiness on this earth.

It must have been in May, the month of lilacs, when our yearly picnic to the Rhine (hampers with all kinds of delicacies, ice cream, wine) took place. Among the guests was a young woman from Paris in airy, stylish dress. I did not take my eyes off this elegant, truly precious creature, and my mother felt obliged to put her badly behaved boy in his place. (Now it seems to Kassianov that there was some rivalry between Anyuta and the beautiful visitor.)

"Why does he look at her like that?" I heard my mother's agitated, indignant voice—speaking of me in the third person. "Why does he keep staring?" And her voice trembled with fear (as it would later tremble when she chased me off the conveniently arranged chairs).

Bewildered, the child backed away and, hiding behind some benches, continued from there to admire the blithe summer guest. Was this the awakening of lust, or was it the first worshiping of beauty, harmony, love? I would not know, Father Nectarius. The Gnostics, of course, condemn every kind of seduction.

9

But now Kassianov is eleven years old and another critical period awaits him. . . .

New (cruel) faces have turned up among his mother's friends and she has taken to going out every night, elegantly dressed and perfumed. The boy has to stay home, left to his own devices. Sandra, the maid, plump, pretty, with a turned-up little nose, sympathizes fully with Anyuta: to placate Kassianov she promises that, once they are alone, they will play "their game" to his heart's content.

The game, Father Nectarius, consisted of this: we would write down the most indecent words on a piece of paper and read them aloud, backwards, repeating the awkward sounds and roaring with laughter, until the partner guessed. She, for instance, would read out "esra . . . ," to which I answered "traf. . . ." Gradually we learned to form and memorize whole sentences with these tabu expressions and we secretly conversed in our new language.

Strangely enough, the nineteen-year-old girl was more aroused by this intellectual game than was Kassianov. I now catch again the questioning, pondering look with which she assessed her miserable partner and those organs of his that we had been so assiduously recording "backwards" on paper. However, in all fairness it must be said that not once did she attempt to pass from "literature" to practical exercises. She probably did not trust my discretion.

Going back some years, I see that there was another housemaid before Sandra. She had been brought from an isolated Alsatian village, grew up in our house, and became almost a member of the family. As a small boy, Kassianov would watch her for hours at the ironing board, delighting in her rhythmically moving, graceful bare arms and the smooth, broad, softly-swaying torso.

A blacked-out eternity passed: Kassianov had changed from a three-year-old cherub into a seven-year-old pest, when suddenly Elsa vanished and no questions were to be asked. Soon, however, she reappeared just as unexpectedly, within her arms a live bundle that constantly demanded her swollen, balloonlike breasts. The following morning a mustachioed sergeant came; laughing, he told how for the last months his sister had always been crouching before the stove to hide her condition. . . . He took her and the baby home to the village.

But after some time she showed up again, dressed in city finery, naïvely seductive, and very thin. (Kassianov pitied her profoundly.) A new maid with whom everyone was still satisfied had just recently begun her reign at Anyuta's, but Kassianov insisted that Elsa be taken back.

"Of course, madame," Elsa declared with false detachment, "to dismiss a person without reason is not right, but in a household with a growing boy, it is important to have someone you can trust." Anyuta realized that Elsa would not remain long with us, but she had to give in to her spoiled offspring.

And so Kassianov spent his vacation in the kitchen. . . . Going in and out I would abstractedly run my hands over

Elsa's broad (magnetic) haunches. What visions the boy saw during the night I cannot now reconstruct—in any case, this infatuation did not last long and, soon after, Elsa disappeared for good.

Now I know, Father Nectarius, that it is quite useless and unnatural to try to live twice through the same illusions—like stepping into one's old footprints in the sand or snow.

10

Father in Heaven, is all this really lust? Caused by the fall of the old Adam? And how and at what time does childish play inadvertently turn into mortal sin? Is there a quantitative or qualitative gradation in our carnal yearnings? Some Gnostics taught that sin is a kind of "vapor": "natural" water having come to a boil. So where does sin actually start: at what temperature? and with what instruments can it be measured?

One should assume that our true fall takes final shape with the appearance of a tangible partner and accomplice (seducer or seduced). But to his horror, even then Kassianov rarely felt guilty of any offense or crime.

Here is the first "accomplice": Margo. For all of one blissful summer we exchanged passionate kisses. She supposedly had magnificent legs that won her the nickname "Margo with the legs." (A namesake of hers was simply Margo, although her shapely muscular calves seemed no less attractive.)

Furthermore, "Margo with the legs" had large, fearless, greenish eyes with long, dark lashes. We spent a whole summer night lying on a cliff above the lake, caressing each other, while in the sky the full moon described with unerring precision its accustomed trajectory.

Margo must have had some previous sexual experiments, for she assumed the lead in our game: she thrashed about, sighed passionately, arched her back. But it did not even occur to Kassianov to touch her secret places. And so this incomparable feeling burned itself out—was wasted on the stones without blossoming any further. And yet, dear Father, Kassianov was genuinely and with youthful innocence in love with this Margo.

Autumn came; on dreary evenings, in cold and rain, he walked up and down the faintly lit boulevard in hope of catching a glimpse of her.

Margo lived in a nearby small town, where the express from Strasbourg never stopped but merely slowed down at a bend of the high embankment and sent forth its drawn-out, old-fashioned, demanding call into the surrounding hamlets. In the summer, she often watched for this train: a colored kerchief pushed down to her fearless eyes, she looked into the flashing windows of the cars. Once, returning from Paris, Kassianov jumped off the moving train at this spot and, as he rolled down the slope, it occurred to him that other romantic youths before him had probably jumped in the same way into Margo's embrace. . . . And the express, having voiced its call, sped on impetuously with its plushy interior and with the ghost of Nekhlyudov smiling behind a window.

No, dearest Father, I swear that lust had not yet revealed itself, although I did have a partner at hand. But after that there was Olivia.

We dropped all inhibitions and gave free play to our darker instincts. As a matter of fact, after the first initiation she continued on her own to perfect herself and exhibited a rare inventiveness. Came a terrible night—February, in Paris. We were alone in a brutally affluent apartment, a fire dying in the grate and in a corner a concert grand covered by a blanket (like a throughbred after its victory).

Kassianov had long ago acquired a primitive rubber condom. Now he put it on. It was an antediluvian Swiss gadget with a special little sack at the tip, intended, according to the inventor, to collect the abundance of semen. But before Kassianov could so much as touch the embarrassed Olivia, I had already exhausted myself. After that I relentlessly continued to torture us both in an effort to embrace the unembraceable.

Yes, there was something degrading, deadly sinful in this dissolute duel of ours; over and over we tried, adjusted, learned, moved away from each other in revulsion. It all resembled an agony, or the attempt to resurrect a dead Lazarus (without the knowledge or the right to do so). That wet, clammy, sticky, paralyzed little worm looked like a puny and already stinking corpse as Kassianov desperately tried to pull the indecent rubber on again. Olivia, on the couch, was waiting in disgust and horror; every so often her eyes would fall on me with hostile curiosity while she continued to listen with trained ear for steps in the hall. (Here, it seems, I was confronted for the first time by that base Vishnevsky within me, who, since then, has scarcely ever left me.)

Gradually our problems resolved themselves and things proceeded quite naturally. At that point, the forbidden became for us a genuine release: as if a summer storm had drenched some arid steppe, discharged the accumulated electricity, and satiated earth, trees, and corn with reviving moisture. (Right afterward, saintly Father, we would begin to laugh and talk, almost yell—from joy, I suppose.)

11

Alas, I still think that even in this there was no real, unequivocal, premeditated lust. We allowed ourselves the essentials only, without any extravaganzas or variations. We rid ourselves of accumulated poisons (brought into being not by us) and felt happy and grateful. On one occasion, in the park, Kassianov attempted from sheer boredom to come up with something new, and afterward apologized, very embarrassed. Olivia reassured him, "Well, obviously, something like that had to happen sooner or later." How much wiser, more mature she was than I, and how cheerful and enterprising.

Here, then, it seems lust was finally reigning supreme. But in Kassianov's consciousness there remained no signs of inner struggle, remorse, reproaches. (Although it is true that, from then on, Vishnevksy took to visiting me more and more often and to enforcing his will.)

We made love in the most unsuitable places, at the most awkward hours. I used simple, cruel means of contraception. We did not realize then, at least I did not (and I repent), that she too had to come the full circle of pleasure. The whole point seemed to be that Kassianov had to blow his nose—as fast as possible. For this, saintly Father, would you believe it, I now reproach myself.

Once Kassianov stayed the night in her family's town house. Except for the servants, who lived on the upper floor out of earshot, there was no one in the deserted and pitilessly splendid apartment. Olivia could have joined me without any danger. But such luxury did not even occur to us. And if the beginning of concupiscence is overindulgence, variety, conscious savoring, then we were still almost innocent.

The repugnant crude battle with the primitive rubber, the many other torments, had united us with all but legitimate, imperishable bonds. So that, several years later when he was already in love with Zora, Kassianov still sometimes slept with Olivia, considering it completely natural (while with other women he did not permit himself such license). But was it lust? How well I remember the stretches of joyful regeneration in the wake of each such meeting. Yes, it was precisely as if a noisy thunderstorm had revived and cleansed the soil and liberated the imprisoned sap.

Only much, much later, when there was hardly any sap left in reserve, when my cells, overcome by panic, were blindly struggling with the specter of death and, not wishing to give in, exuded noxious fumes, only then apparently came the time for unvarnished lust, the Lust that, according to Saint Paul, cannot (perhaps because it need not) be satisfied.

But it is hard to see now when this drought set in. I assume that, between the youthful elementary release from surplus and the wretched semisenile attempts to make use of the sorry remainder, there was a long period of both the abundance of vital forces and the avid ability to exploit them. That, then, would indeed be the Kingdom of Lust triumphant, where, however, pride, jealousy, anger, and other usurpers also play leading roles.

I think, Father Nectarius, that the first prerequisite for lust is the complete absence of any personal reference: the incognito or camouflage of the object. . . . I am doing this with you but could continue with someone else—with anybody! As soon as personal—eternal—relations are introduced, the possibility of choice and love arises; and love seemingly transfigures or eradicates lust. (I'm afraid the great Gnostics would object to this last assertion.)

12

We were taking our fourth-year examinations. Kassianov went every day to the Sorbonne to listen to the answers of his classmates who were undergoing the ordeal in alphabetical order. Since there were several thousand students, these visits to the auditorium proved the best way of preparing for the perfidious questions of our eminent professors. Every one of them had a hobby that he treasured inordinately. And many esoteric realms of the natural sciences never came up during the lectures, so that familiarity with tricky questions of this kind could only be gained among the milling throng of worried students.

There Kassianov saw her for the first time. Evidently she had seldom, if ever, come to classes in the course of the year, for I could not have failed to notice her: this elegant apparition with the face and figure of a thoroughbred Parisian. She stood at the rail separating us from those who were being examined at the long table and, leaning forward, as if about to take flight, listened to the candidates' timid and confused speeches.

No, she was not a true beauty; but young, fragrantly elegant, and obviously from another class or world. Her smart light summer dress both enveloped and set off all the convexities and concavities of her body. . . . In a word, spiritual Father, Kassianov was spellbound: she attracted him magnetically, promising immediate earthly (paradisial) bliss. *Une femme d'intérieur,* but with an extraordinary gift *pour le couchage,* on the side and if opportunity arose.

And I thought, literally: "Lord, I do not want to be a bother, but if your punishment for fornication were to be no more than twenty years of forced labor (and then full rehabilitation), I would immediately sin with this ravishing stranger."

"But what more could befall you?" I heard Vishnevsky's voice—my flesh, my common sense speaking up in indignation. And to his shame, Kassianov, in his stunned condition, found nothing intelligible to parry this voice, although he sensed that the danger threatening him—and the world—was far more serious than twenty years behind bars. I always thought (o heresy!) that precisely because one wants to do *it* so much one must not do it. . . . But to get oneself a girl for ten francs—that is excusable.

She looked back over her shoulder (so powerful with many poisonous fluids was Kassianov's gaze). And although he was probably very poorly dressed according to her standards, she smiled at him, frankly flattered.

"Is this character," referring to the venerable professor, "always so bloodthirsty?" I asked nonchalantly, trembling like Raskolnikov on the verge of his crime.

At this time young Kassianov lived completely alone (not counting Vishnevsky's appearances), in Paris, in an unheated hotel room. At night he would dream of entering a butcher shop and asking: "May I have a pound of female meat, please?"

In those days we considered it an irrefutable fact that if you accosted a young girl it meant one thing, and one thing only: that you wanted to go to bed with her immediately. This shameful arrangement was supposedly understood by all, and in vain did Vishnevsky try to reassure me on this score.

"I don't know, I've never seen him before," she answered readily, with a coquettish movement of her narrow chest (two diminutive hillocks directly under his nose).

She wore a simple low-cut dress that offered to view a slender neck, thin collarbones, and that part which the French call "*la gorge.*"

Nervously checking the wallet in his pocket, Kassianov inquired in a conspiratorial tone, "When is your turn?"

"Tuesday, I believe. And yours?"

"Oh, I still have time," he answered with inordinate gratitude, and, as behooved a gentleman, added, "My name is Kassianov."

She stretched out her hand: her fingers in a tight kid glove, and the palm, the wrist, the elbow, everything tender, fragrant, candidly bared to the shoulder. This hand with its tightly squeezed fingers was, it seemed to Kassianov, created exclusively to caress a man.

13

In silent accord we walked toward the door, made our way down the ponderous staircase, and stepped into the medieval courtyard of the university.

On the street around the corner, in front of the entrance to a small hotel, she said, "I haven't seen my mail yet. Would you like to come up?" and she looked at me with simple, frank intimacy. To our honor it must be said that neither of us even so much as attempted a smile.

The lobby, with its heavy plush curtains, was hot and gloomy. The mail lay on the desk next to the telephone.

"I have to make a call right away," she said, attentively studying a small blue envelope. "Go up three flights, room number two."

In those days people could be *comme il faut* without an elevator (and somehow did not seem to need one). Kassianov ran up to what in Paris is called the fourth floor and, without knocking, entered a room furnished with several small upholstered pieces. Lolling on one of the sky-blue sofas (Tilsit style) was a pretty young woman, plump and fair, in a lacy negligee. "And Monique?" she asked, showing no surprise at the unexpected visitor.

"Monique is on the phone." Kassianov cast a suffering glance at the girl's legs that, one thrown over the other, were exposed to the hips. She followed his look with her eyes and gave him a guileless smile.

A little later Monique came into the room. Kassianov, who was straightening up his clothes, did not recognize her at once, she looked so pale and drawn. "Oh, you have met already," she said almost inaudibly.

"Tell me, for God's sake, what punishment could have befallen me?" he howled in despair.

Of course Monique did not understand; in any case, she did not answer, and so he deemed it fitting to bow exquisitely, à la Vishnevsky, and, waving to the girl in the negligee, he departed.

Much of this, holy Father, has remained unclear to me up to this day. One thing is certain: instead of the nourishing, desired, paradisial food, Kassianov hastily swallowed a vulgar slice of sausage.

Something quite different and yet, perhaps, related happened on another occasion. Kassianov had finally come to an agreement with a prostitute and was following her into the hotel. He had just begun to undress when a cat jumped onto the bed: an ordinary gray house cat, familiar from childhood—it stretched its neck and began to purr. The girl petted her and then, businesslike, chased her off: "Go away, sweetie, don't bother us." Under her human voice and the human purring of the cat all my carnal cravings instantly evaporated. In this case it seemed appropriate to Kassianov to buckle his belt, pay politely, and be gone (hurting the honest professional to the quick).

So, Father Nectarius, I have come to believe that true lust excludes whatever is personal, well-known, familiar, customary. The partner is an abstraction, a symbol. The less human, conscious, close the relationship, the sharper, the more sensual the sexual pleasures. . . . (In vice, fetishism is not an exception but, rather, the rule.)

14

Now, twenty-five years later, Kassianov is attracted by exotic women—women from distant isles, creatures of an unaccustomed breed, incomprehensible to him and very tempting.

One morning, late for work, he rushed into his office and there, among the bookshelves and test tubes, came upon a new lab technician, a yellowish girl with the facial expressions of a pretty monkey. Judging by her size and bone structure, a Polynesian. She turned out to be a Filipino from the mountains who had never been to Manila.

Hardly a beauty: her face, broad, flat, concave, presented what might be called an antiprofile. With her thick, short, flaring nostrils and the equanimously smiling, gently oval eyes under a mane of bluish horse hair, she was enigmatic and imposing, bringing to mind the house gods of ancient, long-extinct tribes. Everything about her struck him as strange, unexplored, miraculous. Hard to guess: was she twenty or forty? intelligent or stupid? good-looking (according to their standards) or homely? The souls out there in Oceania express themselves in their own way, and this must have excited Kassianov's imagination.

After a moment's pause I decided (in close cooperation with Vishnevsky) that she was beautiful, well-bred, and, above all, most appreciative of my scientific and pedagogical activities.

Her skin, Father Nectarius, was altogether special: soft, slippery, fusing with the muscles below, not a separate, exterior covering. Her sinuous yellow arms seemed to bend in the most unexpected places. And yet the grasp of her semi-transparent hands was of amazing strength: apparently relinquishing, they took back everything on the spot and with interest. (Like bright tropical plants that feed on insects and birds.) Her name was Fey, and Fey smelled of a mysterious Micronesian perfume that probably was already in use at the time of Atlantis or Pacifides (Limuria).

Her birthday was in July, and Vishnevsky, having struck up a conversation about the zodiacal sign of Cancer during lunch in the cafeteria, was lavish in his praise of women born under this constellation. Fey seemed intrigued by the topic (I say "seemed" because Kassianov was unable to state anything about her with certainty).

She got hold of a popular introduction to astrology and a few days later brought up the question of horoscopes. Whenever she was about to say something, she would break into a wide smile and make an odd, butting movement with her flat head; and even though she never said anything very funny, everyone around always reacted with the same indefinite kind of chuckling. Now Fey, smiling her sleepy, happy smile, her large teeth glistening, butted with her heavy head, stretched out her soft prehensile hands toward me, and finally said, "Please tell me all about Cancer!"

Kassianov thought she was referring to the disease and his face fell. (We were at the time engaged in the general statistics of this contemporary scourge and, having thrown men and women, old and young, Negroes and Chinese, rich and poor, into the same basket, had ended up in a complete muddle.)

When it became clear that she had the sign of the zodiac in mind, Vishnevsky adroitly countered that for the discussion of such a rich topic one ought to get together at leisure and in a more comfortable place. "What are your plans for the weekend?" I interrupted rudely.

"Good Lord, no!" Fey laughed soundlessly, butting her heavy head on its fragile neck. "Oh no!"

But in Oceania, Father Nectarius, they have their own logic, with all its legitimate contradictions.

(On the map the islands look like bread crumbs in a huge tub of water, scattered to feed the birds. Fey told me, grinning, that an American archaeologist once found some ashes in one of the caves near her native village and, through radio-carbon dating, gave them an age of about twenty thousand years. He subsequently reported to a scientific congress that small personal fires had been in use on these islands since time immemorial.

Actually, Fey's father, returning from a fishing trip, had spent the night in this rocky cave and, to keep himself warm, had burned some old driftwood.)

15

The talk about the constellation of Cancer took place on a Monday; on Thursday, spiritual Father, as she was leaving Kassianov's office after having brought him the mail, Fey smiled with her two-dimensional antiprofile, butted, and, bowing deeply, inquired, "Where was it you wanted to go for the weekend?"

I was surprised, but Vishnevsky boldly took her up. "You wonderful girl, of course, please, listen. . . ." And Kassianov explained that he owned a modest little cottage, a mere shack, on the tip of Long Island: we could leave Friday night and spend two days together there.

"How is that?" She butted with her tiger head, laughing embarrassedly. "Alone in the cottage, day and night?"

"Not indoors—on the beach, at the boundless ocean! We'll only go back to the house late at night. Of course, I shall try to kiss you or some such thing, but I'm a gentleman. And think, we'll have the ocean, the dunes, the smell of pines, and there will be a full moon besides."

I do not know what convinced her: that Kassianov was a

gentleman or that the moon would be full above the sea. In any case, immediately and very soberly, she accepted. We set the time and place for our meeting (it turned out that Fey had long ago identified my old green Buick and was well-acquainted with it).

As luck would have it, on Friday afternoon Kassianov ran into the head of the department in the elevator and was held up for an extra hour (for some reason the chief always exhibited great administrative zeal at the end of the week). After that he still had to dash home to make the last arrangements for Zora: paralyzed from the waist down, his wife was still perfectly able to move about in her wheel chair. Besides, Father Nectarius, a kind neighbor comes in to check on her twice a day for a modest sum. (Our marriage and Zora's subsequent illness could be the subject of a quite elevating old-fashioned novel; but since this has no direct relationship to Kassianov's confession, I shall refrain here from superfluous details.)

It was already growing dark, notwithstanding daylight-saving time, when Kassianov arrived at the appointed place; before he had brought the car to a complete halt, he saw Fey's small, predatory shadow sliding, as through the jungle, toward the door and next to her a silhouette, also feminine.

"This is my sister, Sarsava," said Fey, and with exaggerated giggling the two installed themselves in the back of the car, leaving Kassianov the whole front to himself.

Recalling this dreadful trip, heavenly Father, I feel, as I have felt so often before, the evil unreality or the flimsiness of the material that makes up life (with my participation, yes, but not quite according to my wishes).

As soon as the sisters realized that Kassianov had no intention of making a scene or of turning back, they brightened and grew quite jolly. Sarsava, a gentle flower, a colibri, went into peals of childlike, birdlike, and promising laughter. Sweet and educated, she had even heard of Tolstoi (Anna Karenina) and, more important still, possessed a great sense of humor most welcome under the circumstances.

On the girls' initiative we stopped at the other end of the bridge and they joined Kassianov in the front, leaving their raincoats and blue flight bags in the back seat. We reached our destination late at night. There was the ever-present ocean, there was the bottomless dark sky with the pale Milky Way, and there was the full moon in its assigned quadrant, all visible through the enormous window that took up one entire wall of the cottage.

Kassianov lit the fire, set the table, and brought out some snacks. I had prepared everything for precisely such an occasion during our last stay; from the wheel chair, Zora had followed my movements with her serene, radiant, sand-colored eyes. . . .

Father Nectarius, why didn't I die with you, when I was good, when I saw a certain light? Remember how we lay next to each other? I could hear everything but was no longer willing to respond. If it were not for Zora, who climbed onto the scaffold and touched me with her hand, I swear I would never have parted from you.

16

The sisters admired everything, praised my foresight, approved of the microscopic kitchen with its many electrical appliances. They ate with earnest concentration, carefully biting and chewing as if there were a secret or a danger in the very process of digestion. They especially liked the wine; it was hard to tell whether their cheeks had become flushed, but their shining eyes bespoke a love of life and a readiness for adventure; Sarsava showed particular enterprise.

Kassianov's aim was to maneuver things so that all three of them would end up in the same, the only comfortable, the master bed. The dear little sister understood at once that this was quite natural under the circumstances and agreed courageously, without any fuss. This brought about a succession of Fey's soundless titterings and the butting of her invincible tiger head that flooded Kassianov with a wave of blind passion.

At long last, having switched off the lamps, we stretched out on the low, oaken bed (which resembled Ulysses' couch at home in Ithaca) illuminated only by the plastic (three-dimensional) light of the moon. Through the window the triumphant satellite poured her cosmic shower over us, weighing us down with her tangible, material particles.

During the ride Kassianov (or was it Vishnevsky?) had waited only for this moment, had tasted in advance the many, apparently unlimited, inebriating possibilities. Now he took advantage of the situation and all but finished himself in the process; the sisters, too, received their full share.

But lust, Father Nectarius, lust, of all things, I cannot recall. Unless I simply do not know what lust is. There was toil, an accursed duty, agony, death, a night one had to pass through in order to see the sun and day again. Desire, though, had apparently been left behind, together with the fantasies, the preparations, the scheming. (So, as Kassianov knows, is the aroma of brewing coffee more enticing than its taste, and the herring in cream sauce more tempting on the plate than in the mouth.)

To this day, when a new vile affection comes to trouble Kassianov's soul, the lesson of that night often brings him back to his senses. My little partners, I'm afraid, suffered even more during this monotonous, businesslike work shift (else they would have had no qualms about coming along for another ride to the sea).

In short, imagination is the main requirement for sinning: without it, the most skillful love-making is nothing but tortuous gymnastics.

Thus it was that Kassianov reached the heights of sensuality and inventiveness with the Starling whom he only knew by way of the telephone. (When he finally touched her "for real," the enchantment was over, immediately and completely, and there was no trace left of temptation.)

She lived in the apartment house next to ours, on the same floor and facing our windows. When her lights went on, her room seemed to stretch out its hands toward Kassianov. But touch each other we could not. We communicated by signs; only at the end by telephone. Kassianov did not know her name or how she smelled, and saw her only in parts, in movement—limbs, a torso—later assembling the separate pieces as in a jigsaw puzzle. But I think that, at the beginning of this uncommon acquaintanceship, Lust, the Lust described by Saint Paul, presided over our ideal copulations, passionate pantomimes, abstract orgies. (Yes, spiritual Father, you will have to absolve Kassianov from yet another voluntary sin.)

The Starling must have only quite recently moved into that apartment, since nothing had ever attracted Kassianov's attention to it before (nor had Zora ever looked into the windows across the way). The previous inhabitants had somehow remained unnoticed—and this too is wrong.

Then, suddenly, almost next to us, appeared this small spare "starling" with the sensual, mobile, lithe silhouette. Almost at first sight, that Sunday, Kassianov (or was it Vishnevsky?) submitted without thinking to a power similar to gravitation and nonchalantly waved to her. Easily and with humorous exaggeration she waved back. (In the Kingdom of Heaven there will be no gravitation.)

And that same evening, both probably having waited with equal impatience for the moment, they began, by the light of their table lamps, to assume the most outrageous poses, displaying themselves shamelessly and giving their lewd imagination free rein. Come to think of it, dear Father, the first night was not altogether dissolute. But at the second or third session we already behaved like a couple of professionals, performing, stark naked, a dance of love with the most intricate figures, and reducing ourselves in the process to a state of complete senselessness.

17

Coming home from work in the evening, Kassianov, after a short visit with his paralyzed wife, would turn on the light in his bedroom. Instantly, having been waiting for the signal, the Starling drew open the curtains and seated herself decorously on the sofa that she had pushed into the center of the room. He wanted to see her breasts, legs, hips. Obediently she would take off her clothes, sometimes hesitating in embarrassment and demanding his participation, his help. She liked to place her head on his naked body and let her hair stream down over it. (Often he had to make great efforts to guess her latest whim and to assume, finally, the position she preferred or considered most comfortable.)

Afterward they "chatted" peacefully; Kassianov asked questions that she either answered or shrugged off, secretive in all that concerned her private life (name, apartment, or telephone number). At the accustomed hour they had a snack they prepared jointly. He uncorked a bottle of white wine and they gleefully toasted each other. (Kassianov bathed his starling in champagne; Valerik's lessons had not been wasted.)

To make the illusion complete, they sometimes quarreled, upbraided each other, withdrew into their separate corners; Starling had a most natural way of hurling a glass or plate at him. But she stubbornly refused to divulge her telephone number, even broke into authentic tears when he pressed her too much. He finally talked her into telephoning him. But it took a long time until she dared to speak: at first she immediately hung up in response to his "hello"; later she would listen, in silence, to his passionate whisper. With breathless speed Kassianov described all the possible delights that a meeting—soon, this day, now!—might hold. It seemed as if, at the other end of the wire, a wounded but curious little creature was sizing up, and trying to get used to, some terrifying and tempting sounds.

One day she answered—in a lively, musical, boyish voice. "Yes. But I am frightened. . . ." She sounded like a spoiled child, used to ordering a household about. She spoke rapidly but with long pauses between the separate sentences, as if searching for a rational, honest basis to her confused thoughts and emotions.

So their dialogue began. From hints and disconnected remarks Kassianov gathered that she had been married and divorced, had since had some short-lived and unsatisfactory affairs. "Is it always so painful and such a bore?" she inquired with inordinate, morbid interest.

At first Kassianov did not understand her question and answered in generalizations such as: "There is a grain of suffering in every person's life. . . ."

But obstinately she kept coming back to the subject, until he realized that she was not alluding to some high-flown suffering but to the most basic, vital kind. The Starling, all atremble, was waiting for an explanation, and it appeared that she had entered into the relationship with Kassianov for the specific purpose of finding a solution to her agonizing sexual problems. "Does it have to be such an ordeal, so disgusting and tedious?" she would ask over and over again, in different variations, until he came to understand fully what an important part this question played in her life.

She was twenty-six years old. Already. When mentioning her age she invariably added "already" (the assumption being that there was precious little time left for tempestuous pleasures).

For some reason she considered Kassianov a specialist in the realm of sex and he, realizing, with the help of Vishnevsky, that this was precisely what attracted this particular partner, never dissuaded her. (Some fashion their fetish pure and innocent; others prefer it debauched, or famous, or rich.)

But, frightened by her previous humiliating experiences, she still refused a face-to-face meeting. Besides, after her prolonged sexual despondency she probably found the highest kind of gratification in our surrealistic embraces. It is worth mentioning, spiritual Father, that it was the Starling who took the leading part in these abstract saturnalia; Kassianov only played obedient second fiddle.

18

Gradually Kassianov came to regard the Starling adventure as a symbolic battle for the insulted and injured. (You must believe him, Father Nectarius: quite often in life he got caught on that devilish bait.)

And so he decided to avail himself of an old plan of his—one he had tried to work out years before and under entirely different circumstances. The idea was to "skip" psychologically the initial, difficult, and unavoidable stage of a new field or study. . . . In the case of the Starling, for instance, we had to pretend that a happy, intimate relationship of long standing existed between us, that we had already, many times, done everything possible together, had appreciated it, and now had no more fears. Actually, Kassianov had carried over Lord Keynes's theory from the realm of economics into psychology and even the bed. Just as in a country with its industry paralyzed the population must first be provided with the means to purchase all kinds of appliances and industrial products, after which the economy will prosper . . . so, in the mysteries of love, a couple must, as it were, decide that they have already attained adequate bliss and thus create the conditions favorable for a genuinely happy marriage.

Starling listened to all this, sighed comfortably, gave little sobs—of impatience or excitement—and, putting in an occasional question of her own, enthusiastically helped work out a scheme to fit her own case. This was the plan: she would retire in her accustomed way, but with the door unlocked and a light burning in the hall. Kassianov would enter as if he belonged, go to her bed, and begin to caress her, unhurriedly, as if it were his firmly established right. Should she speak, Kassianov answers; should she push him back, he gets up and leaves quietly, without a word.

And still, Father Nectarius, the temptation did not come from me alone. True, Kassianov painted glowing pictures, piled on the colors, embellished, but she always started these talks: wounded and vanquished long ago, now touched to the quick, she constantly reverted to the subject.

One Saturday Kassianov did not come home at the usual hour. (We had been devoting Saturday nights to our intimate pantomimes.) Having spent the better part of the night somewhat promiscuously, he returned home in the early hours of Sunday morning. He had hardly switched on the light when her green lamp lit up and, a moment later, her anxious voice came over the phone: "Where have you been? I was so worried. Why didn't you let me know?" She sounded like a frightened child. There was something splendidly familiar, comradely, and intimate in her jealous whisper, as if indeed we had for the longest time been engaged in that activity toward which, so far unsuccessfully, I was trying to bring her.

Suddenly she said: "If I asked you to come over now, would you promise not to say a word, would you leave as soon as I wanted you to?"

"Absolutely! I promise," Kassianov replied sonorously. "You just give the sign and I'll vanish, dissolve. But, you know, it's four o'clock, almost five, time to sleep and not to wander into strange boudoirs." He tried to turn the whole thing into a joke while at the same time becoming aware of a loathsomely rapturous surge in the pit of his stomach.

"As you like," she answered casually, and after a pause added, "In any case I'm leaving the door unlocked; perhaps someone will stop by."

19

Needless to say, Kassianov rushed over. At first everything progressed according to plan: it was even somewhat degrading to see how reality can at times so easily match fantasy. However, when at long last Starling trustingly pulled him closer, it became apparent that he was in no condition to take part in the action. How vile, how stupid, and how familiar to every male is this feeling of one's own uselessness and the sheer absurdity of the whole undertaking, intensified, as it is, by the awkward, ridiculous position. And to think that for many years such silly gymnastics occupy the center of human life, crippling and deforming our state of mind.

To bury my head in the pillows! to go to sleep forever! pounded in Kassianov's temples. Why can't she leave me alone, the fool!

Oh, how enviable the higher, angelic echelons. It is so hard, so unrewarding at times for us earthlings to sin! In short, Kassianov did not derive a trace of pleasure from this dismal dawn. He was, above all, ashamed—for he could not be sure what the patronizingly docile Starling was feeling and thinking.

And this, saintly Father, is the point. Inundated as we are by the boundless ocean of lust, it is not the elementary desire to tickle oneself, to bite off a sweet morsel, that is so sinful. . . . No, pride is the crime! We want to possess, subjugate the other person, we want to mete out pain and joy, satiate, satisfy fully and by our own means alone. And always this unquenchable greed: I, here, more, all.

Thus, in his search for the sources of lust, Kassianov stumbled upon other foul-smelling sins that feed it. . . .

At this point Kassianov had to interrupt his narration to go into his wife's room. Her paralysis had been undergoing changes, deteriorations followed by apparent improvements, that led the specialists to suspect hysteric simulation. But I have known Zora for a long time, ever since she was a young student, and have never doubted the seriousness of her disease. For the last few years there has been a definite aggravation: now she can hardly speak and swallows only with difficulty. Before long the sclerosis will reach the respiratory and cardiovascular centers—and that will be the very end. There, alas, Father Nectarius, you and I are both utterly helpless, and without blame. And if this be heresy, then our entire life is heresy!

To preserve the patient, the doctors advised passing a rubber tube through her nose and esophagus into her stomach—to feed her. Since milk and gruels tend to clog the catheter, it must be changed occasionally. At first Kassianov used to call an intern from the hospital for this purpose, but soon he learned to perform the entire operation himself. The hitch is that Zora, unable to make normal swallowing movements, cannot cooperate: one has to use force—and her eyes, still the old, golden-sand color, become bloodshot. Sometimes the tube slides into the trachea instead of the esophagus—not only a danger, but torture as well.

I continue with lust, heavenly Father (how petty it all seems). . . . So Kassianov became convinced that a man will very often chase a skirt not from lust but from greed. (Women, by the way, also have their form of eternal dissatisfaction and unquenchable thirst.)

Greed. Greed, with its inordinately big eyes. Greed, which makes well-bred people heap Homeric portions onto their plates, fill their glasses to overflowing, buy two coats at once, and sell their souls to the devil at the roulette table. On his deathbed a man may still ruefully recall that he never managed to see Venice, that he missed a magnificent painting at an auction, that he did not invite a charming woman up to his rooms when he still could have done so. And this last regret, what has it to do with lust? Is it not rather a mixture

—as when gluttony is mixed with liquor? (And everywhere, in everything, that unbridled "I, for me, myself, give!")

In his professional work Kassianov is always aware of giving honestly, by the sweat of his brow, without stinting—and he insists on prompt and full remuneration. If for some reason the administration does not pay punctually, he is invaded by a wild anger, as if someone had spat in his face, had mortally offended him.

Yes, saintly Father, in our primitive anger lies another sin: pride. I did my job. I helped. I was denied. I was cheated. Furious indignation, blind rage grow from such an exaggerated, blown-up consciousness of one's own worth and personal uniqueness.

This intimate connection of the capital sins brings to mind an ancient toy: a wooden egg, colorfully painted . . . you open it and inside is another, smaller one, just as colorful; you open that and there is a third. So it goes with my trespasses: as I peel off shell after shell, I discover every time a new mortal fault, and it is never clear which single one at any particular moment brands Kassianov. May Thomas Aquinas forgive me: all sins are indivisible and unfusable, imitating in this the heavenly image.

20

To tell about Kassianov's pride would mean to go over his entire life, day by day. For were some fearful giant or an archangel with flaming sword to strike down this pride, there would be nothing left of Kassianov but a pallid, smiling mollusk.

His real life—which means his actual existence, not a possible or desirable one—has always been directed by pride. And yet, heavenly Father, I was not happy on this road, and I did not succeed in producing anything noteworthy.

There is the boy, playing with other children in the garden. It is Sunday, a holiday. His mother calls, "Come in, we'll put on your new suit!" Kassianov runs into the house and a few minutes later emerges, scrubbed, in a blue sailor suit with short, cuffed trousers. He does not rejoin his companions. "He is shy," Anyuta declares. The children, however, have their own opinion about Kassianov and begin to pelt him with stones. Later in life he will come to realize that his playmates were right in punishing him for his vanity. For what else is this famous shyness of ours if not pride in disguise? The fear of not being appreciated as we deserve or desire. A morbid self-esteem, approaching hysteria, hallucination. And since most of all you fear that, instead of being taken for a genius or a hero, you may, God forbid, be taken for a shit, this is precisely what happens. Those others (in the garden) are very shrewd, as well as vain, ambitious, and vengeful in their turn.

Not to make a fool of myself!—this was Kassianov's only concern when entering a crowded drawing room or meeting some public figure. "I, me, here." So much that is ridiculous, stupid, even cruel, stems from the avid desire to prove something special about oneself and for oneself, above the others.

Entire periods in Kassianov's life have been spent in the melancholy savoring of past "mistakes," of situations in which he played a ridiculous or cowardly role. Ever since his youth Kassianov, like some Tolstoi character, has grimaced, fidgeted, and cried out at the most inappropriate moments when remembering or becoming aware of a blunder or a humiliation. And while he thus grimaces or clenches his fists, someone else is performing all his customary and complex duties for him.

If a past offense suddenly dawns upon him, Kassianov, invaded by a belated and vicious rage, is ready to destroy the perpetrator of this real or imagined humiliation. (Pride too is not completely autonomous; it thrives on anger, is reinforced by it.)

Kassianov is at the wheel of his green Buick. A man in a broad-buttocked Pontiac makes a sharp turn and cuts right in front of him. Kassianov's face swells with indignation: he speeds after the broad-haunched offender, at the first opportunity squeezes into the other lane, and, zipping by the arrogant driver, puts him in his place. Only then does Kassianov calm down and forget—for the time being. (Had he not been able to take immediate revenge, he would have kept up an endless inner stream of abuse.) Spiritual Father, tell me, if you had to drive a car across the limitless expanses of New York, would you be able to bear humbly offenses and humiliations of this kind?

Kassianov figures that his character would improve by a full twenty-five percent if he had no car. If he weren't obliged to make a living (that is, use his elbows), Kassianov would be yet another twenty-five percent kinder, better, purer. Then, of course, there are the women, who force us to run after them and to tell lies: without this encumbrance he would be more perfect by still another quarter. And finally (last but not least), if God answered our prayers more often and gave us direct instructions, then Kassianov would lose the last fourth of his bestiality, inherited and self-acquired. (Or do I only fancy all this?)

21

And so, on the basis of his everyday experience, Kassianov has become convinced that it is futile and naïve to speak of the notorious sin of pride without simultaneously mentioning anger and envy. Perhaps this is the deadly sting of pride: that it leads quite naturally to fratricidal and suicidal anger, which, in its turn, is stuffed with other passions and failings.

In rage Kassianov forgets himself and out pops another ancient creature, differing very little from the double of his neighbor in the broad-buttocked car. I would put it this way: these doubles are rather alike in everyone; we simply become replicas of each other whenever we give free rein to these, our natural companions. Thus, in addition to "I, mine, for me," there dwells in every individual a blind, collective monster that rears up obediently whenever pride generates anger, lust, or envy.

He, this faithful monster, I call Nape. It is his characteristic trait that he does not recognize himself in the other Napes and rushes into the melee (like a gorilla who has seen his own image in the mirror). I understand, if belatedly; but he acts, instinctively, artlessly, automatically—defending himself (and me).

Nape differs from darling Vishnevsky (who, by the way, bears an amazing resemblance to Valerik). Vishnevsky knows how to flatter, to whom to tell jokes, for whom to think up a dirty story . . . he knows how to smile, bow, make a dubious proposition, tell a lie, read a letter meant for someone else, fondle, eat, drink, pound his fist on the table, and retreat or give in at the right moment.

And so we were speeding on, trying to catch up with our latest enemy: Kassianov, almost paralyzed; Vishnevsky, ingeniously cursing; and someone, lodged in the nape of my neck, stubbornly and accurately driving the car and doing everything needed to keep pace safely with the other monsters. "Dearest Father," Kassianov thinks, as he does so often, "having lost my wholeness, I can hardly pretend to holiness. . . . And yet, by Jove, there exists in me besides Vishnevsky and Nape a certain Holy Ghost Who joins us together and sheds His one light upon us." (And this, after all, is no heresy. . . .)

Luckily, the incident with the broad-beamed Pontiac has been settled: we are again in front, rolling along without a care in the world. Now Kassianov wonders who has turned on his headlights—he had not noticed when it was done or by whom. . . . Suddenly, as if from the outside, he sees his gestures, his distorted face, the whole ugly race with the other car, and he is mortified: his face turns green, he is ready to cry out—to shake off his past (remake it). And here Nape comes to his assistance. Raising his voice, whistling, laughing loudly, he protects Kassianov by diverting his attention. Through such exhausting scenes of contrition I am partially returned to my original self. (In pride and anger, Kassianov loses his personal profile.)

On the job, if anyone dares reprove Kassianov, I, holding back a flow of abuse, howl in a fury: "Don't you (son of a bitch) interfere in my business. . . ."

If another man pays court to a girl who has caught Kassianov's fancy, he immediately and resentfully drops out. "Aha, that's how it is," he thinks (or even says to her). "For a minute you had your doubts. In that case I have no need of you and all your charms. . . ."

This, Vishnevsky assures him, is simply jealousy.

Why call it jealousy? It is pride, injured vanity, morbid conceit, envy. It is "I, for me, mine. . . ."

22

On a Quatorze Juillet Kassianov picked up a Swedish girl on Montparnasse. Upon closer inspection he did not like her at all and even tried to pass her on to Ainer. When this did not work out, he resigned himself to spending the evening in her company—as behooved a gentleman. Since it was still too early for dinner, they entered a movie house. The theater was crowded and they were given seats in different rows. Presently the young man next to whom the Swede had been seated began, in the dim light, to write something on his newspaper, which he then handed her; she read the message with difficulty and shook her head. He again wrote a few lines and this time she took his pencil and wrote a longish answer: I assume she gave him her address. Kassianov sat, bathed in sweat, his heart pounding in his throat. "She's a bitch," explained Vishnevsky. "Kill him," proposed Nape. Indeed, I was close to homicide (or suicide). And note, dear Father, the Swede did not really suit Kassianov at all; secretly he wished only to be rid of her as fast as possible.

Thus, all this celebrated jealousy is actually nothing but one more incarnation of hurt pride . . . resentment, mortal resentment, stemming from the conviction of one's personal uniqueness and exceptional quality. (To put *me* on a level with just anybody!)

As to envy, envy in which Kassianov has been wallowing from the very first day of his professional career, it too is a reply to some presumed injury—done us by God, fate, or our brothers. If Kassianov had reached the heights to which he (and not without reason, of course) aspired, if he had quickly and elegantly surmounted all obstacles, without humiliating compromises and kicks in the behind, oh, what an ideally unenvious, unselfish, benevolent, tactful comrade he would be. (But meanwhile he feels cheated whenever someone else achieves easily what he, Kassianov, was able to get only after decades of effort.)

A winter evening in a big city. P, a pudgy, bald-headed mathematician of the slippery-brilliant kind, enters the auditorium; the students rise and applaud. . . . He has been awarded a high academic honor for a work that by no means surpasses Kassianov's discovery in a related field. P has evidently just acquired a resplendent modish overcoat and, with his short stature and enormous head, now looks exactly like a rhinoceros or a bison. Vishnevsky and I stand crushed, poisoned by the stream of rage, malice, envy that rushes through us as if we were hollow pipes and empties itself over this comical beast. Oh, how we desire his immediate and complete ruin! (It was then that I realized for the first time to what depths we can fall on this earth.)

Saintly Father, if you covet your neighbor's ass or his wife, it is, of course, bad but it is not envy. Envy is to wish for your neighbor not to have an ass or a wife (or not to receive the Nobel Prize—even if such a bauble does not interest Vishnevsky and me at all).

It is envy when you hope that Z will not pass his exam, not win in the lottery, not go to Rome on his holiday (even though you yourself have long ago passed all examinations, never gamble, and have no intention whatever of going to Italy). It is envy that pushes us to play a dirty trick on our neighbor or to spoil his pleasure (at times even at some small sacrifices to ourselves—sacrifices that in such cases are entirely without self-interest).

Jealousy asks for full and exclusive possession of the object: complete submission. Envy (in the name of justice) wants everyone in the whole hostile world also to suffer before achieving a measure of success. Jealousy links Kassianov disgracefully to another being in the center of the universe; envy underscores his loneliness on the periphery.

But be adivsed that we are not born with envy (or with lust). Only gradually, with the growth of our glands and instincts, appetites and failures, does our envy flower and wax stronger. It would be possible to avoid this sin (as well as lust) by remaining a child forever. . . . Pride, though, and anger are already with the infant, unadulterated: they are innate, not the result of warped or hampered development.

In the last analysis, pride derives from a legitimate awareness of our unique—godlike—quality. But this sacred feeling, this consciousness, became deformed when we ceased to recognize that our neighbors too are miraculous, holy creatures. Pride is a disfigured but basically valid acknowledgment of man's great role in the universe. Envy and lust are merely the acquired fruits of a polluted world.

23

Here we are, our cars blocking each other at an intersection and neither of us willing to back up; he curses wildly and Kassianov counters with an obscene gesture. At this point the challenger gets out of his car but, the light having opportunely changed, Kassianov squeezes through. Even now, remembering this shameful flight, Kassianov flushes and cries out or grimaces (in spite of Vishnevsky's joking). "Bastard," I yell, trying to wipe the foe off the face of the earth, erase him from my memory. I cannot forgive him the humiliation.

Kassianov knows: murderer, adulterer, envier, inveterate hog—he is all of them! And only on account of excessive love for himself (for his godlike image). And so, mighty acedia invades him—and it, too, is a sin. He begins to doubt all human values and the uniqueness of man's destiny.

Early in the morning he gets up to the ring of the alarm clock—bugle of the city barracks. In winter it is still dark, and Kassianov automatically flicks switches and presses obliging buttons as he gropes his way to the bathroom.

Immediately Vishnevsky starts shaving him, propping up the fleshy jowls with his tongue (like Chichikov) while Nape, eagle-eyed, watches the stream of hot water: as soon as the neighbor above turns on the faucet the pressure in our pipe decreases and, although there is usually quite enough water left, Nape takes instant, rigorous measures to keep the opponent in check. Looking at myself in the mirror, I suddenly remember how, the day before, I had asked the chief accountant "to stop cheating me" . . . and, recalling the incident, I grimace and yell out. (To be *ridiculed* is just as frightening to Kassianov in contemporary Manhattan as it was to Prince Andrei on the road near Esselsdorf in 1805.)

The dispute with the business office is a long-standing feud that has made Kassianov into something like a Cain. Please, holy Father, note: Kassianov's fee is given him only after the students have paid their full tuition. If, for instance, one of them has paid nine hundred of his thousand-dollar fee, the office informs Kassianov that his share is still to come. Revolting! For in all reason it would be legitimate to assume that ninety percent of what is Kassianov's due has been collected.

On this score I had frequent and noisy arguments with the accountant, each time deepening further the deadly rift between us. A thief who would wring the necks of a dozen orphans for a quick buck, the accountant virtuously robs Kassianov of hundreds of dollars in the interest of an anonymous multimillion-dollar institution. All this is beyond question—but why did Kassianov compliment him on his tie at the beginning of a decisive talk? Now my pride (I, mine, for me) cannot forgive God and the world and the wretched accountant—who is a homosexual to boot—this flattery. For some time, while Vishnevsky props up the massive jowl with his tongue and deftly wields the razor, I have been shouting in Nape's voice: "Why? What for? Don't! Why, why?" (In this way Nape tries, roughly and unceremoniously, to muffle my inner, self-critical voice.)

Then Kassianov busies himself with cleaning and scraping his teeth; only after his coffee will he glue the dentures firmly into place. In all these acts there is a need for strict consistency, and faithful Nape unerringly supervises the sequence of operations.

Here, usually a soft scratching can be heard from Zora's

quarters; Vishnevsky, Nape, and I cautiously look into her room. (Not too many years ago all of us still shared the same bed, and while Vishnevsky was his own vulgar self and Nape honestly fulfilled his obligations, I pondered the sordid metamorphoses of the soul. Heavenly Father, you remember, don't you, how I loved Zora!)

Thus we enter my wife's room. (From the bureau the big portrait of Markali smiles at us triumphantly. Dead, that glorious gypsy still seems to watch over her.) Zora is awake and expects her first cigarette. Her toilet and tea take up another half hour. It is only fair to note that Kassianov hardly ever grimaces or shouts during these procedures: "I, mine, for me" is relegated to the second or third plane. (And Vishnevsky and Nape stand motionless along the wall—two obedient, dumb sentinels.)

24

At last Kassianov goes to his car—with a bitter foretaste, particularly in fall and winter, of the many complications that may arise, what with cold, humidity, and an old motor. In such cases he is wont to invoke the Holy Trinity: automatically, as if Vishnevsky and Nape had now taken over the job of prayer and glorification.

But frequently he has to run to a garage for help. Then curses, angry outcries, and reproaches take the place of the laconic hosannas. The soul's keys reverberate, with full use of pedal, in an established scale, and, except for slight variations, the tune is always the same. There is nothing personal, conscious, life-giving in Kassianov's rage, despair, and supplications. He feels all the while that reality, full and sober, will take over further on—after the motor has started. But this too turns out to be an illusion: he still has to arrive at his destination, has to walk in and begin to work. Only then, supposedly, will he at long last be reinstated into his authentic existence.

So it became apparent that Kassianov's life, his real life, kept retreating in the face of a multitude of artificial, preparatory stages (and this too is a sin, but one for which I do not know the name). He had to wrestle endlessly with a host of imaginary monsters: entangled in an indestructible web of causality, he argued, raged, and cursed. And this struggle by no means satisfied him, for it transformed him into a hired hand, a slave, a gladiator. So that the question arose: why did Kassianov continue frantically to defend and affirm himself and all he stood for if it brought him no happiness whatever?

Once the car has warmed up properly and gets rolling, we again laud the Trinity. And again, this practice, taken up long ago, Kassianov without further conscious participation leaves entirely up to Nape & Co.—like a lesson that has been learned by heart once and for all. . . . It must be owned that, for the last twenty-five years, God has simply made no response to these tiresome calls. From all this, however, do not deduce that Kassianov is a nonbeliever. Quite the contrary.

Shatov, in *The Possessed,* deals with the problem in this way: "I . . . shall believe." Kassianov ought to say: "I . . . once believed." This former belief is an imperishable reality that has marked my life forever. (So does an old man, who has become too feeble to swim, still know that to abandon the shallows is possible and pleasant.)

Anyhow, such a weighty, complex question as a man's belief should have more than two mutually exclusive answers: yes or no. In contemporary physics, Father Nectarius, matter is wave and particle, and not wave and not particle—and still something else. Thus it is permissible to retort to the old-fashioned, inquiring voice (old-fashioned as a waltz tune): "Yes *and* no, and still something else that is neither."

Sometimes I wonder whether it is not with God as with the rest of our reality: love, matter, gravitation, time. We can conceive of worlds (some form of pocket or hole in the cosmos) where there is no matter, no gravitation, no time. Kassianov now lives without God because a sort of air pocket has formed in our cosmos and has swallowed up his entire sacred inventory.

By and large the best thing about God was said by a five-year-old girl: "Of course God exists, but I do not believe in Him."

Saint Augustine's is one of the possible experiences. . . . He struggled in silence and in darkness, he plagued God, he cried out, and suddenly The Other answered him. This proved sufficient for the saint once and for all.

As for Kassianov, a rather absurd thing happened to him: at the very beginning of his path, and quite undeservedly, God answered his lament. But before long the voice ceased to reach him, thick weeds overgrew the path, and now it seems impossible to break through.

That, in short, is how matters stand regarding my faith. Kassianov is by no means an atheist, quite the opposite; he is merely a heretic. And the Church needs heretics too—if only in order to bring them back to their senses. Yes, I believe in God but God does not always believe in me—and can you blame Him?

25

Having warmed up the motor, we (Vishnevsky, Nape, and I) are finally on our way. Around the corner, at the end of the block, we hit the first traffic light. In the summer, hidden by the heavy foliage of maples and chestnuts, this signal can only be detected right at the intersection. But now the days are getting shorter, the clouds in the sky thicker, and "the raucous caravan of geese has passed on southward."

Each time when, on turning the corner, he can again see the red or green light from afar, it is brought home to Kassianov that "a rather dismal season was approaching." The trees, grown bare, stand bony and shivering, anticipating no good from the days to come.

The next turn brings the first crisis. All in all, the entire way to the office (and what goes on before and after—life as a whole) consists of critical links, joined to each other by inexpressive hyphens.

Crisis Number One is the turn at the bridge where hosts of cars leave the expressway and enter the thoroughfare leading into the city. Here trucks have already created the usual traffic jam, so that one change of lights will certainly not be enough to let him through. In addition, all sorts of maniacs who have lost both patience and reason bear down upon you from the side streets. The torture of the ride is mainly this: one has to rely upon the common sense of an assembly of madmen, trust their judgment, have faith in their agility. If one had to adjust one's ideas about God or life or art to the whims and tastes of these people, what mortal collisions would occur at every turn! But here, armed with lethal motors, we all somehow adapt to each other—and make it. Considering the prevalence of stupidity and brutality, it is amazing how few accidents there are. Could Descartes be right when he says that man is gifted with perfect reasoning which he puts into action in crucial situations?

The next crisis occurs as we are drawn into the main artery: here a certain squaring of the circle has to be accomplished. . . . Suddenly the outpouring of six or seven roads has to find room on three lanes. You can imagine how the Vishnevskys in the other cars behave; as to our Nape, he bares his teeth threateningly, keeps turning the steering wheel sharply, and, undismayed by the cursing around him, pitilessly carves out his monolithic track.

It is hard to say where Kassianov himself dwells during this time. Only after the "knot" has been disentangled do I suddenly find myself and, by grimaces and other means, attempt to shake off and forget (erase) our fratricidal words and maneuvers. Meanwhile Vishnevsky is already winking at a girl in a Triumph, paying her ambiguous compliments: sitting at the wheel, in her truly minimal skirt, she offers to view the total infinity of her American legs.

I have barely brought Vishnevsky to his senses when Nape steps hard on the brake: another second and, tailgating as we were, we certainly would have caused a pile-up. (Nape distinguishes himself everywhere, fulfilling without delay the most unexpected and intricate assignments; and yet, in our culture, we despise him and barely admit him to the drawing room.)

On a straight stretch Vishnevsky steps on the gas—not evenly, but in spurts, as if ecstatically pumping an atomizer. Vishnevsky lacks sophistication but he is an observant fellow and he insists that this reminds him of an ejaculation: he is, as it were, irrigating the surroundings with a jet of semen, fertilizing the city, the air, the asphalt with himself (with me). So too, he swears, do the other Vishnevskys. It resembles the salmon's process of propagation.

Another critical moment: a railroad viaduct across the main artery. One lane of the road is taken up by the pillars supporting this obsolete structure. The stream of cars has to flow from three lanes into two—like the incoming tide that flows through a narrow neck from ocean into bay.

There are two such viaducts a short distance from each other. One has barely caught one's breath when one has to squeeze together again and seethe in the maelstrom. "You bastard, can't you see where you're going! Son of a bitch, I'll show you!"

26

By and large, Father Confessor, people no longer push each other around (literally, that is) or contrive to "slip through," as do automobile drivers on the road; our civilization has taught even louts to hold the door open and let ladies go first. But when our behavior passes through the filter of a car, it becomes impersonal, abstract. An anonym switches on an engine of two- or three-hundred horsepower and feels endowed with titanic forces; whereas in private life he suffers from piles or cough or sciatica and wheezes when he has to climb a flight of stairs—all of which tend to tame him. But at the wheel of his car he reverts for some reason to a Stone Age mentality (isn't it a paradox?).

There are two kinds of monsters on the road. Kassianov and his kind have only to switch on the motor and it is obvious to everyone that once upon a time they were placed behind the wheel of a car and taught how to drive. In the American wilderness, North or West, one finds the other sort, those who grew up at the wheel, car and driver constituting a whole, formed in one mold: contemporary centaurs of indefinite sex. These creatures are calm and amiable on the road; they let others pass them, certain that they will make it, will arrive in good time. Of course, they mostly travel along endless highways, through deserts or sparsely populated townships. (Extracted from their metal shells for an hour or so, these even-tempered centaurs very quickly change into mollusks or boa constrictors.)

In the meantime Nape has taken aim and now deftly enters the neighboring lane, speeds up, passes the narrow span under the viaduct, and swings back into "our" lane on the outside. If anybody else ever dared to perform such a caper under our very nose, Vishnevsky would be outraged. Here he snickers approvingly.

One can only marvel at the multitude of Vishnevskys and Napes flitting around us. Actually, three quarters of our lives are directed by those parasites. No, Kassianov does not resemble them. He has, from early youth, contemptuously ignored those vulgar people who live only for their own pleasure (I, mine, for me!) or worship some pallid idol such as Marx, Freud, or Darwin. Clearly, their failure in life is due to a false philosophy.

But how to explain my defeat? Dearest Father, Kassianov believed in God, went to confession, and received the sacraments. If now his life, toward its end, has come to resemble a barren desert or a town buried in sand, with only the remnants of an aqueduct visible (and ahead lies inevitable death), does this not mean that Kassianov has either confessed a false god or that he has served the True One badly? Dante's complaint is childish by comparison. Big deal: in the middle of his earthly wanderings he found himself in a dark wood. Kassianov, in the middle of his way, was afraid of nothing. But to find oneself, at the finish, on a desolate island, lost in the middle of a sea of glass. . . . When feeble legs give way, when the heart trembles and flutters and black spots dance before one's eyes—then, Father Nectarius, one cannot help but sink into despondency.

The life of a godless man is built on sand; such is the dialectic of godlessness. But how did it happen that Kassianov got stranded on a sandbank? This cannot be his fault, it seems, or not his alone.

So now I have made myself clear: acedia—(doubt and boredom)—deadly acedia is invading Kassianov. And perhaps this sin represents the sum, the fruit of all our vices put together.

27

Wherever in the flow of traffic brother Nape happens to be, within a few blocks, he, spurred on by Vishnevsky, will have taken up the position in which we are most likely to get ahead. So that the combination of my Vishnevsky and Nape can be considered extraordinarily lucky.

Nape would speed off into the distance, were it not for the traffic lights, the scourge of the modern city that curb individual initiative and level the chances of the first and the last. Thanks to the red light, gaps form between separate packs of cars. The green flashes, and the race is on in pursuit of those ahead. . . . (Thus will a new generation of professionals, fresh out of school, fling itself into public life and, given full freedom and sufficient time, is bound to catch up with the graduates of the previous generation; but the conventional red signals paralyze us, force us to step on the brake before catching up with the elders ahead of us.)

Nevertheless, toward the very end we all join the advance guard and merge with it. This resembles the vascular system: at the center arise separate waves and pulsations, but on the periphery, in the capillaries, the blood flows in a steady, unvarying stream. (Probably somewhere in the cosmos there also beats a mighty heart, ejecting the plasma of life in separate systoles—but at the outskirts these spontaneous explosions assume a viscous, homogenous character.)

Vishnevsky, shallow creature that he is, constantly complains that there are too many cars and that they make it difficult for him to concentrate. He is unable to grasp the fact that only thanks to the production of millions of cars can we, Vishnevsky and I, afford one. Everything—spare parts, service, gasoline—is easily available because the demand for it is so great. There are fewer airplanes made, and they cost ever so much more; as to a submarine, no private person could possibly afford the upkeep. Vishnevsky is by nature incapable of accepting this state of affairs: any generalization makes him sick. Whatever is unclear or contradictory he considers a fraud. "I can't understand this," he often says, and says it with such exhaustive impertinence that the challenger is immediately silenced.

"Air holes" (where there is neither time nor gravitation), an unsuccessful personal God (if one has lived by faith and turned out to be a failure), the traffic lights (which divide the generations), such creative thoughts satisfy and inspire Kassianov for a while. But they never effect a true transformation: at the next critical stage he again resents, rants, and reviles in the usual manner; and Nape and Vishnevsky immediately pop out like jack-in-the-boxes and chase after the foe in order to mete out punishment.

We approach the next danger point. Here seven roads merge and, by an evil magician, are turned into three. The vast plaza roars and trembles. Underground, beneath the grills, trains hiss and steam; above, on the viaducts, endless freight cars rattle along; and in the sky, just overhead, planes labor upward on their way overseas.

Heavenly Father, this deafening square of iron and concrete is surely the most senseless place in our universe. No medieval hero, no Roman, Greek, or Persian warrior would dare cross it without abundant sacrifices to the fickle gods. But Kassianov, quite casually, performs the trick twice a day. Every so often, however, painfully shrinking from the grating and grinding, his soul taps out its automatic praise of Father, Son, and Holy Ghost.

Characteristic of such critical junctions is the over-all feeling of insecurity they create in man. If only one could be certain to get through safely and on time, one's heart would not contract with such morbid impatience—Kassianov would not be in such a frenzy to overcome this particular unpleasant obstacle. Of course, Vishnevsky and Nape show their usual verve and spare no effort. They claim that if you don't push, you won't make it at all.

28

Anticipating somewhat, I want to say that returning home by way of this same screaming plaza in the evening, and faced with the same saturnalia, the same currents, whirlwinds, noises, and foul smells, Kassianov—one in an army of taxpayers who have finished their shift—often does not recognize it. Although still formidable, the plaza looks more lyrical, more spiritual, almost human.

One might say: the sun has set, the day is over, the exam is passed; some new plans have been conceived, poems written, dwellings constructed. . . . Consequently one is no longer the same, and the entire world, this plaza included, has changed too. In the morning we but strive to accomplish; now the job is done and, having added something to the universe, we can rest on our laurels or indulge in pleasant, painful, sinful games.

All this is so. Still, it does not fully explain why the terrifying plaza should seem different, transfigured, on the way back . . . why Kassianov actually admires the lyrical way in which the roads radiate from it. One begins to suspect that it is not the place in which we find ourselves but the direction (the tendency) that gives meaning to our life. (Heavenly Father, why is it that Kassianov wants so much to understand Your creation and to bless it? But every day Job's wife—or Vishnevsky—whispers to him: "Curse God and die.")

Having ordered Vishnevsky to keep quiet and assigned the driving to Nape, Kassianov, in his illusory solitude, gives himself over to reveries: he is engaged in the construction of a model of the simplest stable universe, a game that has attracted him from youth and even helped him in his academic career.

He sees life, or a day, an hour, a minute, as an unbroken, harmoniously spreading sphere; but life—every moment of it—also consists of separate, solid, critical points that war with one another. If matter is wave *and* particle, if light is wave *and* photon, if continuous time can be broken down into chronons, then human life, which, as a whole, is a blown-up wavelike balloon, also consists of the limitless quantity of our critical movements: actons. And the same for personality: on the one hand it is a continuous presence expanding into eternity; on the other it is a hive of microscopic particles, personons, rotating around their own axis.

In "The New Sociology," a short course for advanced students, Kassianov formulates his theory as follows. Personons are the quanta of personality, the smallest units of the true essence of a person. Actons are the quanta of a person's external actions. If the personality is a harmonious whole, its actons are essentially equal to its personons—or at least approximate them. But as soon as we become fragmented, our actons no longer correspond to our personons; they become nothing but the sad reflection of the Vishnevskys and Napes who dwell within us.

I suspect, Father Confessor, that this kind of philosophizing is sinful, but I do not know to which sin it should be accredited—as to vanity, there is no trace of it. I guess it is all sounding brass. But sounding brass will also be useful in the chorus of the seraphim (once light and love have established themselves throughout).

More than anywhere else, Kassianov is seized by a philosophical mood, by a yearning for imaginative elaborations, on the narrow, fenced-off lane that is part of the bridge crossing the river. This isolated lane, where a long-defunct trolley car used to run, has been given over to passenger cars exclusively. The special feature of this blessed section of the road is that, having entered on it, cars must proceed in single file: no passing or cutting in! Thus, all competition, ill will, envy, and pride, all fighting, cease for the duration of this sanctuary. For a while we can be peaceful travelers, pilgrims on our way to holy places. Neither Marx nor Darwin nor Freud-Adler-Jung hold sway. It is as if some healing balm has been poured onto our souls, bringing with it the promise of a complete cure.

But the fanciful improvisations, the bay below, the skyscraper windows smiling from afar (where free photons choose their way of reflection, similar to those personons in me that spontaneously bless life), this whole miracle of real existence, seen from the narrow lane, turns out to be surprisingly shaky. As soon as we reach the ramp of the bridge where a new crisis awaits us, we immediately, as one mob, begin to snarl at one another in accordance with our ancient dog-nature. Cursing, Vishnevsky joins with Nape and nimbly leads us into the wide bed of the traffic stream; we are all in a rush to get on, to get it over with, heavenly Father, for here nothing makes sense.

If people were engaged only in dignified, ennobling activities, they would most probably rid themselves of the dubious need for using their elbows and clenching their teeth in such a wolfish manner.

29

The last crisis of the beginning of the working day approaches; one more outburst of atoms, photons, chronons, actons, personons. Vishnevsky searches with one eye for a suitable parking space while evaluating with the other the seductive legs of the young girls who are rushing to their offices (the older ones come a little later). Nape turns the steering wheel with deft precision, and Kassianov can barely manage to restore some order in his unique and, after all, immortal soul.

Because our institute is a privileged one, the city has reserved a minuscule parking lot in the center of town for the use of the employees. But there is not room for everybody. It is very simple—even in antiquity, to judge by the Scriptures, many were called but few were chosen.

The cunning arrive early, only to encounter the cars of private citizens, since it is apparently legal to park there for the night, until 8:00 A.M. From this ambiguity there ensue explosive situations, limited in time but fraught with many dangers, from violent arguments to fist fights (all recklessly promoted by the Vishnevskys and Napes).

And so our trip, broken up into a multitude of critical knots or beads, can, in its entirety, be considered as one necklace. Now the working period begins, which, in its turn, is fragmented into separate links. And then: the trip home, the evening, the night, the weekend, all of them new strands of beads. Holidays are supposed to be outside the usual fatal necessities and causalities; at such times a workingman is meant to be free to choose any trajectory, any direction. . . . Yet, once his goal is fixed, the city dweller begins his murderous pushing and snarling and again he crumbles under pride and anger and envy.

Those who travel by bus or subway have to pass through their own particular series of critical tangles (like astronauts on their way to Mars in a multistaged rocket): from house to subway—cross busy thoroughfare; first train—wait for it, get on; change to express—don't miss this one. (Why is it our earthly habit to call the train we have missed "ours"? It would be so simple and so much more in accordance with reality to say, "My train is the next one!") Then to office or workshop—push through the crowded streets. Every block, every crossing and traffic light is a critical point, a bead, an acton. Of course, those who take a cab are subjected to yet other accidental explosions and crosscurrents.

Having arrived at the Institute, one must first of all reach the right floor. Here I again ask Nape and Vishnevsky for assistance. They maneuver with such persuasiveness and grace that Kassianov floats up in the very first express elevator.

At work, the chain of paroxysms and breaking points, reinforced by competitiveness, ambition, greed, and even lust, has been so firmly established long ago that one would have to be a saint (or in love) to free oneself from it. I, along with Vishnevsky and Nape, have professional rank. In the past, our talents contributed to a scientific journal, a geriatric club, and a church-affiliated philanthropic organization. Wherever we went we brought with us, apart from the desire to earn as much and work as little as possible, the classic elements of pride, envy, and ill will, which, by the way, were shared by our colleagues.

Against my own egotistical actons move all the actons of animate and inanimate nature: we paralyze one another. Only rarely does a person appear who knows how to synchronize the flow of his personons with our actons. (When you were near me, saintly Father, I was always aware of this synergy.)

30

Periodic crises are inherent in the activities of a professor, too. Different strands of the professional yarn are forever getting tangled into "knots." Kassianov teaches only five hours a week, but at every point, at every single step he makes, undercurrents and hidden reefs manifest themselves in the form of competition, violent ambition, malice, and pride.

Preparing himself for the lectures takes another fifteen hours or so. The library and the seminars in their turn are riddled with characteristic explosions (where personons and actons are emitted). To reach the reading room on the seventeenth floor, one has to pick the right elevator: the choice lies between express and local. . . . By taking the express to the eighteenth floor and then running down one flight of stairs one could save time and energy. However, by capricious orders of the police or fire department, not all the doors leading to the stairway are always open, so that some poor wretch could wander about the endless gray corridors for hours, if not forever.

Any meeting with colleagues—especially with one's superiors—is yet another hurdle that can be cleared only by bringing into play all seven mortal and a dozen venial sins. This, spiritual Father, thoroughly upsets Kassianov's inner peace and later, in front of the mirror, leads to moans and painful grimaces.

The cafeteria, too, is a spawning ground of crises . . . to be there the moment it opens, to get a seat both comfortable and removed from the gossips, the arrogant and vulgar—else there is no keeping Vishnevsky in check! (To find oneself at the same table with some tooth-picking handyman is no joy either.)

Two or three hours a day are devoted to meetings with members of the administration or heads of research departments. Here the critical junctions are especially fraught with danger, since the careers of all participants are directly involved. The same principle as that in automobile traffic is at work. . . . On the road, the flow from five lanes suddenly has to find room in three; here, it is projects, grants, endowments: quite simply, there are not enough funds to go around. Yet everyone wants to grab a juicy morsel for himself and for his dear ones—without delay.

The work with the students—tests, correction of papers, encouragement of talented youths (and hanky-panky with the co-eds)—also abounds in crises.

All these activities fit neatly one into the other, like toy eggs of various sizes that eventually are placed into the one basic, brightly colored, absurd, huge egg.

The constantly changing barriers and obstructions on our path can only be cleared in a satisfactory manner if a certain timing is maintained, that is, if they are taken in the established tempo and proper order! (The traffic lights installed at every turn in a civilized society prevent a young upstart from quickly and unobtrusively overtaking his competitors.)

Sex assumes a special urgency in our institution. Around every corner you come upon bevies of young secretaries, lab workers, co-eds, most of them somewhat dependent on Vishnevsky and, like true gamblers, ready to risk their all in the hope of winning the jackpot. In addition there are young girls from private schools who attend special lectures. All this, of course, creates an atmosphere of rampant temptation, so that the administration feels obliged to assume the role of guardian and suppress the most innocent flirtations (thereby only further inflaming the carnal instincts). Incidentally, those young girls from private schools and from very wealthy families have all been long since initiated into the basic biological mysteries. Meeting them in the corridors, Vishnevsky outdoes himself in glowing descriptions of "our shack" on the shore. (You remember, dearest Father, that when Kassianov invited the Filipino girl, he was not quite certain who actually had set that dubious adventure into motion!)

While the spluttering Vishnevsky weaves his trite intrigues and Nape stares coarsely, I try to create the impression of a man of the world, a man of culture and charm. Above all, Kassianov wants these sweet girls to walk off thinking: what an interesting man! How intelligent and sensitive! It is this praise that his distorted pride craves for some reason.

31

Pride is always the same, but it appears in different forms. Thus a tiger's aggressive instinct manifests itself in quite another manner from that of a weasel or a buffalo.

The lust of one man is nourished by a plump, stupid blonde, another is inflamed by an aggressive dark-haired floozy, while a third will be aroused only at the sight of a high-heeled, well-worn pump. So it is with pride. There are those who want to be considered intelligent, others crave the reputation of being kindhearted or generous, while yet others seek recognition in some out-of-the-way realm with which they often have only the most tenuous connection. Pride is one, and lust is one, and so are anger, envy, gluttony, avarice, and sloth, but the expression of these passions varies. And so the question arises: are not perhaps the separate mortal sins, those seven or more iniquities, only different reflections of the one eternal cardinal evil—self-love? (I, for me, mine!)

Yet, in the course of the leisurely examination of his daily activities, Kassianov has arrived at the conclusion that it is only thanks to passions and trespasses that his life (in symbiosis with Vishnevsky and Nape) has preserved a certain minimal amount of meaning. Without his harmful proclivities he would probably resemble nothing more than a piece of dough, a lump of unleavened bread, a half-cooked pancake. As a result of such thoughts, Kassianov is overcome by acedia, by a complete, if only temporary, disgust with both his own nature and with that of a universe riddled with empty holes.

I repeat, most virtuous Father, acedia—boredom and doubt—is a mortal sin, not because it is in itself bad for Kassianov to question his own worth, but because acedia always follows in the wake of our intimate participation in all available sins. It is the avowal of our complete helplessness (mine and the Lord's). We declare, as it were, Yes, the stuff of man and of the world is rotten at the roots and can never be set right again.

From this muddle Kassianov has often been saved by postquantum physics. Only think: the world as wave can be perfect; as particle, repulsive. (And there is still a third possibility.) It is true, God is omnipotent and all-loving. But in separate settings! As "particle" God is omnipotent; as wave He is all-loving. In His aspect as particle, the Creator is a personal, living God; in His wave form He dispassionately embraces nature as a whole and completely merges with it. And there is still a third possibility.

Incidentally, it is impossible to inoculate Vishnevsky and Nape with this new point of view. (Even I myself, in the heat of the struggle for survival, often ignore these new revelations.) Note, Father Nectarius, that more and more often Vishnevsky slips us some wine or vodka. . . . His favorite expressions: Take it easy, enjoy yourself, forget all that!

Forget. . . . There is a lethal poison in this prescription

of Vishnevsky's. By some strange coincidence, Kassianov has too often forgotten precisely that which for his salvation he ought to have remembered, and has remembered firmly that which should have been quickly forgotten (which perhaps never really existed).

It appears that we are dealing with an unhappy combination of two complex mechanisms, memory and oblivion. There seem to be two centers in our depths, two focuses (as in an ellipse) connected with the past.

We know there are two custodians of sleep: one that pushes us toward the state of unconsciousness, the other stimulating us to wakefulness . . . and we can achieve and preserve sleep by influencing either of these control systems.

Kassianov believes something similar happens with memory. One of its centers prompts an account of the past, conservation of what existed; the other center obscures, smooths out, washes away what has been—all this supposedly serving the notorious mechanism of self-preservation.

Of course, there is also a third element: the paths, channels, and branches along which memory from its subterranean depths delivers past events up to the light of consciousness. This is why we are able, by concentrating during confession (as if forcing our way through clogged pipes) to remember what we seemed to have thoroughly forgotten.

Due to our unchecked "progress," we no longer notice what we are doing when pressing the infinitude of switches and buttons by which we are surrounded. It is not that we *forget* whether we pushed the elevator button or properly locked the front door: we simply never carried out these acts (in a meaningful way). Thus there is an ever-increasing accumulation of holes, "vacuum pockets," in the consciousness of contemporary man, a piling up of shadows and ghosts, of hulls of ships that never sailed, and of skeletons of imaginary, prematurely delivered babies.

While on the other hand, we tenaciously preserve somewhere on the bottom age-old worries, atavistic dreams, and cave-men habits—an arsenal that ought to have been buried long ago for the harmful odious trash it is.

Kassianov gets out of bed and gropes his way to the bathroom. While he is shaving (between the first and second lather), I decide to brush my teeth and . . . the brush is wet and shows traces of toothpaste. Heavenly Father, wherein lies the secret? Why does this frighten me as if it were some horrid animalistic perversion? Who managed, when, and by what means, to wash and comb himself, in my presence, with my hands, but without my notice?

Nape only does what was assigned to him long ago; as to Vishnevsky, he is probably not able to make any sustained, worth-while effort. So it was done by them and not by them, and by yet another, a third, in Kassianov who unites them all (and at the same time somehow distorts everything).

32

How many more such mysterious spirits are buried in our depths? How easy for one of those blithe fellows who orders me about to make a fatal mistake! And in the end it looks as if it were Kassianov who has broken the Ten Commandments and been tempted by seventy times seven mortal sins and must therefore personally answer for everything. One more heresy, most serene Father: could it be that even his selfless, disinterested acts were not performed by him either (or not only by him)?

I know of course that there is a conscious participation in our good, loving, human (heavenly) acts: Kassianov remembers very well indeed the occasions when he chose the narrow path, remembers, too, that there he was not involved with push buttons and automatic gadgets.

In the morning Kassianov gets out of bed—and it seems that it is not I who have awakened! Half the movements and maneuvers that follow this awakening are accomplished by one does not know whom. For the information of a remote and happier posterity, it might be useful to draw up a list of actions we execute in passing, unawares.

Literature has preserved Homer's account of the ships that sailed to the walls of Troy; there is also Melville's description of the different kinds of whales; these are sublime pages, pages that can inspire the young to heroic deeds. But the list of Man's Automatic Actions fills me with fear, heavenly Father, like some bestial vice, some loathsome heresy, like fire and brimstone, like castration (not Origen's straightforward castration but a new, spiritual and intellectual maiming). Automatism, apparently, is the eighth mortal sin, and of this one Kassianov is wholly guilty.

Much that goes on in bathroom or marketplace escapes our consciousness (Kassianov is often uncertain whether he has paid for his newspaper or received the change).

In a movie theater, he always wonders how it happened that he has landed on the seat he is occupying (to the left of the entrance, without fail).

Embracing a woman when no special feelings are involved, one does not know how it all came about (actually, one does not see the lips one is kissing).

Running into the frigid surf—into a lake or a river—we do not understand who urges us into this agony and why. But for some reason one stubbornly dives in. And all the other agonies that await us also result from the interplay of autonomous centers that were meant to protect us from annihilation. (This is why Kassianov has come to hate the notorious mechanism of so-called self-defense, and considers it an obsolete relic.)

In church we bow and cross ourselves at the appropriate parts of the service, all the while aware only of how dexterously the old man next to us crosses himself: like a jockey wielding his short whip in the home stretch. And all around is the strong familiar mixture of faith, festive boredom, and hypocrisy.

Without thought you down a jigger of vodka and then bite off something salty or smoked—always in the same way; or automatically you prepare the accustomed cocktail, adding twice the gin. This same "absent-mindedness" causes you to dial a telephone number leaving out the last digit (or "feeling" that you have left it out).

The letter is written, the envelope addressed, sealed, stamped, and deposited in the mailbox; suddenly it hits you —did you put down the town, the street number . . . ?

Who started the engine and turned on the radio?

Bringing his car to a halt, the city dweller stacks away his glasses, turns off the lights, rolls up the window, crawls out with much grunting, newspaper tucked under his arm, locks the door, deposits the keys in his left pocket, and trudges the several blocks home. Next morning he has no idea where he has parked the car.

At solitaire, you do not recall how many times you have laid out the cards—is it twice or the third, the last, time?

Smoking . . . Kassianov once was about to light a cigarette while another, freshly lit, hung from the corner of his mouth. (It was then that he finally renounced this slavish habit.)

When looking for a job you ask for information, fill out forms, and wait. You wait—in offices, airports, hospitals—always with the same undifferentiated boredom and impatience.

Sawing wood, shoveling snow, cooking, washing, ironing, knitting—are we doing it or someone else?

You build a fire in the grate—always with the same feelings. Skiing, sailing, tennis: anything demanding precision excludes delay (and reflection).

In chess: the manner in which you move a piece or take one is always the same (repeatable)—whatever kind of game, and whoever your opponent.

The thought cycles before sleep, while slowly fading out: lust, karate (power, strength), applause around you (fame). The same, always the same.

You court a woman, using your charm and power of persuasion—the same style, the same handwriting.

33

At exhibitions and auctions, in the zoo among children and animals, you enter into a many-times-experienced, specific milieu and immediately start behaving according to a set pattern (as if on ball bearings).

You deposit money and checks in the bank as if you were an automaton; you do what is asked of you—sloppily and with aversion you sign your name on seven different slips.

At a reception, a gathering of friends, you hold a glass and a cigarette and you chatter: you always say the same things, although the words are different—certain ones for the beauty, others for the celebrity, still others for the misfit.

At lunch and dinner, you chew and drink away as usual, most of the time quite unconsciously. You fulfill your professional obligations blindly, automatically—at least in those areas where the technical side predominates.

You trim the Christmas tree and set the holiday table according to a once-and-for-all established routine.

Ceremonies, parades, public occasions, *Te Deums*, weddings, funerals—we take part in them mechanically; without thinking we listen to a foreign national anthem or an unfamiliar funeral service with respectful indifference or only slight curiosity.

Thus it is that three quarters of our lives fit into a rigid mold. And Kassianov has little room and time left for free, personal moves. (And yet only those acts of ours that cannot be classified and calculated in advance will eventually be considered the genuine measure of our lives.)

The young bride has not yet learned to answer to her new

name; each time it surprises, elates, or saddens her . . . but soon she will get used to it; there will be no more surprise or elation. During the entire course of the year we mechanically date our letters with the current anno Domini; only directly after New Year does one write down that figure consciously, with a mental effort (wondering or ruing).

We walk, as we breathe, without thinking about it, mechanically: soldiers are known to have fallen asleep on their feet. (Kassianov has sometimes nodded astride a horse, and even on a bicycle, at night.)

You are ill—you cough, you take your temperature, gargle, swallow some medicine, and eventually get well again (or die), all according to an established routine.

We hand a beggar a coin, hastily, absent-mindedly, to be rid of his bothersome presence, and manage to inject charity with a cruel automatism.

Even indifference is automatic! It is possible that all our fixed behavior patterns stem from indifference—to the surroundings, the passers-by, to all the ordinary and miraculous reflections of photons. So that indifference assumes the proportions of a supreme sin. Did not Saint John the Divine wail: I would thou wert cold or hot . . . ? (Heavenly Father, is it possible to commit a mortal sin consciously, really knowing what one is doing?)

Kassianov dresses automatically: trousers, shoes (when and by whom was he taught to tie his laces?), shirt, jacket, then deposits the necessary objects into their appointed pockets. Wallet, left back-pocket; check book, right. (Thus all his life: only instead of the checks there used to be a gun.)

We often take over some odd mannerism from an acquaintance, copy a facial expression we consider original or attractive. At first this borrowed tic (a sigh, perhaps, or a gesture) is a conscious act of imitation, but soon it too turns into a dead reflex. And then comes the moment when Kassianov suddenly realizes: he bought the hideous yellow pullover after seeing J in a canary-colored vest; picked up the sarcastic sigh plus bellow from his friend T.

I'm afraid our entire image is composed of a multitude of odds and ends gathered at different periods of our life. Kassianov says "I'm sorry, but . . ." exactly the way a famous political emigré usually began his speeches; he moves the piece on the chess board à la Alekhine (screwing it into its square); leads his dog on the leash like the late Prince S.

Alas, the older a man and the wider his interests and connections, the more artful a collage of alien, acquired habits he presents. Not only external mannerisms but inner traits too: sympathies, convictions, beliefs. We sin, and it is as if not we had committed the sin: Kassianov is being punished and yet it is not he for whom the punishment is intended.

Here he is, picking his nose distractedly; the purpose accomplished, he experiences the same feeling of gratification as after the conclusion of some important business deal. (So, too, in the bathroom!) And the practical joker who has deafeningly broken wind afterward behaves for a whole hour like a conqueror.

How absurd all this is: a well-accomplished mechanical act rises to our consciousness as a creative achievement. The feeling of satisfaction, whether from a copious evacuation or a well-played game of bridge, lingers long in us (or in the memory of our cells).

34

We tend to consider as generally valid, typical for mankind as a whole, what is, in fact, individual or unaccountable in ourselves. So Vishnevsky childishly asserts that we all experience the same feeling of boredom and annoyance when signing our names; that we all, with similar absent-mindedness, lock our doors; all copulate in the same rhythm as Kassianov. . . .

Perhaps we could be compared to the latest edition of a standard dictionary: the same words—but the examples are different; or to a new textbook of orthodox arithmetic: the same four rules laid out in the usual sequence—only the problems are changed.

The accustomed is reality to us and the unexpected seems fantastic. . . . If we think it over soberly, it is precisely what was assimilated long ago that is madness. Truly, it is hard to imagine anything more absurd than starving children, prisons, wars, and exemplary bordellos—and yet they have been with us from time immemorial.

We are ready to accept any established nightmare, but if we are suddenly confronted by an unexpected reality we do not recognize it as authentic. This is unbelievable! No, no, it can't be! (when the president of the Republic is assassinated. Or during other eruptions of eschatological forces).

Automatically we execute many acts while engrossed in unrelated (sometimes important, sometimes petty or dirty) thoughts. But there are also "mechanical" actions in which we lose ourselves completely and experience something akin to celestial bliss. This happens in the fever of gambling, hunting, and love—our last available forms of catharsis. Father Nectarius, we are haunted by two categories of automatism, one characterized by boredom, sloth, death, the other by elation and inspiration. (But in both one loses oneself—partially or fully.)

We do not *forget* what has been performed mechanically. No, it is outside of us or beneath our existence. And we do not *remember* acts of rapture, ecstasy, creative upsurge, because they are above, beyond, us. (Vishnevsky is whispering in my ear that I ought not to hold forth on such tedious subjects.)

In order to clarify matters Kassianov began to unite various quotidian expressions of human nature into different groups. For example: struggle, defense, taking examinations —order of trials. Another group: boredom (waiting). A third: games (women). So that Kassianov's life could be reduced to five or six groups of occupations requiring only mechanical activity (and that is sinful!).

Anything solely automatic (doglike, conditioned) lacks fantasy and inspiration, and therefore has no real weight; for, whatever he does, man in his entity must also simultaneously create, imagine, and uplift himself mentally. A prayer mechanically produced, a job accomplished without inspiration, even an act deemed heroic or saintly, if automatically performed, cannot possibly attain its end and so is wasted.

And meanwhile our civilization keeps multiplying the legions of buttons we press unceremoniously, without paying them any heed. Afterward we try in vain to remember: what happened? what did I do? and it is impossible to dig up anything from within our consciousness. (Similarly, a man who suffers from cancer cannot find the cure for the dread disease in himself: his cells, too, do not know what they are doing.)

Without imagination, without memory and consciousness, and without thoughts of immortality there can be no full reality. Rather, there is hell.

The first paradise was natural, childlike (before experience and memory); the last Eden, which cannot be described since the needed words are buried deep within our cells, will be a full elucidation, complete consciousness, the triumph of incarnated and nonincarnated reality.

Our self-defense mechanism has long since become distorted and therefore we often forget what is indispensable for a happy life. The memory of it has drowned in the depths of our cells and vegetates there in a state of paralysis. And it may be that an answer to what is most important and necessary, a life-saving answer, lies close by, lost on the bottom—like a sunken, disabled submarine still waiting for help from above.

The never-ending succession of artificially linked, automatic maneuvers creates a certain psychological chain reaction that explodes the living entity of a person. This string of instinctive acts relentlessly chokes Kassianov: this automatism is evil, Father Nectarius. It is the supercardinal, the besetting sin. The play of those blind systems is nothing but an expression of that famous self-defense instinct which more often than not leads man toward his ruin. Only imagine a drowning man "fighting for survival" pulling to the bottom the friend who tries to save him.

Yes, the primitive (acquired) subconscious self-defense mechanism must be abolished if we are to overcome sin and sickness, old age and death. The older the reflexes and associations, the more heavily they weigh on us and cripple us. This entire biological apparatus is no longer needed, it is time to crush it.

But what, holy Father, will then be left of us (in us). . . ?

35

In order to remember what was forgotten (and important), Kassianov must as it were haul up a parchment scroll from a dark vault and attempt to read it in full daylight. Here the following elements come into play:

1 the underground where, either in order or disorder, the decaying papyri are stored;
2 a clear mind able to decipher hieroglyphics;
3 the channels of communication through which the secret writing is transmitted upward; and, finally,
4 a medium, some putty or plasma, evenly distributed on all layers and inside the channels, uniting Vishnevsky, Nape, and me (and every single cell of ours), branding this particular creature with one indelible mark, one sign, one charge.

Watch Kassianov trying to remember something: it is on the tip of his tongue (on the border of consciousness) but does not yield. . . . And suddenly, miraculously, it rises from the dust, floats up in its entirety, smoothly emerges into the open, into full daylight.

Does this not mean that all along, while Kassianov was

trying to find it, it had been lying, squashed, weighted down, stirring and whimpering in the darkness, striving to float up but unable to make its way?

A network of cables and channels stretches between the blind memory of the cells and the center of consciousness, a network through which the quanta of memory, the memoirons, have to pass. If these passages have become clogged —through neglect, old age, sickness, or stupidity—the memoirons, ever-present in the cells and full-blooded though they are, will not be able to rise to the strata of consciousness, clarity, and light.

After all, Father Nectarius, it often happens that we forget our diverse voluntary and involuntary trespasses, only to remember them much later . . . does this not prove that the lines of communication can be interrupted temporarily and, possibly, forever?

My cells grab everything, preserve and remember everything. . . . This is their self-defense mechanism functioning *ad absurdum:* not to lose anything of what was acquired in the past (even if it has become superfluous or harmful ballast)—that is the device! For the cells, too, are greedy, egotistic, lecherous, envious, irascible, and brimful with pride.

If, ages ago, this self-defense mechanism helped preserve Kassianov (at the stage of mollusk or amphibian), it is now completely outdated, and whoever continues to use it is preparing his own doom. For what benefited a crab may well turn out to be man's ruin. . . . He who loves himself too much condemns himself to death.

Kassianov feels that already a catastrophic fragmentation has taken place in each of his molecules. There we are—Vishnevsky, Nape, and me. . . . For the longest time now, each of us has been singing his own boring aria (and we are hopelessly out of tune). Each of us would like to expand at the cost of his neighbor, and every cell of ours in its turn tends to invade the neighboring plot like a malignant tumor.

What if we were to abolish, uproot those forms of self-defense we have accumulated throughout the ages? What if we were to go back to the sources of confidence and love that nourished us at the dawn, in childhood?

Death and sicknesses and horrible sins set in because we obliterated something of ultimate importance (while preserving intact all the ancient reflexes that have become useless or harmful).

I seek to correct this fatal mistake, but Vishnevsky and Nape, active in every cell of mine, march down the banal path and paralyze my well-intentioned beginnings. And so acedia invades the stage! Kassianov envisages a classical Greek tragedy with Vishnevsky, Nape, seven furies, and a pack of dogs (falsehood, sickness, death) tearing the doomed "I" to pieces. Only a single guardian angel still defends it—against all odds.

According to the ancient Orphic myth, the Titans murdered and devoured Dionysus, son of Zeus; Zeus retaliated by burning the Titans with lightning. Then, from their now semidivine ashes, he created man. (And I, created from inspired dust, am for some reason again being devoured by Titans.)

Kassianov thirsts to do good; he does not want to do evil. Nevertheless, he daily multiplies the evil in our world and is not able to sanctify his life. An impasse! And Saint Paul cannot convince me that all this is for the greater glory of God. (You, Father Nectarius, I have never doubted.)

36

The effort to "remember" the essential (unchanged) can be likened to the effort of recovering from an illness, getting back on one's feet, overcoming an attacker; this Kassianov knows, this he vaguely recalls. But, tired or in the clutches of sloth, we surrender: we no longer strive to re-establish what was lost (stand up, get well, save ourselves). . . . What is more, this condition of complete defeat no longer appalls us: we have reconciled ourselves to it.

Once, dear Father, Kassianov lost a certain word and, over a period of five years, tried vainly to retrieve it. . . . Then he gave up. In emigration, language withers and the first words to fall into the abyss are those connected with some old, abolished way of life. (So, with advancing age, does one suddenly become aware of the blurring of the secondary sexual characteristics.) And this is particularly hard on those who cultivate their language (or their sexual life).

Isn't it ridiculous? I forgot an outdated word (some heraldic term or other). What of it? Who cares? Tomorrow I'll remember or try to find it in the dictionary. "Why this tendency to make a tragedy out of everything?" (Vishnevsky).

No, dearest Father, it is not a question of one obsolete noun. It is a question of the pathological, senile changes that lead toward the twilight, toward a no man's land.

And, all along, that little word from the age of chivalry is on the tip of my tongue; just one more effort and Kassianov will fish it out from the murky depths, bring it back to life and illuminate it. (One more resurrection in our dying world.)

Vishnevsky ever more insistently claims that after a day's work it is normal to finish a bottle of wine and then sleep peacefully without need of pills or capsules. But quite possibly Burgundy played a crucial role in the story of the vanished word. Alcohol dulls our faculties. But alcohol is not alone in producing this effect: life in general, with its poisonous residues, works in the same direction. Waste products settle down and gradually clog our consciousness (the central, the master-consciousness, and that of every cell in particular).

Many "incurable" diseases are only the result of a damaged memory. The organism as a whole and certain groups of cells in particular forget some vitally needed sequence of activities and begin to rush about chaotically, in a panic, intent only on their own limited comfort and welfare. The result: ulcer, coronary, cancer. The cause of these disasters does not lie with the Creator of the universe but with ourselves. He continues sending us His signals but we no longer struggle to register, decipher, and understand them, muffled as they are.

Finally we run to the pharmacy, buy medicine and gulp it down, and if we are lucky the mixture brings our cells back to their senses. . . . In the same way, having forgotten a name, an expression, a formula, I can set off for the library to look up in an encyclopedia the familiar, lost definition, the one that, I know, lies in a rusty casket somewhere on the bottom (like my youth, my love).

But what do we achieve by this method? We must carry the fight to the roots, to the causes of this paralysis or semi-consciousness, instead of attacking accidental, external manifestations. (It is Vishnevsky who always comes out in favor of palliatives. Nape hates all medications. As for Kassianov, he is equally revolted by the fact that he has forgotten the now so important word and that, should he remember it by chance, it would not make him happy.)

The word lies in me, reposes somewhere; only the lines of communication are interrupted—temporarily or perhaps forever. Between my center and my periphery there is no longer any intelligible exchange: and this is sin, sickness, another fall.

It was not the medieval term Kassianov wanted to recover, not only that. He wanted to overcome sickness, death, the faintness of body and soul. A library is a temporary salvation; it offers from the outside a milligram of life-giving (alien) sap, similar to an injection of insulin or cortisone. But it will not renew silty tissues or make them whiter than the snow.

37

Heavenly Father, Kassianov remembers perfectly the nature of that word and he cannot conjure it up. A term from the days of chivalry, it refers, I believe, to a coat of arms, an emblem, escutcheon, seal, signet, or some such thing. As a matter of fact, it may well be one of the above-mentioned terms (which, isolated from its natural milieu and only mechanically pronounced, is unrecognizable and useless to me).

Being of foreign origin and belonging to an alien social structure, heraldic terminology is not included in Soviet reference books; there is no need for it. Russia never was a feudalistic country in the Western sense; the boyars were flogged at times but, not feeling in the least dishonored, continued, loyal and faithful, to serve their tsar. So that this word can hardly appear in the works of Tolstoi, Dostoevski, or Chekhov. . . . It definitely appears in translations of Sir Walter Scott, or in other novels of tournaments and knights in armor. But there are few such books in our (portable) emigré libraries.

If Kassianov had a Russian copy of *Ivanhoe* he would surely dig up the term there . . . it lies at the bottom of my every cell, while above, as over silty pebbles, the waters of consciousness flow without touching, without noticing it.

Kassianov does not hear a sound from the lost one, but he constantly senses it, as he senses you, Father. . . . In the same way we discern the faces of faraway, lost friends, of beloved companions, dead and gone: it seems we have only to stretch out a hand to reach and touch them. But thick dull glass inexorably separates us, and Kassianov, like some ugly tropical fish that strikes the dark-green walls of an aquarium, is continuously stopped by this translucent but very real barrier.

I repeat, it is not merely a question of one insignificant word. I have also forgotten and keep forgetting many other things. In vain I strive to retrieve, ravish, incarnate (what formerly I achieved beyond all merit). About and within us whole systems gradually die off, are covered with dross—and there are not enough pharmacies and Sir Walter Scotts around to solve the important existential problems.

Of course, one may say that we humans must reconcile ourselves to losses, to oblivion (and to death); legions of honest citizens have accepted such a point of view and continue zealously to work for the common weal.

But Kassianov is a stubborn and probably a stupid man. He still does not believe that his father (the third, as the count goes) was killed twenty years ago, that M really disappeared without trace, and, lastly, that someday he, like all his contemporaries, will be lowered into the damp soil and be left there alone. I suspect, heavenly Father, that this is precisely what *will* happen; I even understand; but I do not truly believe that this same dirty trick will be played on me too.

There is a certain similarity here with the vanished "heraldic" term. Kassianov has forgotten it temporarily but that it has vanished for good, that it will never be incarnated in him again, to this he cannot consent. (What if he were to strain once more, very hard . . . ?)

Because Kassianov's anxiety at times assumed pathological proportions, Vishnevsky, behind my back, consulted a physician who prescribed the latest tranquilizers—those medications that lull the mind and paralyze memory and will. But Kassianov knew he still had to make the ultimate effort to raise this word from its grave, this word that already stank after its three-day sleep; that he would have to suck it up through clogged pipes and capillaries. (Up and down are only symbolic expressions in this case, like east and west for astronauts in space.)

And suddenly this covert search for the word turned into an epic struggle with death, evil, and sin. . . . This is what Kassianov understood as his duty! Anything else seemed to him only sounding brass. By the way, Father Nectarius, all along I continued to care assiduously for my paralyzed wife and, of course, to love her (as well as a few others).

The resurrection of Lazarus, spiritual Father, or your future resurrection and mine, is indeed only the re-establish-ment of a "word": perhaps some other word (not the one from the time of knight-errantry) but still a word . . . or an act, or a situation, a nutritive process, normal metabolism, eternal loving relations. The important thing here is the principle of ultimate reversibility: it was lost—but not forever; and here it is again—found! I lost consciousness, I fainted, but then I came to. . . .

To search for a noun that has fallen into a chasm is like fighting poverty, leprosy, evil, political stupidity, dark forces from Asia, from Mars, or from the subconscious. Thus Kassianov's temporary defeat was for him actually a time of intellectual and biological blossoming. After all, this confession came about as a result of the loss of that word (and of chastity and vigor and joy).

38

For an emigré it is a special kind of punishment to lose a word: not only is he losing his language, but himself as well. And yet decades of exile irrevocably lead to linguistic collapse.

There was a time when people stayed in their native places and dug familiar loam. Now there are countless millions of exiles in the world. Entire nations flee vile regimes or are forcefully deported by them. Half the United States is inhabited by immigrants who neither speak English nor remember their native tongue. The mysterious process of alienation, of losing one's original country, syntax, family and community, and the old rhythm of existence—the replacement of one environment by another—is a painful, critical process. It is symptomatic of our era.

From Asia alone there stream hosts of bewildered, suffering beings; peaceful, undemanding folk (not Huns, not Goths). We see the beginning of an era of a multilingual, multivocational, nationless, polygamous society of illiterates from whom certain historical humanistic traits have been removed in order that they can be more readily joined and fused into one organism. These martyrs are no longer capable of recollecting a needed word; they cannot even reconstruct their accustomed way of feeling and thinking. And herein lies perhaps their triumph: that they continue to live in expectation of a miracle. Thus it is with the carpet of floating weeds covering the Sargasso Sea: according to tradition they tore themselves loose from ancient Atlantis and now, in the ocean above their long-drowned continent, find certain familiar, nourishing substances that are indispensable for their existence.

Subjected to these trials (for how many years, heavenly Father!), Kassianov began long ago to experience a deep nagging pain, as of an ulcer slowly gaining ground. Not a clean wound, but a festering sore that will never form a scar, never heal . . . that can only be removed, cut out, extirpated.

There were days when he resigned himself, when he was no longer aware of the drowned word (device?). If it crossed his mind, he saw it in the form of an inevitable natural catastrophe to which all resistance was in vain.

And Vishnevsky, naturally, was lavish with cheap advice: Why use force? Develop a strategy, encircle the enemy, take him by surprise! This is how one conquers (remembers). In the meantime there is nothing wrong with having a little fun.

In this way, Kassianov wore himself out: he yielded, then again took up the fight, forcing himself to continue the search for the God-created word that, he knew, was inside him waiting for deliverance.

During the last phase of his dissertation (on statistics) Kassianov became desperate and for a while even dropped all doctoral aspirations. Now, however, I see that somewhere, in the center of his every cell, there dwelt the conviction that a solution was possible and would soon, and in the most elegant manner, come forth.

Oh, if only he had enough courage and love to continue with the same stubbornness his search for the obscured word, then much would be forgiven him, I believe. For all forms of rebirth are but manifestations of Your unified spirit. . . . Creativeness, imagination, memory, the exploration of new poles and planets, life, agony, transfiguration, and, above all, resurrection of the dead, all, all are Thine, Father. Verily, if we shall not remember, we shall not respond in time to Your call, shall not be reborn, not enter the Kingdom of Heaven (where the past is plain as day and where it will be washed whiter than snow).

Possibly, the longing for the word—the abrogated one—the memory of lost youth and of life eternal, is a kind of phantom pain, like the one the proverbial invalid experiences in the toes of an already amputated leg . . . a salutary inner (mute) restoration of ties with a sacred, nourishing continent from which we were cut off, somewhere, sometime.

39

Job among the ashes, scraping his boils with a potsherd, was also trying to *remember:* why You (Love and Omnipotence) had so cruelly punished him, a just man. To understand is only to remember everything; and to forgive is to remember. So is to love.

An aging *bon vivant,* noticing the first signs of approaching impotence, will immediately attempt to correct the condition and improve the weakening circulation by remembering (imagining) his former powers. And sometimes he succeeds. If, poor wretch, he loses courage and accepts defeat, the channels become clogged and the natural capacity, along with the desire, atrophies.

The same with other gifts of body and soul. . . . One must throw oneself against the bars, fight for deliverance, pray or curse (no matter which), and ceaselessly ram one's head against the wall. Or—this is possible too—in untangling the eternal Ariadne's thread, find someday a narrow, winding side path and escape from the maze. (So does a cardiac patient sometimes survive a massive coronary occlusion by developing a collateral circulation that feeds the stricken heart muscle.)

Along with the restoration of a forgotten word or lost health and waning strength, there also occurs a miraculous resurrection of relationships with people who left long ago, faded, sailed away. . . . Of course, as we land the golden fish we also may bring up from the bottom a tin can, a rusty key, or a doll drowned in distant childhood.

All this Kassianov intended to accomplish through his own inner resources, not mechanically like a mnemonist or a computer. He did not couple objects through external associations; he did not call "information" or thumb through reference books (did not run to the surgeon with his abscess). His assignment was to revive not an isolated area but an entire environment, his old familiar surroundings: he had to make the old chopped-down birch grove stand again (had to reconstruct the network of nutrition, metabolism, circulation). . . . Such protracted effort may lead to sudden collapse (just as the old *bon vivant's* reckless pursuit of his aim may end in a brain hemorrhage). For in the restoration of one system of relationships (or one definition), contiguous areas and centers may be violated, crushed to death.

But what is death? Who understands, who remembers this word? . . . What if beyond the grave our organs eventually reunite, revive, and gradually fall in with the rhythmical pulsation of another, mighty heart, in this way recovering ancient forgotten channels of communication (nourishment and circulation) on a cosmic scale?

Man instinctively searches for answers. . . . If grownups are no longer inclined to cope with weightier problems, they at least find satisfaction in their daily crossword puzzle. The interest in intellectual games is a universal phenomenon. Kassianov, too, adores all kinds of puzzles.

It so happened that at the height of his struggle to remember the "chivalric" term he came upon a brain twister in a newspaper that completely took hold of him. So that both efforts—the search for the word and the chess problem—were linked into one. For almost a month he suffered over a seemingly simple mate in three:

WHITE: K-KB1, Q-QR1, R-KB5, B-QR7, Kt-QKt2; pawns: QKt3, KB6
BLACK: KQR4, Kt-QR6; pawns: QR3, QKt5, QKt4, QB5, Q4, KB2

At the end of the fourth week of struggle, doubt, hope, and genuine despair, he finally solved the problem, that is, he found the only possible (the real) combination of moves. Then he saw that the answer had been slumbering in him all along and had been bound to come to the surface in the end.

Afterward, for several days, he played with the pieces on the board like a cat amusing itself with an irrevocably captured mouse. . . . But the word, the word from the tournaments, the accursed word (emblem? . . . gules? . . .) still would not emerge, and imperceptibly he yielded to indolence and the instinct of self-preservation (which actually is our ruin) and for weeks at a time abandoned his quest into that inhospitable and forbidden thicket.

40

Is all such babbling perhaps nothing but the pastime of a proud and restless mind? Are we like the ambitious Martha who strives to put her earthly household into perfect order, the saintly woman who every evening, despite her exhaustion, still scours the copper pans until they shine, while dreamy Mary sits at the feet of the only Word that is necessary for salvation? Faith and prayer are supposed to replace the thirst for knowledge and a lucid memory (sounding brass). The Kingdom of Heaven belongs first of all to the children (the unreasoning), to the poor in spirit, and the holy fools.

In short, Kassianov resigned himself. Renouncing the idea of a cure effected in splendid isolation, he ran to the library like a repentant heretic runs to the church. But, as he did so, the unanswered prayer rose again in his soul. (So does a man with an abscessed tooth on the way to the dentist fervently whisper: please, Lord, let it open up before I get there!)

Who is to say whether God helped Kassianov or whether He simply did not hear his supplications? . . . The old Russian encyclopedias, all the chapters about tournaments, coats of arms, and heraldic beasts, clarified nothing.

"Listen, is there such a word at all?" Vishnevsky asked, frankly annoyed. (He was usually the first to express doubts about spiritual matters, about anything concerning God, saintliness, and the Good.)

But still, I do, I do remember, as through an acoustic curtain, the outlines, the music (the glimmer) of the word, in the same way that we sometimes discern (as through a veil) the paradisial landscape of full life.

"Yes," Kassianov repeats firmly, "I remember."

"Do you remember or do you imagine that you remember?" Vishnevsky insolently persists. "Soon you will be claiming that you hear the voices of angels, see Joan of Arc on her steed, and can exorcise archdemons."

"Listen, was there really such a word?" asks Nape, who is often influenced by Vishnevsky's speeches.

And Kassianov is almost ready to yield, to deny his reality. (So do many of us, as we grow up, renounce the convictions and heroic aspirations of our youth. . . . He, too, it seems, has now matured enough to betray the sacred image that once inspired his struggle against night, oblivion, and non-existence.)

But I do not give up completely: as I sink to the bottom I flounder about somehow (like that frog in the cream) and float up again. I take a deep breath, still feeling in my mouth the bitter taste of the soft, viscous silt that covers everything down there.

Spiritual Father, help a man about to fall! These days it is rare that Kassianov tries to resist. (He is like a horse that has bolted and tears along, heedless of the way.) The old wound in my memory aches in bad weather and sends dreams of bygone, valiant campaigns to the tired veteran. A scar formed long ago, an ugly purple scar, but one which is in a way a perfect creation: irreversible, eternal.

In the meantime Vishnevsky fabricates his own little theory. He says there is no need to torture oneself, no need to strain to remember. The word will incarnate itself; effortlessly, freely, by grace, it will reveal itself like the beautiful lady in the fairy tale. (So does an unemployed, despairing of ever finding work again, dream of winning two hundred thousand dollars; and a man afflicted with an incurable disease listen to accounts of miraculous recoveries at Lourdes.)

I know all that is generally known about grace. However, so long as grace, with all its implications, has not manifested itself, it is for all practical purposes absent from our path. It will either meet up with Kassianov somewhere, at some obscure railroad station, or else they will miss each other irrevocably. But for the time being I have to push on, consciously and actively, with my last (supernatural) resources.

Nevertheless—in retreat, subjugated and maimed because he had lost the word forever—Kassianov could still feel happy at times, similar to a soldier who has lost a limb in the storming of an historic citadel. (The same kind of bitter joy is known to the wretches who on the advice of their doctor have managed to give up smoking.)

Quite another comparison also suggests itself. My wife Zora had a child who died at a very early age. He would be grown up by now, but she still sees him as a rosy bundle on her lap, remembers the smell of diapers and baby powder, and weeps over him. Our friends, the few we have here, try to reassure her in their own way. One says: "We'll all meet again up there!" Another: "Listen, was there really such a child?" A third: "Do you know how ungrateful children are nowadays? They dump their parents into old-age homes."

(All of which is meant to comfort Zora.)

41

And so Kassianov gradually reconciled himself to the loss of this word and many others—a surrender of which he now heartily repents. This semiconscious state actually pleased him, and he trained himself to protect his rare and precious, if unnatural, peace. After all, a sick man gets used to the rubber tube in his stomach and ends up cherishing it.

But sometimes, in the depth of my cells, in their memory or consciousness, something would erupt and float up. . . .

Then I would grow sad and anxious, and in a fury would accuse Vishnevsky of criminal negligence. (A vacationer probably experiences the same when, having paid no attention to a small scratch, he suddenly notices that his whole leg is swollen and throbbing.)

"Enough, there is no such word!" shouts Vishnevsky. "You have dreamed it up. Where could it have gone? And anyway, into whatever hole it has fallen, the word will stay there, it won't get lost." (Why worry?)

Something like this had come into my mind for the first time while I was engrossed in the chess problem, and immediately after that it was solved: the answer appeared out of nowhere, as if born of the foam. Everything worked out so naturally, so simply, that it was hard to believe in the reality (the logic) of the tormenting month-long search that had gone before.

Herein lies the temptation. "Exactly the same thing will happen with the vanished word," Kassianov whispers, and he smiles like a man drugged. "Suddenly, gratuitously, unsolicited, it will show itself!"

My word (the limited one) lies together with other lost valuables at the bottom of a pond and, given the right conditions, even Vishnevsky could easily recognize it among other vague shapes . . . recognize it and haul it up, selflessly submitting to the promptings of original virtue. . . . The buried word is here and has been in our possession all along. The task is not to "remember" mechanically but to reinstate communication between the different time layers in man.

It is as in the old prophetic tale: the cut-up pieces of the toad grow together into one whole, the toad revives, and, to our growing delight, turns into a glorious prince. Human planning, age-old experience, and our inspired dreams as well, take part in this metamorphosis.

However, Father Nectarius, as I have said before, modern technical achievements prod us at every step to act automatically, without discrimination or understanding. Our ancestor in his cave had to rub sticks together skillfully and patiently so that the dry leaves would finally burst into flame. He knew what he was doing at that moment, knew why he was breaking into a sweat—and afterward remembered (could not forget) that this day he had made the blessed fire.

But when Nape gets hold of the matches and turns on the gas (in the midst of the morning shave or a telephone call), Vishnevsky and I do not know who has done it and why. It is not that we *forget:* no, we simply had nothing to do with that act in the first place.

A man's life only attains full reality if all of him is involved in it: his hands, legs, senses, reason, memory, plus all the powers of his soul, including love for what he is creating. Then the world becomes a livable, happy place where there is unity between nature and God. No more "empty holes" in a vacuum—hours, days, and months of which we are not aware, that we do not accept or assimilate. Automatism is a deadly sin; and our instinct of self-defense, which out of greed and sloth produced this automatism, will be our ruin.

To retrace *post factum* Nape's blindly performed acts is exhausting, disgusting, and, above all, useless: like praying without sensing the presence of God—praying to a wall. (A vigil without grace.) Prayer, too, is remembering: an inspired memory of God Who, even when temporarily forgotten, is still next to us or deep within us. (Communion is "in remembrance.")

"Simmer down, pal, you are boring us," Vishnevsky whispers. "Come down from the empyrean. A man needs to have some fun, a change. It wouldn't hurt, either, if you looked after practical matters. There is so much to be done around the house: here a nail, there some scrubbing or a coat of paint. . . . And to keep Zora comfortable you'll need money, money, and more money!"

This is what they preach—and how they drive us into the grave! Relax. Don't be emotional. After all, the word Kassianov is searching for belongs to the vocabulary of chivalry and will hardly be of use to anybody within the near future. "It can be lost without much harm."

There is suffering that is useless, extraneous, and there is suffering that belongs to us, that is sacred. The former, imposed from the outside, debases; the latter, if freely chosen, is life-giving. But it is difficult to realize with which particular pain we are dealing—until we have left it behind on the road or ground it up into powder. And something else is important: do you accept the fateful ordeal humbly or in a spirit of rebellion? Poverty, destitution, for instance: to fight them all one's life is petty and degrading; but to accept this or any other yoke voluntarily is a heroic deed, a victory, a transfiguration. Is it perhaps the same with the knightly "emblem"—should I *voluntarily* forget about it, give it up, sacrifice it?

Sometimes it seemed to Kassianov that he had found his word; then, with feigned indifference, he would begin to play with it (as the cat with the mouse, or as I played with the black king on the chessboard). But he was not convinced: something was lacking for complete triumph, for the triumph of authenticity (as the pressing of a hand or a kiss —incarnating the reality of love).

I know, spiritual Father, that at some time, after "everything has happened," perhaps after "death," the living word will suddenly liberate itself from its bonds and spontaneously, easily and gracefully, float up to the surface of the soul—mine or a universal one. Oh, what bliss! (And then we will be able to describe it!)

42

Through his quest for the lost word, Kassianov discovered that our memory is engaged not only in preserving the past but that it also fulfills the apparently reverse function of erasing, blotting out, what supposedly is no longer worth remembering. This too is an aspect of self-defense.

What has been "forgotten," saintly Father, is in fact preserved in an unadulterated form, "canned" inside us, in emptiness and cold. That is why sound, well-balanced persons often "forget" what is most important for them and thus save it for eternity. After entering into one's diary (an act similar to confession) some experience worthy of note, one immediately loses it, for there is no longer any need to store it alive in its "active" form.

In this way, little by little, I came to understand that there are two kinds of memory: one resurrecting, the other interring, casting into oblivion. (Similarly, there seem to exist two kinds of nerve fibers: one for the reception of pleasure and one for the transmission of pain.)

It is of great importance to develop and train the obliviating memory so as to "forget" with inspired consciousness, not with blind passivity. There are memory cells gathered together in the brain; and there is the memory of the separate cells with which that center has long since lost its living connection, allegedly because there is no longer any need for it. Cells have a memory that memory no longer has. (*Les cellules ont une mémoire que la mémoire n'a plus.*)

Just as it is possible to reproduce an entire organism from a single cell (there is no absolute need for spermatozoids), so it is possible to re-establish from the memory of one cell all that has been accumulated in the central memory of the brain. This applies to the buried word as well: from it we shall be able, eventually, to resurrect the entire universal tongue.

Furthermore, I believe there exists yet a third memory, outside of us and, akin to Your Spirit, penetrating and illuminating the infinite continuum, and uniting Vishnevsky and Nape and Kassianov with the Maker of the Universe. Like Anaximander's *apeiron,* perhaps, something undefined and unlimited: not proto-substance or proto-matter, but a proto-consciousness. This too is probably a heresy (but I trust not a dangerous one).

The memory of the cells is unaccountable and shapeless; the central memory expresses itself distinctly; and the cosmic memory flows evenly—everywhere—between us and You, Father. This memory, inherent in God, reaches us here on earth, one may suppose, by way of a net of capillaries that have become obstructed throughout the centuries. Probably, and this seems more complicated, there are also two kinds of cosmic memory: one peripheral (in every "cell") and the other at the center—with the Creator. This, Lord, is why all the separate organisms or "atoms" can gravitate with such precision toward goodness (similar to the magnetic needle that unerringly—and inexplicably—pointed north on the rafts of the seafarers of old).

Our consciousness, in submitting to a cosmic form of self-defense, erases much that is important so as *not* to lose it in the general hurly-burly, to keep it safe in the depths of the cells and bring it back untainted to the Creator.

To order memory, to bid it remember this, that, or the other thing, is as senseless as to order it to forget. (When a bicycle rider tries to avoid a piece of chewing gum or some dog dirt, he will most likely run right over it.) To bid living tissue to overcome weakness and the ills of our body is absolute nonsense. Quite the contrary; in this way we only freeze and fixate forever the errors and defects of our organism.

The same applies to failing memory . . . no direct approach is possible. In order really to remember, it is sometimes necessary to *exclude* all that surrounds the forgotten; uproot the wrong deduction, the persistent association or metaphor in which the apparatus of memory has, for reasons of comfort, safety, or profit, become entangled.

Our salvation, Father Nectarius, may lie at times in the loss of memory; for now our main source of ruin is the primitive self-defense mechanism that bears imprinted upon it the no-longer-needed pre-Cenozoic experience of an amoeba, reptile, triton, or other incidental and alien fellow traveler of man.

What advantage is there for a salmon to swim across an

ocean and ascend a torrential river so as there to spawn in agony? It could enter the delta of the river nearest to it instead of crossing the seven seas (if the spawning does, indeed, have to take place in fresh water—which I doubt). And European eels for some reason set out for the Sargasso Sea and by spawning there oblige the larvae to swim back over a period of three years to their "native" shores, evading hordes of hungry foes on the way. Who could truly call this self-defense?

Or let us consider heart transplants: in principle they could be life-saving; but blindly, brutally, man rejects the beneficial organ, only because he has become accustomed in the "struggle for survival" to spew out every foreign body, to free himself of it without discrimination. Kassianov thinks that in many of our physiological, economic, aesthetic acts we too often exhibit such an absurd, suicidal selfishness.

43

Kassianov stood at the edge of a high precipice, on a desert island surrounded by an undulating sea of glass. His condition was truly pitiful, for he had just realized with absolute certainty that he had lost God or (what amounted to the same) that God whom he continuously confessed could not or did not wish to grant him a rewarding and productive life.

To add to his distress, hideous horned monsters were rising up here and there from the green foam of the sea. "I am thy god," they bellowed, and flung themselves at Kassianov. In his terror he began to run, faster and faster, and farther and farther from the shore, but soon—as in a bad dream—reached the other, the western edge of the island, where again he saw the seething, glassy rollers and heard the blood-curdling cries of fat, many-headed bulls.

Arrested at the land's very edge, Kassianov saw before him the semblance of a bridge floating over the abyss, its artfully wrought steel ends resting on the air. Suddenly, far off, a dark peaked cloud appeared. . . . Dilating, growing like a tornado or whirlwind, it fell from a great altitude, now resembling in shape a gigantic flat chalice. The black whirlwind (or disk) swept with unimaginable speed toward Kassianov and finally hit the metal platform so that the entire structure shook. But it did not collapse; instead, the chalice split open and out of it, as from an egg, stepped the familiar figure of a stooped old man: of enormous, unnatural height, as if on stilts, in black cassock and small skullcap, with a thin, silvery beard (curved like the sickle of the new moon). Leaning in Kassianov's direction, hovering above him, Father Nectarius asked sternly: "Did you love God, you heretic?"

Timidly Kassianov said: "Saintly Father, if it can be done, please grant me absolution before we are again interrupted."

But Father Nectarius demanded even more insistently: "Did you grumble against God, you heretic?"

And Kassianov answered: "Between me and God stands life. If it were not for life I should probably be wholly in Him and He in me. But as it is, we see each other through a glass, darkly: the glass distorts like a prism, both ways."

The priest raised his pale hand to make the sign of the cross over him and it seemed to Kassianov that he could hear the whisper from long ago: "Numb and dumb, numb and dumb."

Kassianov broke into tears of joy and awoke. It was dark in the house and quiet, as it was every other night; but for some reason he was frightened by the silence.

"It's still early," Vishnevsky obligingly, coaxingly remarked, ready to curl up again.

But Kassianov switched on the light and went barefoot along the corridor to his wife's room. There, on her back, drowned in the pillows, lay his former beloved, looking like a beetle in an old herbarium. She was still warm.

"Never hit a man who is down," ran the old saying from Kassianov's school days. It was exactly as if some idle and capricious being had flattened her body, compressed and wizened as it was, with one stroke of the palm.

Nape was already busying himself with the corpse. He pulled the rubber tubing out of the nostrils, closed the sand-colored, impeccable eyes. Vishnevsky was speaking quite coherently to someone over the telephone.

It was getting light in Zora's room. Someone had flung open the window. Free photons ricocheted from the half-open panes and came to repose in a rainbow wreath on the opposite wall. (Why they had chosen precisely this path remained incomprehensible.)

Part Two (or One)

A Certain Light

"I see a certain light . . ."

A. Pushkin

1

The two-wheeled cart, drawn by an aging but obviously thoroughbred gelding, advanced at a walking pace across the baked, crumbling ground; the land, rising and falling monotonously in all directions without sign of any road, was crisscrossed by deep fissures and covered with a bluish-gray dust. In the cart sat a young man, completely gray as if powdered with ashes. He seemed not to have shaved for several days: a sparse, monastic growth of hair that went well with his manly appearance sprouted on his lean cheeks. Next to him on the seat perched a thin, graceful young girl who fidgeted incessantly, trying to take in every detail of the countryside at once. Wrapped in a drab windbreaker and enveloped in clouds of dust, she yet appeared inordinately fair, even radiant.

The driver, who in spite of the heat wore a sheepskin vest over his shirt and a heavy woolen muffler around his neck, trotted with a peasant's imperturbable and concentrated look beside the sweaty horse, every so often straightening the traces or taking hold of the bit. Slowly the cart rolled through the parched, rippling wasteland. The winding gashes frequently barred the way; when they were narrow, the wheels could make it and the gelding scrambled gamely across on his thin, nimble legs. But some of the rifts were so wide that the driver had to turn aside and make his way around.

These crevices, winding, repeating themselves, divided the mounds and hillocks into almost equal quadrangles, so that wherever the eye looked, it saw a limitless, ash-strewn checkerboard.

At the more dangerous places, the driver all but embraced the gelding, clasping its long neck in his arms, and both advanced as one, in silence, only emitting occasional guttural sounds. The intelligent horse apparently had no difficulty understanding the driver. In fact, it often turned its fine head around as if to encourage the passengers. Sometimes, however, it froze in its tracks: a statue, with only its ears twitching nervously, expressively. And indeed, one might lose heart at the vast, uneven surface ahead, cut up by a network of trenches (bringing to mind transparent chessboards haphazardly nailed one on top of the other).

The natives were thoroughly familiar with this conformation of the soil; they accepted it, but they knew of no definite explanation for it. In any event, the inhabitants of the settlements in the valley, who suffered most from this natural phenomenon, had no idea what really caused it. Some claimed that during periods of great heat the earth gave up its moisture unevenly and immediately after began to crack and slide. Whatever the explanation, at every new serious obstacle the driver took the gelding by the halter and, without entering into scientific speculations, led him around the dangerous precipice.

It was no wonder that in such a fashion a journey that anywhere else could be accomplished in ten hours here took several days—particularly since it was not advisable to proceed over such terrain at night.

They were descending a slope where dry, stunted undergrowth threw a pale shadow when the horse stopped short. The driver began to unharness it. Between the ragged vines a spring murmured: a trickle of water, thin, transparent, and cold, apparently breaking through to the surface from a great depth.

The bearded driver deftly, deliberately, got out the feedbag and hung it around the horse's neck, after which, in the same skillful and deliberate manner, he made a fire from the dry vines and roots; almost simultaneously with the smoke, the aroma of Oriental coffee began to rise. Out of nowhere appeared a rough, homespun cloth and on it scones, hard-boiled eggs, ham, and a straw-covered bottle of impressive dimensions.

The landscape around them resembled the surface of the moon. The dry undergrowth clinked like stone. The only moving, live thing was the shadow of the stalks. Everywhere was a mist of bluish dust; filtered through it, the sun—no longer a perfect sphere—shone in bizarre, brown and violet colors. No birds, no insects, not a blade of green grass. Only the hard, dead earth covered with scars. And, looming in the distance, dark-gray basalt mountains and, above them, gloomy, bloated clouds.

"It's interesting," the young man said. "I wonder how you travel here in the winter."

The girl threw up her hands and laughed. "Philolai," she said to the driver, "the Professor wonders how one travels here in the winter." But Philolai was muttering to the fire and only shook his head disparagingly.

"Please, just coffee for me, I don't want anything to eat." The girl continued, no longer laughing—yet the impression of joy brimming over persisted. She was tall and slender, even fragile. There was nothing special, nothing arresting about her delicate, fair face, only this glow of happiness radiating out and infecting those around her with a feeling of spontaneous joy. (So Philolai attempted a smile as he handed her a cup over which hovered an aromatic cloud.)

"Thank you. And a sip of slivovitz, please." Everything she said seemed only to serve the purpose of producing yet another wave of unexpected, God-given joy. "And you, Master, aren't you hungry?"

"What should I call him, your fiancé?" Philolai asked with another awkward grin, as if this information were a prerequisite for sharing a meal.

In answer, the girl looked up with her laughing, golden eyes, sand-colored (the color of African lions): she had a slight squint that gave her a somewhat abnormal, inhuman look (the look of a deer, an angel, or, perhaps even more, an inhabitant of ancient Atlantis).

"Master Kassian, lunch is ready," she announced.

"Master Kassian," the driver repeated solemnly, and with great dignity nodded his head. "That makes sense."

The guest accepted a drink and some food. He had a habit of jutting his head, with its massive nose, slightly forward, as if he were scowling. Sipping from his glass, he said, "After all, it's probably thanks to homemade vodka and brandy that man has survived the various ice ages and thirty-year wars."

Philolai, grunting approval, emptied his glass.

"And how is the transportation here in winter?" the visitor from the city asked again, and, after a pause, "Is it easier or harder?"

The girl flung up her hands again. Philolai unhurriedly swallowed a piece of goat's cheese and then explained that at times there was no getting through the snow at all. . . . Bitter cold, high winds, everything encrusted with ice, and, of course, the crevices. No horse could pull a cart or a sled through; only a donkey could make it. Sometimes the donkey with the packload came back alone, while the mailman would be dug out of the snow only in the spring. "Our snowstorms are special!" Philolai's weather-beaten face lit up for a moment. "At Christmas we sometimes hear thunder, and hail comes down. Lightning flickers and a rainbow stretches across half the sky. Snow and a rainbow, and on the snow, farther on, another, paler rainbow." He smugly nodded his graying head and turned back to his food, considering the conversation ended.

But the Master was still curious. "And in the spring and fall?"

"In the spring and fall," answered the frustrated driver, holding a piece of bread and ham in his hand, "in spring and fall there is no road here. Just greasy dough up to the animal's belly. No one can get through." And he looked at the visitor with pride. "What is there to tell? Zora knows, she grew up here."

"The Professor is no stranger either," the girl hurriedly explained. "His mother used to live here."

"At the Bishop's?" Philolai asked circumspectly. "He's had a lot of people there; they come, they stay for a while, and then they leave. . . . A good man, the Bishop," he added indifferently, "a clever man. He sees what's coming two years ahead of time."

"More coffee, please!" the girl interrupted, but Master Kassian continued his questioning: "What about werewolves and vampires? Are there many around?"

"He means people who turn into wolves," Zora explained,

looking with the same joy at the talking men, the sky, the amber ball of the sun, the ashen earth, and the small lizard sticking out from under a stone.

"Yes, it happens here," listlessly affirmed Philolai, for whom this topic was of little interest. He was impatient to tackle the ham and slivovitz in earnest. And the horse, too, had to be watered.

The girl said—and again it sounded as if she were sharing some joyful news—"How strange. Here people turn into wolves. In other places they become cats. Is there some kind of law at work?"

"Still cause-and-effect reasoning," Kassian said didactically. Zora seemed to break into laughter, but without a sound, smiling only with her sand-colored eyes.

"You're right," she corrected herself. "How difficult it is to overcome age-old habits. There should be a textbook for beginners."

"Will the gentleman have some coffee?" Philolai asked patronizingly.

"Yes, Master, yes, you must get to like our coffee," the girl joined in. "You won't find such coffee anywhere else." She spoke softly, quietly, yet giving the impression of elatedly clapping her hands.

Philolai poured coffee for the guest and himself and filled Zora's cup a second time: a smell of the Orient, of oases and drowsy siestas rose over the dusty undergrowth.

The guest sipped, swallowed, caught his breath (the coffee was hellishly hot), and said: "Actually, the smell of coffee is more pleasant than its taste. So it is with many fruits of the earth."

"Do you hear, Philolai?" the girl exclaimed. "Coffee should be smelled, not drunk."

The driver shook his beard disapprovingly. In accordance with the local custom, he had expected to drain about fifteen of the small cups, but now he saw that he would not get the chance. . . . Indeed, Zora soon inquired whether the gelding was rested.

Philolai answered with an endless monologue wherein figured a mythical gypsy who was always in a hurry and an impetuous general who landed his army in quicksand. Nevertheless, clanking the bucket and dishes, he slowly began to gather up everything and then harnessed the horse.

But here an unexpected circumstance complicated the advance of the travelers. The intelligent, good-tempered gelding, having drunk his water and politely shaken his tail, was straining forward in his harness, ready to pull, when suddenly, as if a string had snapped inside him, he froze in his place, the muscles under his taut, silken skin trembling convulsively. Animated and alive a moment before, the horse, though still on his feet, all at once grew cold, withered, seemed to stop breathing. His eyes sank deep into their sockets and glazed over with a dull film.

"What is it, my friend, what is it?" roughly and gently said Philolai over and over, aimlessly fussing around the horse. He loosened the traces, took off the bridle, and held a handful of oats to the gelding's soft muzzle. But the horse remained as he had been, only guiltily lowering his head more and more. . . . Finally he fell on his side and was still.

The newspapers sometimes tell of public figures, Hollywood stars or Nobel Prize winners, who have expired abruptly while stepping into a taxi on Montmartre or leaving the Coliseum. The same had happened to the venerable gelding. (But there would be no mention of it in the press.)

The horse lay, turned away from the travelers and the

cart, his entire appearance indicating total separation, detachment. His belly had already begun to swell up and became hideously distorted. Philolai tried to force some slivovitz down the horse's throat, then (sacrificing what is most precious on the road) he poured half a bucket of water into the animal's transparent ear. The gelding did not stir.

"He's dead," said Zora, mechanically defining this absurd condition with the generally accepted but completely meaningless, unenlightening term.

Recognizing a note in her voice that was by now familiar, Master Kassian quickly turned around. The girl was cowering on the ground, her knees drawn up almost level with her face. The attack apparently was a mild one: she was not shaking—only her hands were bent spastically at the wrists. Her face, which had momentarily become ashen, was already lighting up. A moment later she had overcome the seizure and got to her feet. (As he had so many times before, the Master asked himself: from where does this eternal joy come, this joy she so steadily radiates . . . ?)

"Strange," he said aloud—half to himself—"usually such attacks begin with an aura, a momentary, intense feeling of inexpressible cosmic happiness, and end in a state of depression. . . . but with Zora it is the other way around."

"Really?" the girl asked, shining.

"Yes. A reverse process," he explained gently. "As if for you time were turned inside out."

Meanwhile Philolai had taken the harness off the horse and covered the wagon with canvas, which he tied down with a rope. He handed Zora the almost empty food basket, Kassian his light suitcase, and, loading himself with the mail, slivovitz, and water, set out with a firm, even step.

Again there were the dry mounds encircled by crevices as

by the rings of a giant boa constrictor; and the oblique sun that (beneficial only in small doses) continued to burn down on them despotically. Suddenly several ugly birds, predators with enormous, red, hooked beaks, floated low overhead; then a pack of dogs (looking around fearfully) ran silently by, a short-haired, insolent male in the lead.

All the while, on the horizon, a dire transformation was taking place: the farthest ashy-blue strip of naked earth, almost touching the catastrophically inflated, deep-orange sphere of the sun, seemed to contract and jerk up, half covering it. Immediately insects began buzzing and there was a breath of cool air; a prairie dog, standing on its hind paws, whistled.

Philolai trudged steadily ahead, carefully avoiding all obstacles. At particularly dangerous crevices he waited for his companions and helped the girl across. Soon, however, a change in his behavior became apparent. Whistling a tune, he strode faster, with more assurance. Maneuvering skillfully around the fissures, he entered a narrow, stuffy gully, rather like a tunnel hewn in the rock. Now Zora, too, began to hurry and soon overtook the guide.

First they dove into bluish dusk, then into dark night, and finally the light of the waning day again glimmered ahead. Smells drifted toward them—of a village, a river, and gardens; the smell of smoke, of onions. They entered a wide lane with wattle fences on both sides, and a few minutes later found themselves in a large piazza paved with pinkish stones, an ancient fountain in the middle.

Bordering the piazza were austere two-storied houses with flat white roofs (like terraces); only the upper story had windows, shielded by an ornamental latticework of soft stone. There was also a church with an Eastern cupola; another building, clearly of an official nature—the village hall, three stories high, with a clock on the tower and wide stairs leading down from the porch; and several stores and workshops. Beyond all this lay pretty gardens and a valley, sloping down, unequally divided by the zigzag of a foaming river.

In front of the stores merchandise was still on display: sickles, earthenware, rugs, sweets, boots. From the workshops came the lively thunder of a hammer, the insistent squeal of a saw, the sharp hiss of a blowtorch. In front of the inn, an elongated, two-story building with a covered inner courtyard, the natives gathered, apparently puzzled by the return of Philolai without his wagon. A gendarme, in a blue uniform lavishly adorned with leather straps, stepped from the official-looking building, treading firmly in his locally made boots; he took off his coarse blue kepi and wiped his sweaty forehead with his peasant's palm.

The regular customers, all much like Philolai, dressed in sheepskin vests, bearded, stocky, and dignified, poured from the courtyard and from the terrace in front of the taproom. They surrounded Philolai, questioning him about the gelding, sighing in sympathy, and trading far-ranging technical explanations, none of which prevented them from attentively examining Zora and, even more, the stranger who had arrived with her.

The peasants all held small cups of coffee, glasses of transparent slivovitz, or mugs of local brew. Behind them, at a proper distance, in doorways and windows, clustered groups of women in colored shawls, with infants in their arms. The older children raced screaming around the piazza. Farther back, as if at an agreed radius from the inn, packs of dogs, peered inquisitively through bushes and fences. They too seemed to study the new arrivals curiously.

Zora held joyous reunion with the women. Master Kassian walked up and down in front of the inn, delighting in the feel of soft live soil. The natives followed his movements as if trying to guess their secret meaning.

Presently an old American jeep, freshly painted, drove up, and from it, as from a toy, stepped a gigantic, handsome, gray-haired gypsy. He was in festive, colorful dress, bedecked with silver and gold coins that jingled and shimmered at every step. He bowed to Zora, his teeth and earrings gleaming. She gave him her small hand, as everyone around watched with the same approving smile.

"This is Markali, my nurse and friend," Zora introduced him. "How are things at home?"

"Thank God, all is well," Markali answered, laughing as if playing a part in a theatrical performance.

Taking hold of the guest's suitcase and the bag the girl was carrying, he strode to the jeep, where he stood at attention, without however removing his hat with its long peacock feather.

"I'll walk," the Master decided. "It isn't far, is it?"

"Two kilometers," said the gypsy confidingly, making his medals jingle and shimmer. "There, across the bridge and through the park."

"I must hurry," Zora said, smiling with her eyes. "Don't be late, Professor." She climbed in beside the towering Markali.

The peasants chuckled in unison; then their women began to shriek with laughter, the children squealed, and, far off, from the darkening ravines near the river, the dogs echoed the laughter in separate choruses.

2

The stranger ambled slowly across the pink piazza. The stores had closed; in the windows above, candles and kerosene lamps glowed and distorted shadows moved awkwardly about. (The man from the city looked up and thought: there lies happiness. From the houses the people watched him—also with envy.)

Motionless, on the steps of the church, stood a thin black figure, stooped and very tall—a sickle, in cassock and tiny skullcap. His long, narrow silvery beard curled like another, smaller sickle. From the still-open door of the workshop facing the church came sparks and the energetic voices of people who work with fire. Apparently some tinning and soldering was still being done.

A flock of children accompanied the visitor to the bridge, now running ahead of him and then, cutting back through the gardens, trailing behind. The river, roaring and splashing below, sounded powerful. (In the gloom, in any case, it inspired fear.)

After crossing the long, narrow, and now completely deserted bridge and climbing a steep, stony path, Master Kassian soon found himself in plowed fields where late-planted corn was just pushing through. From the south came the smell of rich earth, early flowers, and cherry blossoms; to the north, seemingly near, loomed bare mountaintops. Zora's estate probably lay to the east, where a cedar grove blended into an old park of neglected linden, chestnut, and oak trees. Those clumsy giants, hundreds of years old and covered with thick gnarled bark, resembled mammoths, elephants, rhinos, and pinkish-violet hippopotamuses.

Turning onto a sandy path that cut through a dozing herd of the gnarled, pungent-smelling monsters, Master Kassian suddenly found himself on the edge of a wide, well-kept meadow from where he could see an impressive, illuminated manor—the castle. It was an elongated, four-storied, rectangular structure of white stone, with many embrasure-like windows; low wings had been added to both sides, and a number of sturdy dark buildings squatted around the whole. A vast lawn with enormous flower beds ran up to the castle, while on the left and right the meadow stretched on toward blossoming fruit trees, orchards, gardens, and, beyond, again to the woods.

Surprising in the tableau were the electric lights (they seemed a fugue intervening in a lyrical passage from a shepherd's pipe).

The park was separated from the lawn by a white stone wall. The gates to the courtyard were locked, but an oak wicket remained open. All around was silence, smoothness, not a soul to be seen; only the crickets chirping. But Master Kassian could not shake the feeling (it had begun in the village) that he was being watched. He headed straight for the white-columned portico. Shadows of what were probably dogs appeared and vanished. The visitor's movements lost their naturalness; tensely, stiffly, Kassian continued toward the landing.

There stood the familiar freshly painted jeep. Only then, seeing it was no taller than two of the stone steps, Kassian understood that the castle was of much larger dimensions than it had at first appeared. "This way, please," someone said, and the swarthy, giant gypsy, having apparently waited on the landing, stepped up to him with an angelic (and predatory) smile.

Women had gathered on the landing and greeted him, giggling behind their hands. From the lower windows, from doorways, even, it seemed, from cracks, heads and torsos stuck out: almost exclusively women in colored shawls. Somersaulting head over heels, a gang of children passed through the courtyard, dogs raced around the luxuriant flower beds, and a bearded goat appeared at a gate, avidly studying the new face from a respectful distance.

The guest walked into a bare two-storied vestibule and from there into a vast room decorated with old portraits and neglected suits of armor. In the corners, marble statues held up candelabra. A fire glowed in the oversized hearth. But despite all these sources of light and heat, the room was cold, damp, and dusky.

A majestic elder met Kassian. He was clean-shaven, with hair neatly parted in the middle and with a large, powerful nose. In profile, his face, of yellowish complexion, resembled that found on Roman medals.

"I am Zora's grandfather," he said with the experienced smile of a man of the world.

"Ah, the Bishop!" Master Kassian shook the dry, hot, well-groomed hand.

"Yes, they still call me that although I haven't been a bishop for a long time." Again he smiled, certain that the guest would consider this circumstance amusing. But the Master listened respectfully and remained silent. "Zora and her father are exchanging sentiments. They will be down presently. You would probably like to wash up after your journey. This way! You still have time before dinner."

A Certain Light

A woman of youthful appearance (as far as could be ascertained, wrapped as she was in a white shawl) led the guest up the wide, gently rising stone stairs. On the landings slumbered marble lackeys, unlit torches in their muscular arms. The sparsely distributed electric bulbs shed a scant, reddish-yellow light.

A gang of children tumbled down the stairs, led by a raven-haired girl who resembled a little snake. They were in hot pursuit of a dirty-white swan with clipped wings. The bird was hastily waddling down the stairs, from time to time turning around to let out a menacing, ineffective hiss. At the sight of the stranger the procession instantly vanished. The Master and the woman, who seemed to be laughing behind her shawl, continued their mountainous ascent up the stairs and along spacious oval landings. Having long ago lost count of those monumental floors, the guest, catching his breath on the last, unkept and uncarpeted landing, asked without any special curiosity, "What is this place—a woman's kingdom?" In answer, his companion only put her hand to her mouth, to show that she considered this question very funny. Notwithstanding her grimaces and old-fashioned behavior, she seemed no fool.

The room assigned to the guest was furnished with only the bare (and rather decrepit) essentials. The woman showed him where the conveniences were located—a sort of toilet at the farthest end of the corridor. She thoroughly inspected the bed, plumped up the pillows, noted the lack of towels, and fetched some as well as a pitcher with water and a cake of sandalwood soap. Then she vanished, as if she had fallen through a crack in the stone slabs.

His suitcase was waiting for him on a stool. Master Kassian washed, put on a clean shirt, a tie and jacket and comfortable shoes—all of which took no more than two minutes. Through the deep and narrow windows he could see lanterns far down below moving in the courtyard: probably servants scurrying to the granary, cellars, and larders.

Suddenly a gong rang out, daring and gay. That, thought the guest, is the gypsy calling us to dinner! But why must it be the gypsy? the Master asked, dissatisfied with himself. Always those deductions and associations. Cause and effect! We must do away with this slavish habit. No, it is not Markali beating the gong. There are many people in this house. And the most modest, subdued creature can, once in a lifetime, ring out in a triumphant major scale. To miss such an exception from the statistical norm is a mortal sin!

So he stood for a moment, listening to his thoughts, checking them out. Then he moved toward the call of the gong, vaguely following the direction that for some obscure reason he considered the right one. And of course he lost his way among the corridors and missed the big central staircase. To all appearances the castle must have been laid out many centuries ago. The walls were moss-grown—and not only on the outside. The narrow embrasures bore scars from the Middle Ages; but in some places ulcers of more recent times, craters and holes of artillery and automatic weapons, were also visible.

Master Kassian descended a small wooden staircase (a contemporary addition) that led into a large, high-ceilinged room with numerous somber stained-glass windows. There, in front of a candlelit icon, the imposing figure of a woman wrapped in an earth-colored shawl lay prostrate on the tile floor. Sensing the intruder, she jumped to her feet and raised her arms in a passionate yet restrained gesture, emitting angry, unintelligible sounds. The brown shawl, slipping from her head, revealed her completely gray hair; but her eyes shone with a rebellious, young (or mad) fire. One thing was certain: she was outraged by the intrusion and did not hide her feelings.

The guest backed out precipitously, intent only upon escaping as quickly as possible from the enraged matron and her birdlike noises. When he had chosen his direction, he had lost his way; now that he proceeded without thinking, the familiar landing with the stone giants appeared immediately before him. . . . Like river rapids, the majestic stairway swept him down. Women and cats roamed about, but the Master did not ask questions, running confidently, two steps at a time (more than two was impossible). Finally he arrived in the vestibule and from there entered the dining hall.

A very long and, because of its length, seemingly overnarrow oak table was richly laid with china, crystal, and silver that shone dimly in the yellow light of two chandeliers. These, and a few candles, burned above the table. The rest of the enormous room was drowned in darkness out of which women and girls hurriedly appeared with bottles and deep bowls, to disappear again into the gloom, into nothingness.

Zora was already there. Taking the Master by the hand, she led him to her father who, however, did not express any particular pleasure. He merely scowled and showed his teeth, which made him resemble a mature and somewhat hungry wolf.

"This is Master Kassian, my teacher and friend. Please, Felix, do like him," the girl said, addressing her father by his first name.

"Certainly," said Felix, "I always appreciate young academicians."

"Master Kaz Yan," the Bishop repeated politely. "I knew some Kaz Yans in Constantinople."

"No," the Master explained, "it's Kassian, not Kaz Yan. My mother named me for your local saint."

"Oh, I see," the Bishop replied, not without regret. "Well, Cassian is a great saint—"

He was about to continue but Felix cut in, "I understand you have founded a new religion?"

"No," the guest answered cautiously, "Zora exaggerates. It is more a matter of philosophy . . . our contemporary problems demand a new approach."

Their eyes met, the guest's adding, as it were, "You may dislike me, but you have to behave," and Felix's answering back, "You are probably very clever, but I couldn't care less." Strangely, at that moment, they both resembled predators of the same species, if of different age.

Suddenly, like a whirlwind, a woman burst through the wide-open door into the room. The Master recognized her as the monumental Fury who had chased him from the chapel. With her mane of gray curls, fiery eyes, and dark, thick brows, trembling with passion, she conveyed an impression of extraordinary beauty; only gradually, in the dim light, did the guest realize that she was old, deaf and dumb, and perhaps even demented.

"Soup, soup," Zora announced, imitating the expressive gestures of the imperious matron, who was apparently the housekeeper.

But yet another person entered the dining room, so that again they all had to turn their attention away from the oversized tureen from which enticing vapors were rising.

"I completely forgot about Chako," Felix remarked with an amiable smile. "Chako, meet our guest."

Exaggeratedly slender, as if in a corset, the youth was dressed in civilian clothes, but his entire demeanor suggested that a hussar's uniform would suit him better. (His passionate, pale, melancholy face with the narrow mustache resembled Lermontov's self-portrait.)

"This is Chako, the cousin I told you about," Zora explained, radiant.

Finally they were seated; even the deaf-mute settled at the farthest end of the table. But she hardly touched her food; instead, she directed the servants like an orchestra conductor. Some of her gestures were understandable even to a stranger. Others could be interpreted only by the initiated, particularly the women and girls who, dressed alike in kerchiefs or shawls, with the eyes of fallen nuns, rushed chaotically between kitchen, pantry, wine cellar, and dining hall. With such an abundance of servants, one might have expected some division of labor. But here they had not yet come to that: one girl carried a bottle of wine, a second brought another straw-covered bottle, while a third uncorked still more Tokay or slivovitz; the first returned with fried fowl, the second appeared with fried fowl, the third came running with fried fowl. All of this lent the scene an irrational, spontaneous force.

Felix, as everyone called Zora's father, mumbled a blessing in Latin and they all turned to the thick soup rich with mushrooms. Swallowing a first spoonful, the guest, his eyes bulging, immediately and without waiting for an invitation, emptied his glass of wine. The red-hot greasy concoction could be eaten only with precaution. The others knew: they chatted leisurely, chewing bread.

"So you are a professor?" Felix asked.

Master Kassian frowned and Zora, who sat across the table from them, implored, "Please, Father, let us eat."

Reluctantly Felix turned to Chako. "Let's have a drink, hussar! A real one!" he said airily.

"We are ready for a taste too," the Bishop seconded.

From behind them the women, smiling like idols, began to pour the transparent liquid into the glasses.

"This," the Bishop explained, "is our bread and butter. In the past our slivovitz was sent to the Imperial table in Vienna."

"And to Constantinople," Zora added joyfully.

"Yes, also to Constantinople," the Bishop confirmed. "By way of the Patriarch this slivovitz even reached the Sultan."

"One has to get used to a drink to really appreciate it," remarked the guest somewhat didactically. "As Tolstoi once said, dismissing a beautiful sonata, 'This doesn't remind me of anything.' "

"I think it's very simple. You just have to drain an entire bottle—and the morning after, any fool will understand why this is excellent slivovitz," Felix said curtly.

Chako laughed. Everyone looked at him with surprise, but he did not say anything. The deaf-mute raised her glass and with an expressive gesture poured its contents into her mouth: directly into her stomach—or so it seemed.

"Curious," said the Master, "when we had vodka, my mother drank it exactly the same way. Bottoms up!"

No one was listening; they were all busy eating, as is proper after slivovitz. Only the deaf housekeeper, the old woman with the high young breasts and the passionate, burning eyes, looked at the guest with a peculiar smile.

The inhabitants of the castle consumed with pleasure the molten mass that passed for soup—it seemed like a trick of magic. Even Zora managed to swallow this lava (albeit in tiny portions). The guest blew at a spoonful, took a sip of wine, blew again, but all he could do with relative safety was lick his spoon.

"One can tell immediately that you are a stranger," Felix said.

"His mother lived here," Zora retorted with her usual elation.

"Is that so?" Felix said, unconvinced. "To whom was she related?"

The Bishop raised his large predatory head.

"I don't know," Kassian answered quietly. "She was running from the Tsar's police and stayed here until the Revolution."

The women, in a group, apparently at a signal from the deaf-mute, were carrying off the soup bowls and began changing the plates. Although he had not finished, the guest was happy to be rid of the soup. There was already a meat dish on the table, something with a lot of gravy. It smelled like mutton. A special bottle was brought in; the Bishop examined it and nodded.

"This wine is of Austro-Hungarian vintage," he said, addressing himself to the Master and politely, even elaborately, clinking glasses with him. Then he continued in the same tone: "I wonder what the students of today think about religion?" (Now he was the benevolent patriarch, celebrating the return of a beloved grandchild.)

"That is both very complicated and very simple," Kassian said with a sigh. "I'm afraid Zora makes it sound too exciting."

"How could it be anything else?" the girl said severely (and yet joyfully).

"Yes, perhaps," the guest agreed. "But we are not particularly interested in the Church or religion."

"And what are you interested in?" Felix interrupted with his usual harshness.

The Master took his time answering. "We are interested in reality. The reality of the visible and the invisible world. The macrocosm and microcosm. And studying this reality, we noticed that the new data of the so-called postnuclear physics often coincide with the old theological canons—even with the Revelations of Saint John."

"It's so obvious," said Zora, "and yet the common man continues to worship the idols of the eighteenth and nineteenth centuries." She seemed to rejoice in this very contradiction.

Chako, melancholy, ivory-pale, looked at her in surprise, almost in horror. (He had dark, shining eyes with long velvety lashes.)

"We must change all this," the guest said.

"That's what I wanted to know," the Bishop said innocently, sucking (with red lips) on a mutton bone. "I want to know how contemporary physics relates to the Credo. . . . This is eaten with paprika," he interrupted himself, helping the guest to a dish.

"Thank you, but I saw some horse-radish on the table."

"Our horse-radish is excellent," the Bishop concurred. "But let's continue. Some time ago I renounced my office because I was tempted by the achievements of scientific thought. And now it turns out that the two can easily be reconciled. It appears I am the victim of a misunderstanding."

"Yes, and you are not the only one," the guest agreed. He spoke slowly. "However, I hope you renounced your office for other reasons as well, and that you do not regret it too much."

For the first time during the meal, the Bishop looked at the guest without his conventional worldly smile and answered earnestly: "All in all, I am satisfied with my life. At least I was until my granddaughter came home." The sharp creases of his face again distorted into a smile. "But you still haven't told us what electricity has to do with the Revelations of Saint John, besides the fact that when we were children we were afraid of both."

In the half-dark the women had removed one set of dishes and, obeying the inspired gestures of the deaf-mute, were bringing in others, heaped with steaming vegetables.

"Today we perceive reality in a complex way," Kassian began without enthusiasm. "Reality is real and it is unreal, and it is still something else. Such a point of view, though it may sound confusing, brings us a little closer to the nature of reality. Matter is particle and not particle, and it is wave and not wave, and therefore there is still a third possibility. This is an established fact. But we have not yet been able to assimilate it." He tasted the fragrant, amber-colored wine, which struck him as exquisitely dry, particularly precious because at the same moment Zora was bringing her glass to her lips. She was sitting across the table from him, silent and shining. Her thin, gentle face was unremarkable, but there was nothing more beautiful and meaningful in the whole world—at least for him. The triumphant joy she radiated—through her skin and blood, her soul and thoughts—was an undeniable reality, a testimony to the ultimate, innate glory of Creation. (But about that he could not speak here!)

"A wave and a particle, and neither a wave nor a particle, and still something else," the Bishop repeated thoughtfully. "That does resemble the Holy Trinity. Indivisible and unfusable."

"The most important thing is that we have re-established freedom of choice," Zora announced. "On the subnuclear level the chain of cause and effect breaks or twists in the most unpredictable way."

"Just a minute," her father interrupted, and, turning toward the guest, asked, "Are you a professor of physics?"

"No, I teach advanced sociology."

"Sociology," Felix repeated with exaggerated surprise. "Really? Chako," he said, sure of the young man's allegiance, "Chako, does sociology deal with matter and waves? Professor, how old are you?"

"I am almost thirty. I was born in November, like you. We are both Scorpio."

"There you have it. No connections, almost thirty years old, and still a pauper," Felix continued obstinately. "The only consolation is that he's a Scorpio!"

Zora rose without a word and walked away, down the medieval hall. When she stepped into the darkness, it was as though the tiled floor had swallowed her up: even her steps could no longer be heard. The deaf-mute and several other women flew after her, like heavy-winged birds.

Rising from his seat and leaning on the massive glittering handle of his cane, the Bishop carefully lit a long cigar on a candle. Chako vanished into the dark for a moment and reappeared, puffing on a Turkish pipe. Only Felix remained seated. He was absorbed in arranging two forks and a spoon into a stable tripod.

Master Kassian approached the deeply recessed window. Outside it was night; a lantern bobbed up and down in the courtyard. The sharp point of an anemic new moon was caught in a fan of poplars. Its palish light fell on the smoothly cropped lawns, on the flower beds, and on bushes that looked like rhododendrons. In the old days sumptuous balls had probably been held here, with strings of colored lanterns and the thunder of Chinese fireworks that had frightened the chamois on the foggy mountain crags. Champagne flowed and countesses were seduced. Beethoven had sat at the grand piano in the far corner, Liszt, and Schubert (perhaps even Mozart).

The Bishop was addressing him: "If I understood you correctly, you are from this part of the country?" he said blandly.

"Not really. I was born a long way from here. But my mother lived here for a while," the Master replied.

"What was her name?"

"Anna. Anyuta."

"There are many Annas around here. What was her family name?"

"She fled from the Russian police and apparently was in hiding. I don't know what name she used here."

"And your father?"

"He died before I was born. Soon after, Anyuta married a civil servant in Colmar. It was an unhappy marriage. Later I had another father, a White Russian officer, an emigré. To him I owe everything. He sent me to Paris and gave me my first start. So in a sense I did not have a father, and at the same time I had at least three," the guest concluded seriously.

"Where did your mother stay when she lived here?"

"She worked on a big estate, maybe even in this castle."

A sudden clatter drowned out the Master's voice: the deaf-mute had swept a pile of dishes off the table.

"I don't know what's the matter with that woman today, she is ready to climb the walls," the Bishop said.

"I want you to know," Chako stuttered, the stem of his pipe gripped between his teeth, "I want you to know that at our academy duels were perfectly acceptable."

"Oh, shut up, for heaven's sake," Felix snapped, retrieving two forks and a spoon from the floor.

"I think that after such a long journey a young man is entitled to a rest," the Bishop announced with his most benevolent smile.

At the sound of dishes breaking, women and girls had streamed in from all sides: some were picking up the shards while others counted the silver, swept the floor, and put the heavy chairs back in their places. One of the older ones, in a red kerchief and with eyes full of mischief, was holding a lighted candle. She motioned Kassian to follow her. Together they climbed the endless, sweeping staircase.

The woman, a gay, fiery gypsy, was the wife of the herculean Markali; she and their young daughter were both called Katerina. Deftly she plumped up the pillows, brought in fresh water, found more towels, laughing and chatting all the while.

"We called your mother Anyuta. The deaf-mute spotted you immediately. Beware of her, sir," she said.

"What is she then—a werewolf?" the Master asked. He had a way with simple people. The woman burst into laughter and finally, with a burning look at him, said, "She can do anything, the witch."

Wandering aimlessly around the room, she suddenly stopped and asked, "Shall I stay, or should I send someone younger? That's no problem around here."

"No," he said heavily. "I won't be needing anything else tonight."

As if she had expected exactly that answer, the woman immediately took wing, disappearing into the dusky empty corridor. Her footsteps could not be heard (just as any screams would be muffled). The thick walls filtered neither light nor smells. The deep small windows were really embrasures. A prison, a fortress, and still something else? The door to his room could not be pulled to completely, much less locked. Kassian pushed an oak chair up against it.

3

The sun was playing in the farthest corner of the room. But the earth was rotating, and a minute later the room darkened, then grew light again: now sunlight fell through the next embrasure. Such an arrangement makes watches and calendars unnecessary, thought the Master.

He dressed without haste and scraped his face before an ancient (eternally dusty) mercury-lined mirror; the cold water dulled the blade.

He pulled a sleeveless sweater over his shirt and cautiously set out in search of the main corridor. Now he easily located the big staircase with the titans on the landing, then the great hall, the vestibule, and the portico with the marble columns.

Unnoticed, the guest crossed the clean, paved, but weed-grown courtyard, where a stork was affectedly taking his morning constitutional, then walked through the wicket into the park. In the daylight the trees looked simpler, more understandable; they creaked and sighed like old people. On both sides of the avenue, beyond the ancient trees, stood prehensile bushes and stunted birches with lumpy growths. There was also a lot of juniper, and a special kind of hardy, lacelike fern. A meadow sloped toward the river, the banks of which were covered with willows and reeds. An oriole whistled, and high up in the sky a lark was exhausting itself in a song of love.

Kassian followed the steep, stony path and reached the bridge: on the other side, clustered around the piazza, lay the picturesque village with its stores and strange semi-eyeless houses. Bright-colored stones and metal ornamentations glittered in the sun. The geometrical shapes of fields, orchards, gardens, stretched to the south as far as the eye could see. Squeezed between violet hills and mountains, all this wealth shimmered in the sun, seeming to float in an eternal sea of light.

The valley was a witness to the continuous miracle of existence. A fairly large river burst out of the mountains at the foot of the stone cliffs and, for thousands of years now, had fertilized this circumscribed region with its seasonal overflow. The village with the ancient piazza had taken root here and flourished, together with a dozen or so farmsteads along the river's banks. The farmers fertilized the grainy, fat soil (which glistened like caviar or a mixture of poppyseeds and honey) with the silt from the river; they also carried it farther up, to the rocky terraces where they grew their melons and pumpkins. In the fall, the rains and brooks washed it all away and after the spring thaw the farmers again hauled their existential dirt across ravines and gorges up to the steep terraces. But as a result of this absurd tenacity they collected, at the end of each summer, a blessed harvest of fragrant vegetables, berries, fruit—bushels of their special kind of prunes—and corn, buckwheat and barley, as well as hay, oats, millet, and other feed for their livestock.

Yet only a short distance away from the river, abruptly, as with the Nile, lay the desert, its crevices resembling pythons waiting to invade and swallow up the fertile earth. Still farther on came bare mountains, some of granite, some of basalt, and in the south the river was sucked back into a dark, narrow gorge where it vanished completely under the rocks. From there on, almost all the way to the sea, its life-bearing gifts were wasted.

On the piazza a donkey was dozing near the fountain and a few dirty pigeons walked about, dutifully picking at the dung. A thin golden cross shone atop the single (Moslem?) dome of the church. Despite the early hour, there was already some activity at the inn: from the front room came the sound of a player piano. Several natives, in sheepskin vests over dirty homespun shirts, were busying themselves around a wagon, loading it with crates and barrels of unusually small dimensions. Horses and donkeys peered out of the back court, apparently interested in the nature of the cargo and in who would be driving that day.

The gendarme in his blue uniform stepped with great self-importance down the steps of the village hall. From beneath his heavy military cap the sweat was already pouring abundantly. He wiped his red forehead with his palm and yelled from afar to the peasants, "The mail, don't forget the mail, you muttonheads!" He had an utterly harmless face. With his stiff mustache he looked like a huge, friendly cockroach.

The natives answered with an avalanche of indecent folksy phrases and complicated proverbs. From somewhere behind fences or from cellars the women joined in with their mirthless, multipitched laughter.

A small white mare with a random sampling of Arab characteristics was led out. She was discontentedly swishing aside imaginary flies with her long silky tail.

At the approach of the guest everyone dropped his boring occupation. Even the mare stopped flogging herself.

"May I have some coffee?" the Master asked after he had greeted them, not addressing anyone in particular.

There was no answer. He looked straight at a big, oily-faced peasant with bulging eyes and said, "I'll pay." The imposing fellow with his dignified beard gaped at the guest's mouth as if antediluvian birds had issued from it. A man in a business suit, who was the owner of the grocery store and also the mayor, said, "That's no problem. We always have coffee. And a good man doesn't have to pay." He was surnamed the Owl, and indeed, his magnificent thick, feathery eyebrows, half circling his eyes, did make him resemble one.

The peasants promptly seconded the mayor: "That's no problem. We always have enough coffee. There's always coffee for an honest guest. Hey, women, didn't you hear? The Professor wants coffee. Wiggle your hips!" And now, frankly abandoning their work, they all sat down on the terrace in front of the inn as if they had been waiting for just such a distraction. Only the white mare remained standing, but she hospitably nodded her delicate, elongated head.

The women and girls, big, strong yet graceful, wrapped in brightly colored shawls, were already in motion, each one carrying a cup of coffee. Promptly there rose the smell of the East, of warm seas, palms, and siestas.

"Black, hot, and aromatic," announced a man with a huge, bony red nose who was called, very appropriately, Pelikan Effendi.

Fragrant, ideally black as the eye's pupil, the coffee gave off tempting clouds, but it was impossible to put it to one's lips. That was how they prepared it here! The guest asked for sugar (the milk, he knew, would be goat's milk).

"Sugar? Sugar is good. Sugar does not spoil the coffee. It only dulls the taste," the bearded natives concurred, holding out their empty cups for more. (To swallow such molten iron, the throats and stomachs of these people must have been coated with tin.)

"What do you say? How do you like it? Have you ever had better coffee?" they asked proudly. "Our coffee is first class. And so is our slivovitz. They don't serve any better in the castle."

"The Bishop's women are better," declared Philolai, spitting contemptuously through his teeth. In a clean shirt, sucking on his pipe, he obviously had the day off.

The natives resembled one another in looks and dress, but even more in an over-all similarity of behavior: their way of speaking and smiling, and, most of all, their unshakable, deliberate slowness.

The village notables—the merchants, the owner of the factory, and the artisans—wore suits; almost the entire bourgeoisie was sitting at the table with the Owl and Philolai's brother Cantemir, the innkeeper. Pelikan Effendi, who was the Comptroller and also the proprietor of the quarry that supplied a rare colored marble for export, sat there with the tinsmith Yovan, who made the very pots and pans in which the molten liquid they called coffee was prepared and served. They were smoking and talking and drinking the slivovitz that had somehow inobtrusively appeared on the table. The gendarme unbuckled his belt with the saber and sat down at one of the tables with the obvious intention of staying, since he ordered a boy to lock his office and to return with the key. (From time to time one or another band of dogs would crawl out of a ravine and, with decorum, cross the bright piazza.)

The laconic, repetitious speeches of the natives abounded in proverbs and folk sayings and, like musical variations, only made sense at the very end, as an entity.

This confusion (to an outsider) was further increased by their names. It seemed that almost all the peasants were called Joachim—only persons of importance and a certain wealth were honored with different names. The older, more respected peasants, however, had acquired surnames such as Joachim the Gray, Joachim the Flogged, Joachim Tobacco. In a way this simplified life, at least for a stranger: one could call anyone Joachim and be right three times out of four.

There were no young men in the village; without exception they left to make their fortunes overseas or in faraway cities. As a rule they never returned once they left, never wrote letters, never sent presents. Every so often, by indirect ways, would come a rumor that the son of Joachim (Tobacco or the Flogged) had struck it rich in a foreign land. But whether or not this was true no one knew for sure, and by tacit agreement no one ever tried to find out.

The women, young and old in colored shawls and heavy brown dresses, kept themselves in the background, in separate groups (or choruses). The children roamed about in gangs, making way only for the packs of half-wild dogs. It was not always easy to guess the sex of a particular child, nor to whom the child belonged. But the mothers had no trouble recognizing their own among the sun-tanned urchins and every night retrieved them without fail. Most of the women were called Anna. One of them had just jumped over a fence and, catching her offspring, was giving him a fast hard blow.

The fathers and grandfathers did not distinguish among the children—they treated them all with the same indifference. They were by now draining their fifth cup of coffee, all the while exchanging profound observations.

"The cicadas have started early this year," one said.

"The prunes will be good," another announced.

"That's for sure," said someone else, "it will be a fine harvest."

"A fine harvest for the Bishop, anyway," the first said.

"He'll fix us all right, the Bishop will," everyone agreed.

"What are they saying in the city about our rights, about freedom?" Joachim the Turk inquired.

Readily putting down his cup of red-hot lava, the Master began to expound on new possibilities for freedom, even managing to get in the concept of reversibility and the bankruptcy of the Second Law of Thermodynamics. But the peasants were not interested in that. They thought of freedom exclusively as the right to dispose of their labor and income without the interference of the castle and the civil servants in the city. Theories could not tempt them, though they listened politely to the guest so as not to hold up to him their intellectual superiority.

"As to your kind of freedom, a new plan has just been

proposed," Kassian said finally, giving up the idea of interesting them by less direct means. And he explained to the peasants, who were looking at him with their imperturbable faces, that it was no longer necessary for anyone to be poor or weak or second-class.

This part of his speech genuinely impressed the Joachims. Exclamations such as "Say that again. . . . How was that? . . . Tell us more. . . ." rained on the guest.

The notables merely listened with benevolent smiles, certain that equality could never be achieved on this planet. There would always be poverty! As for the "arm of the law," without his kepi even more like a kindly cockroach, he was strenuously puffing on his pipe and looking around him in amazement: thanks to the quantity of slivovitz he had consumed, he saw—and also thought—double.

The Master knew that with simple people one should not broach a serious topic until mutual confidence has been established. But experience had also taught him that a moment as opportune as this should be taken advantage of, and anyway, in the end, what he had to say would always sound suspect and foreign to them. (Later, someone else would come along and repeat what he had said. For that one it would be easier.)

The Joachims, concealing their doubts for the moment, wanted further explanations. "Say that again! How is it there will be enough for everybody? Who will give us all this?"

Even the women approached the table and listened intently with sullen, flat (enduring) faces.

"It's simple." The guest was beginning to imitate their manner of speech: short, repetitious, aiming purposely (as a kind of self-defense) not at the bull's eye but slightly to the side. "It's very simple. Would you say a man works for about fifty years out of his life? If he is healthy?"

"Yes . . . that's correct . . . you could say that. . . . Fifty years everybody works, that's simple . . ." the Joachims agreed.

"All right. Now, if he makes a thousand a year, how much will he make in those fifty years?"

"A thousand a year . . . that is correct . . . that's right . . . some years even more . . ." the natives agreed happily.

Bored, the mare had turned her back to the company and was now pensively looking at her sun-drenched, yellow-violet native valley.

"A thousand a year means fifty thousand in a lifetime. Is that so or not?" the Professor went on. But this deduction seemed to them too hasty.

"Yes, of course it is so. But not quite. A thousand a year—that's correct. But fifty thousand—that's big money. That's different."

Philolai put an end to their mulish doubting: "If it's one thousand a year, it has to be fifty thousand altogether. Let the Professor talk."

Cautiously they agreed. "Well, maybe that's right. It seems that way, for sure."

"That means that every baby born here is certain to earn fifty thousand during his lifetime. Now, suppose we gave him half that sum in the cradle?" After a sly pause, the Master answered his own question: "Then it would be easy for him to grow up, get an education, and choose a trade. Later, of course, he would return the advance with interest."

The people were getting excited, giving free course to colorful visions and bright dreams; but they were still wary.

"You mean twenty-five thousand for every suckling?" Philolai asked with elation. "Then you could raise him, educate him, and set him up in a trade."

"And if it's a girl? Does that go for girls too?"

"And who advances the money? Where will such funds come from?" wondered the skeptics (the local merchants).

"Yes. The funds . . . !" This word seemed very significant to the Joachims and they repeated it over and over with many nuances.

"Everyone contributes: society, the government, we all do," the Master continued. "Everybody here knows everyone around. You would give goods on credit to every newborn; thus you would give the funds. Up to twenty-five thousand. He'll grow up, earn money, and pay back the advance."

"What if he runs away with the funds? How are you going to catch the scoundrel? Take the Turk's son, for instance. . . ."

"Where could he run to?" the Master argued. "Not many would run. The government would find them. Besides, we could deduct a percentage as insurance against such crooks."

"That means deducting a percentage for possible loss. But you would really have to watch them!"

The peasants were visibly cheered. But they continued to ask the man from the city tricky questions, trying not only to understand his words but also to get at the secret thoughts behind them.

"It won't work, fellows," the gendarme (a dumfounded cockroach) suddenly broke out. "Because it's funds and funds. . . . People will multiply like mosquitoes. Right away every girl will start having babies."

"It won't work." Mayor Owl supported him.

"It won't work because there is no place to get the money from," Pelikan Effendi, the respected exporter of rare marble, spoke up sadly.

Kassian did not feel like arguing further. To change the subject he asked, "Is that your church?"

The Joachims, glad of the respite, readily nodded their heads.

"It's ours. . . . A good church. . . . Even in the cities there aren't many like it left. An old one, and in perfect condition."

"It looks like a mosque."

"It was a mosque once. Under the Turks. Then the Austrians took it over. Now it's ours again. We won it back."

"Don't worry, we'll harness them," Philolai squeezed in, apparently attributing a special meaning to this expression.

"Sure you'll harness them. In the meantime you go on giving the devils hens and eggs, homespun, and a goat every spring." The Joachims' powerful beards shook like evergreen branches.

"Don't worry, we'll harness them," repeated Philolai.

"Yes, that's for sure," said Joachim the Turk, "it makes no difference to us. The Turks, the Germans, the Russians. They all come to the same end. Even the Italians tried to poke their noses in. They came on elephants, so help me God. Meant to scare us." They all laughed, delighted with the stupidity of the Italians.

"Not really on elephants," said Joachim the Gray, the one whose turn it was to drive the mail to town. "And they were not Italians but Magyars. They galloped with two horses. One they rode, the other they ate."

The driver's speech reminded them of their duties. The merchants and the gendarme rose, tugged at their jackets, and buttoned up, thus giving everyone to understand it was time to get back to work. The mare trotted of her own accord to the fountain and the Joachims pushed their women out of the way and once more began to arrange the goods on the wagon in the most economical way, stuffing straw between the packages and tying the whole down with homemade rope of a truly flaxen color.

The valley lay under the sun, sweet-smelling and luxuriant; the river foamed and seethed, now and then sparkling as if lit up from the inside. Gray sandy banks, ashen blocks of mountains, and in between, shimmering, pinkish, bluish, lilac greens of fields, orchards, and gardens; poplars and cedars amiably making room for the white, flat-roofed stone houses; and the wide piazza casually paved with pink marble, its Roman fountain and medieval doves like a priceless museum exhibit.

Groups of morose farmers walked and rode over the bridge spanning the abyss. Packs of dogs impudently ran past them. Filtered by the wooden planks, the noise of the horses' hoofs sounded oddly quiet, yet distinct. A donkey, laden with two baskets, was conscientiously trotting toward the sun.

On the tower of the village hall, the hands of the round silent clock stubbornly pointed to a quarter of twelve. In the morning, when Master Kassian had come and begun his talk with the Joachims, this hour had seemed absurd. Now, after his third cup of red-hot coffee, it was indeed getting close to noon.

"The clock," the guest said, half statement, half question.

"Yes. The clock," complacently echoed the few who were still sitting.

"It's not working. It has stopped," the Master continued.

"That's right," the peasants assured him, smiling through their beards.

"Why doesn't it work?"

"The clock?"

"Yes. Why?"

"Why should it work?" The Joachims seemed surprised.

Presently Philolai, as a sign of special sympathy for the stranger, explained: "All clocks lie."

The others supported this competent explanation. "At least our clock doesn't lie," they said. "It cannot lie."

Behind the walls and fences the women could be heard: "A professor, and he doesn't even know that."

Now that the guest had proved his simple-mindedness, the Joachims could indulge their curiosity without inhibition and began to bombard him with indiscreet questions. "Are you really a professor? What does a professor do? Are all professors equal or are there professors for professors? Are you going to marry Zora?"

"Zora is a good girl," they declared without particular enthusiasm. "And her mother was an angel. But that Felix, he has a temper. A devil, to tell the truth."

"Listen," they advised the Master, "don't give in to that devil. He'll eat you alive. Felix can do that!"

The women, who were busying themselves close by, giggled but said nothing.

"Now it's homespun. Instead of women he takes homespun," the Joachims complained.

"And hens."

"And lambs," they enumerated indignantly.

"Just beware of Felix," Cantemir advised. "He'll swallow you in one gulp."

"My mother used to live here," Kassian began cautiously.

"Her name was Anna, or Anyuta. Perhaps you've heard of her?"

"Who can remember?" the peasants said. "Sometimes we forget our own wives." From behind the walls or from the cellars came a buzz as if of angry hornets.

"She was a Russian refugee," the guest continued.

"Whenever there is a war or some other calamity, the Bishop immediately gathers them up," they said. "Women, girls, sometimes even children."

The women laughed (from cellars or larders) and contributed a few stinging remarks.

"You had better make friends with the Bishop," Philolai counseled. "The Bishop will tell you everything."

"Yes, now they take our homespun instead of our women," the Joachims complained. (The conversation had a way of drifting in circles.)

"Don't worry, we'll harness them," Philolai closed the topic. "Do you go to church? That's good. We still have our old priest here. Our own."

"He is getting very weak," said Joachim the Turk with a sigh.

The others fell upon him: "Are you looking for a new one? When they send you a new priest, you'll be sorry."

"I didn't say that. We don't need a new broom. The old one is good enough."

They all shook their beards thoughtfully. In the background, like an ancient chorus, the women added something indistinguishable.

The Master had heard that the local church was a strange hybrid of ancient rites: though basically Catholic, it had been isolated for a long time under the Turkish yoke, and when, in the seventies, the Pope pronounced his infallibility, they did not accept the newfangled dogma and separated from Rome. Establishing a communion of prayer with the parishes of the Near East, the local church continued its independent life. The natives considered themselves true Orthodox Christians, which, up to a point, they were.

"We are quite satisfied with our priest. We don't need a new broom," they said again.

"But he is very old. What will happen when he dies?" said Joachim the Turk. There was no answer. All eyes were fixed in the direction of the bridge: Zora, tall, slender, delicate, almost frail, was just entering the glistening piazza. For a moment she stopped at the graceful stone fountain and looked at it with morbidly intense concentration.

In the hot midday air everything seemed arrested—like the clock on the tower. Only the yellow-purple shadows of the poplars near the river trembled. (Perhaps they moved in response to the rotation of the earth.)

4

The girl approached. Some of the Joachims rose, others remained seated but politely nodded their beards. Here in the center of her native village, on the pink piazza with the doves, the young woman who so steadily radiated an austere, serene happiness seemed completely, incontestably, in her place.

"You were having coffee, Master?" she asked, her golden-yellow eyes laughing. The peasants smiled too, sedately. The women surrounded her.

"What a clever one she is! What a pretty one!" they repeated, sincerely and falsely at the same time, stroking and petting Zora. "A fashionable dress. A new hairdo. Ready to be married. And she's brought a fiancé along. A real professor. What a clever girl!"

"And how are you?" Zora began hesitatingly; but, recognizing one of the younger women, addressed her with her usual elation: "Anna, what a joy! Is this your child?"

She embraced the blushing woman in hitched-up skirts and kissed her on both cheeks. The other Annas softly clucked their approval. The Joachims only waved their mighty beards.

"Her mother nursed both of us, we are like sisters," Zora explained to Kassian. "She was married years ago and must have a houseful of children by now."

The women around tittered. Squealing, the children again started to race across the piazza. From the stores and workshops dignified farmers emerged and headed straight for the inn to celebrate the deal they had just closed. People began to gather in the dining room and at the bar. Some came out to the terrace, glass in hand, and greeted Joachim the Old or Joachim the Flogged, after which both vanished together into the inn.

The gendarme, unable to decide where his duty required him to be, ran in and out, wiping his streaming red forehead: whatever he drank immediately turned into sweat.

"How is your husband? Is he good to you?" Zora questioned.

"That good-for-that!" Anna made a coarse gesture. "Tell us about yourself. How is Chako? He must be miserable, poor dear."

"No, Chako is no problem," cut in Joachim the Turk, the

somber skeptic who had worried about the priest's age. "Chako is a good fellow. Felix is the one to watch out for."

"And the deaf-mute?" Anna asked.

"That one! Skin her alive, the witch. Drive a stake through her heart!" came threatening female voices. If the peasants disliked Felix, the women obviously hated the housekeeper.

All the women had husky, aggressive voices and heavy, handsome, but early-aging faces; yet some spark of bitter lustiness remained in their eyes (like embers beneath the ashes of a dying fire that can still flare up and burn you!). Master Kassian felt ill at ease with them. But Zora continued in high spirits the seemingly endless talk.

Meanwhile Joachim the Gray had again watered the mare and was harnessing her. The two-wheeled wagon swayed cautiously at first and then, finally, was on its way. The driver clapped on his fur cap, tied the thick scarf securely around his neck, and buttoned his jacket all the way up, as if he were setting out for the North Pole.

"The mail, you devil, did you take the mail?" the gendarme, running out onto the terrace, managed to yell after him as the wagon, with mysterious speed, vanished behind the natural stone wall separating the valley from the empty, cracked wasteland across which the driver would have to travel for the next several days.

Kassian and Zora, both blinking against the sun, wandered through the piazza, looking into shady courtyards and shops. The girl greeted everyone, exchanged a few words, but did not linger.

"Yes, you are right, it is a miracle," the Master was saying. "A paleontological miracle!"

"Isn't it?" Like a child she ran ahead of him and turned around to look into his face. Hers was serious and at the same time crinkled with happiness (or blinded by the sunlight). "I used to think everything here should be turned upside down. I wanted roads, electricity, telephones, a hospital; I didn't want the women to do their wash in the river in wintertime. But, you know, I'm not so sure any more."

The old withered priest, very tall and stooped, with a tiny black skullcap and a silvery beard that fell to his belt in a thin rivulet, stood on the lawn in front of the church. His legs beneath the tight black cassock seemed about to give way from weakness. Leaning on his long staff, he had raised his white, ancient face—either to facilitate his breathing or in avid admiration of the brilliant summer sky.

They greeted him, but his answer gave no clue as to whether he had recognized Zora. He cast a glance at the Master as if he were a familiar sinner of whom he had wearied long ago.

"This is my fiancé, Father Nectarius," said the girl.

The priest mumbled something that sounded like "numb and dumb, numb and dumb," and then, taking a deep breath, he said in a stronger voice, distinctly and somewhat angrily: "Do you go to church? Do you partake in the sacraments?"

"He goes to all churches, Father," the girl said, as if announcing glad tidings.

"How is that?" the priest asked. "To the Catholics? And to the Lutherans? Do you cheat?"

"No, I don't cheat," the guest answered firmly. "It's true that I have been chased away, even with curses. But the clergy is changing."

"Are there many heretics like you?" the priest asked curiously.

"More and more of them," Zora informed him joyfully.

"Well," Father Nectarius said with a sigh, "if it's done in faith, God will forgive them." He hurriedly crossed the couple with his pale hand and turned his face again to the sky to concentrate on his breathing or steadfastly imprint the image of God's glory in his mind. "Numb and dumb, numb and dumb," he muttered.

From the river the carefree shouts of children drifted up to them, ducks quacked monotonously, and from time to time the dogs let out an ominous howl. All these sounds, unchanged probably for the last two thousand years, filled the stranger from the city with a forlorn sadness.

Kassian and Zora were walking across the bridge. Their steps, filtered through the planks, sounded as though coming from another world. There was the stony path over the ravine; to the left, the imprisoned, seething river; to the right, the forest with its mighty lindens, cedars, and oak trees that parted into the avenue leading to the castle. In the meadows, buzzing flies and bees. The glittering sun. Cold gusts of air from the mountains mixing with the smell of century-old orchards. To a newcomer it was intoxicating.

"Say something important," Zora begged, smiling without a smile, joy shining through her skin. The lark in the green sky was still overwhelmed with love. The Master was afraid to look into the girl's inspired face: it promised perfection or immortality. "I love you as ever," he said.

"How do you know?"

"I can't explain it, but I know. My love has no cause and no effect. It is spontaneous and miraculous, like life itself."

The girl listened to this valuable news, cocking her head sideways and laughing with her golden eyes.

"My heart sings, it is full to overflowing . . ." he continued cautiously, as if probing his way along dangerous ground. "Spontaneously I came to understand that the world is magnificent and that I am good. There are no limits to my inner capacities any more. And I pity the simpletons who never had a similar experience. Impossible to explain to them how real and accessible happiness is. Is there one and the same love for everyone, everywhere? Or is it broken up, so that everyone has his own, separate, and special love? This is the only thing I can talk seriously about these days. And it seems to me that everybody realizes it, sees through me—the Bishop, the deaf-mute, Felix, Chako. They envy us. Last night Katerina the Gypsy asked whether I wanted her to stay with me, and it was like a message from you in code. I never could understand what atheism is, or whether there really is such a thing. But now I know that anyone who has ever been in love must begin to believe in God: my eyes turn involuntarily from you, who are splendid and almost perfect, toward someone greater who stands behind you. The lover believes, even when he is not aware of it," the Master concluded, and caught his breath. The path was rising. A huge ugly bird soared in the sky, peering into the angry depths of the river for something edible. A strip of coarse, rushlike sedge along the bank bowed gently, rippling under the caresses of a silky wind.

"More, Professor, please more," the girl demanded. (During their walk she seemed to have grown still thinner.)

"I am afraid—or ashamed—to pronounce the name Zora. I think of you in the third person, as of someone far away. So that I do not come too close to you, do not take hold of your hand . . . for really I do not need that much: only to tell passers-by about my love, about the transfigurating power of love."

"More, please . . ."

"In the presence of old and sick people, one is reminded of death. Thus, long ago, I experienced my own death; I was even present at your funeral. But there is no death any more. Nor is there a future or a past: on that plane where love and wave mechanics meet, they are all strictly pedestrian concepts."

"Physics here too?"

"Yes, alas. I cannot know your essence without distorting you. That is Heisenberg's equation. The closer I get to you, the more you escape me." He gave a sudden, helpless sob.

"Talk," the girl said softly, "please, talk."

"It is painful to look at your rapturous face. In your presence I lose myself. I can do nothing from now on but affirm my love. How good it is that we are separated by stone walls and locks and fences."

"It is easy to jump over those walls and fences," Zora whispered. "I am bored here alone, Professor."

"I would like to solve the mystery at last. Are you only you or do all the "yous" join into one entity? Is my love really "mine" or is it everyone's love, the eternal, the only one? This love paralyzes me and at the same time it is a blessing, the limit of perfection. I don't exist any more: you are in me—everywhere. Have pity on me, for my heart cannot hold so much."

"What can I do?" Zora cried in joyous awe, convinced that all would end well in the fullness of time. Taking his hand, she led him along an uneven path toward a grove bowing silently at the top of the hill.

"Zora's presence is torture to me, and yet I am forever seeking it. When I think of your pure radiance, all evil in me is wiped out. I weigh less now—as if the law of gravity had lost its power over me."

"How did it all happen?" she asked.

"Love has transfigured and mutilated me. A locomotive hit a freight train and derailed it."

"Yes?"

"I can only glorify you day and night, glorify the angels and the spirits that guard you. You were before the beginning of life, and you justify its end."

"For heaven's sake, don't tell them that at home," Zora begged, laughing.

"When Anyuta was dying, I realized that you and I would someday be transformed into matter too—with no possibility of appeal. Such irrefutable evidence had to be conquered. My theory of reversibility was born out of my love for you. Love taught me immortality and showed me the perfection, if not of nature, then of the origin of nature. It is not we who are doomed. It is the Second Law of Thermodynamics that is dead and waiting to be buried. . . ."

"More about us," the girl interrupted.

"What injustice! There are people who will go through life knowing nothing, hearing nothing of Zora. Just as exhausted tourists leave an ancient city without suspecting that there, in a small chapel on the outskirts of town, is one of the miracles of art, not yet described in guidebooks."

"Dear Master. In a minute we'll be back at the castle. Please, don't mention any of this. Simply ask for my hand—the way it's done. Soon we'll be alone, or with people we feel close to. Then we shall be able to continue this talk."

Looking around distractedly, Master Kassian took a deep breath. After a moment he said, "Tell me about the deaf-mute."

"She is an old romance of the Bishop's. Everything you just said about love she would understand."

"Are you sure she is deaf?"

"That's strange," Zora said, "you are not the first to ask. They say that when she was young she was bathing in the river and there was an avalanche. Such catastrophes happen often around here. Frightened, she dove under the water, and the thunder and vibrations ruptured her eardrums. That's the official version."

"How many wives has the Bishop had?"

"Many," the girl said. Her clear, even voice enveloped him, so that he seemed to perceive it not through his ears alone but through all the pores of his body, or through his soul. The same was true of her sand-colored laughing eyes: their glance was perceived not only visually. . . . A merely optic or acoustic impression of Zora did not exhaust her presence.

In the meadow, bathed in the downpour of sun, squatted Markali, the dashing, graying, blue-skinned giant. He was whittling at something with an ax he held by the butt. Beside him a gleaming, brightly painted agricultural machine stood rearing; spare parts lay strewn around it on the grass.

"This is a trusted friend. He can fix, paint, build, mend, and even cure anything," Zora informed the Master.

Markali straightened up and with a broad smile waited for them to approach. His large, slightly puffed, bluish face made the Master uneasy: as though he were looking at a hanged, or a drowned, man. The hot moist glance of the gypsy, his strong white teeth, his smile and the gleaming earring, all spoke of freedom, passion, recklessness. And yet, sensing some fateful vulnerability, the Master felt pity for him.

Markali nodded to the couple, obviously approving of the way they were spending their time, and then immediately went back to his whittling, much to the surprise of the guest, who had already noted with what contempt and indifference the natives treated their work.

"You remember his wife Katerina," said the girl. "A beauty. And they have a daughter, Little Katerina: an angel, a devil, or one and the other and still something else. Actually she resembles a little snake." She laughed with her honey-colored eyes.

"Yes, there are many enchanting serpents around," Kassian agreed, watching with admiration the deft movements of the gypsy's large (live) hands.

"No. Little Katerina is something special," Zora insisted. "Something very special."

"How he whittles," the Master said quietly, and sighed. "I envy him. That is how great men fight their age-old enemies, discover new combinations of molecules or colors."

"Markali is always busy," Zora confirmed with delight. "I noticed it even as a child—it made a great impression on me. And animals obey him: horses, birds, rabbits, goats. He's never been bitten by a dog—and that is rare around here. Let him inside anyone's house and he'll immediately find the tools or improvise something to patch a leaking roof or repair the chimney. He's a gypsy!" The girl spoke with great emotion, not minding that Markali could overhear her. "They are always the scapegoats in the valley. If a harness gets lost or if it rains on Saint Cassian's Day, they say, 'It's the gypsy's fault. He should be hanged!' He's been beaten up so many times. And he is the kindest, the most honest, helpful soul. When he's sober, that is. He doctors the animals, talks to the birds, has pet names for the cats, the colts, and the puppies. Salty, Fatso, Dumpling, Sugar, he calls them. And they understand, they come, they fly to him.

His daughter is a mystery too. . . . She isn't like anyone around here." Zora spoke seriously, eagerly; Markali calmly continued to move his ax back and forth. "The simplest explanation would be that a fairy brought Little Katerina from another time and sphere," Zora concluded, laughing.

They had reached the park. Tall cedars exuded a dry smell of vinegar and turpentine. Two thin-legged fawns, pawing the ground in exactly the same manner, jumped, first one, then the other, across the path and vanished in the grove. On the avenue with its huge linden trees the Bishop appeared, dressed in a green jacket, a peacock feather on his blue hat: exquisite, old-fashioned, but by no means comical.

"Have you had lunch yet?" he called from a distance. "It's so boring to eat by oneself."

"If I'm not mistaken, we haven't had lunch," Kassian answered cheerfully.

"Go ahead, I'll join you in a moment," the girl said, and ran off.

5

Leaving the sanded path (almost the color of Zora's eyes) they crossed the courtyard and finally climbed the steps to the monumental portico. On the veranda, where blue caravels floated endlessly over large square tiles, they sat down at a marble-topped table that several women instantly and chaotically began to set.

"Is there somewhere on this floor I can wash my hands?" Kassian asked diffidently.

"No," answered his host with an affable smile. "You would have to run up three flights. And between you and me," he added in a confidential tone and so softly that the Master had to bend closer to catch his words, "only dirty people wash themselves constantly."

Kassian did not argue and, without much enthusiasm, put a massive wing of a cold fried bird on his plate; strangely enough, here he had no appetite. As for the Bishop, he was already attacking several different kinds of ham and salami. A cloud of steam hovered menacingly over the coffee pot but it smelled enticing.

"By the way, what time is it?" the Master asked with deliberate, emphasized restraint, repelled by these people who seemed to get drunk at the mere sight of pork and sausages.

"I wouldn't know," the host answered, interrupting his energetic chewing. "Here we live by the sun and by the Church holidays. It is the wisest thing." The Bishop's cup was giving off a wonderful aroma but the Master dared not touch his own. "Anyway, which time would you prefer to observe?" the Bishop continued, savoring his food, his words, and his thoughts. "Summertime, wintertime, Western European Time? Russian, American, Chinese? In the cities there are clocks everywhere and they seldom agree. Perhaps everyone should observe his own physiological time? Or the absolute, mathematical? Such concepts do exist, but what good are they to us in this valley?"

"Yes, I noticed that the clock on the village hall does not work, and the people seem almost proud of it."

"That's it," the Bishop replied animatedly, "our clock is exceptional. I assure you, it is the only clock about which it can be said that it shows the exact time twice every twenty-four hours. Precisely when, we do not know, but we do know for sure it has to happen twice a day."

"Contemporary philosophy agrees with you," the Master said after some thought. "According to this line of reasoning, at least eight percent of reality, unshakable reality, is revealed to us."

"Why eight percent?" For once the worldly old charmer appeared puzzled. But this did not prevent him from continuing to chew, sip, swallow, which caused his mouth to become unpleasantly distorted, resembling a huge bloodless toad (or lizard) with heavy folds around the lips.

"Twice in twenty-four hours," Kassian explained, trying not to notice the circular movements of the Bishop's jaws. "Twice every twenty-five hours would be eight percent. In our case we get eight and a third percent. Is that right?"

"Yes," the host drawled. "But what does that prove—if you are serious," he added hurriedly, politely giving his companion a chance to turn it all into a joke.

"Quite serious. It means that in our world any absurdity, any senseless theory, any imaginable remedy—social, medical, religious—any combination of sounds, colors, ideas, will eight times out of a hundred lead somewhere and turn out to be partially true, beautiful, beneficial, and just. So that those criminals and morons who present us with the latest absurd discovery are always at least eight and one third percent right."

"Amusing," the Bishop approved. "Is this a sample of the new subatomic form of thinking?"

"Yes, you might call it that."

"It was my suggestion not to repair the clock on the village hall," the Bishop said, smiling at a dish of stuffed tomatoes. "It seemed easier to do without information entirely than to use false data. I am glad we are alone and can talk off the record," he continued, without changing his tone of voice. "You are indeed an excellent fiancé. And Zora is rich and from a good family, although of course nowadays all this has become irrelevant." He smiled distractedly with his large lemon-yellow face. (From such faces El Greco painted his portraits.)

The guest was silent, giving him no help, but the Bishop continued with the assurance of a man of the world who knows how to behave under any circumstance or will impose his own rules of behavior. "Personally, I have nothing against the marriage. I like you. I really do. Money is only a convention. And birth? Who knows, you may be of ancient lineage. Zora is reckless, like her mother. There is no reasoning with her. So the best thing for everyone concerned would be to settle this affair peacefully and promptly. However, a ticklish complication has come up."

Since Kassian still said nothing, the Bishop had no choice but to continue: "The question concerns your father. Have you really never tried to find out who he was?"

This was a direct challenge and the Master answered: "My entire life has been directed toward that aim. By studying myself I discover to some extent who created me."

"Yes, of course. But sometimes one would like to know concretely whether one was sired by an ape, a mule driver, or the Prince of Wales."

"I believe the correct answer to that would be: by one and the other, and still something else."

"Of course, of course," the Bishop agreed hastily, "again that is physics. But let's be practical. Your mother apparently lived here in the castle. Then she left and you were born. The deaf-mute says you are my son, that is, Felix's brother. Half brother, if you wish."

"The deaf-mute says . . . ?"

"Yes, the deaf-mute says," the Bishop repeated, controlling his irritation. "How is it that you, with your new mechanics, can't accept such a paradox?"

"Then she remembers my mother?"

The Bishop studied the cigar he was about to light. "After the death of my wife, Felix's mother," he said evenly, "I lost my reason to a certain degree. In any case, I lost all sense of decency and proportion. It was the deaf-mute who eventually saved me. But not before I had made a number of dangerous and frivolous experiments."

The guest stubbornly kept his silence and the Bishop concluded firmly: "So it turns out that you and Zora cannot marry."

"Why?" The Master finally sipped his coffee. It was cool, but it had also lost its taste.

"Why?" the host repeated, surprised. "But it would be against every law of society. Incest is forbidden by the Church as well as by the government."

"To listen to the guesses of a woman who is deaf and dumb and—" the guest hesitated for a moment—"probably demented . . . that, forgive me, is an absurdity. Of course, similar to any other stupid hypothesis, this one also contains eight percent of the truth. Neither more nor less. Which means that out of every hundred couples like me and Zora, eight might turn out to be close relations. But precisely which couples, that we will never know and never be able to predict. Anyhow, we are interested only in our particular, personal, concrete case. General statistics do not concern us." The Master boldly finished his coffee and pushed the cup away.

"I cannot agree with such reasoning," hurriedly objected the Bishop.

"What is the matter? What troubles you? You know perfectly well that all men are brothers. We have one Father. What bothers you? Incidentally, in the Bible and among royalty, marriages between members of the same family were the rule."

"That is a completely different story," the Bishop said.

But Kassian was not easily shaken. "No," he answered, "it is not a completely different story, it is exactly the same thing."

The Bishop smiled indulgently: "You know of whom you remind me? Of myself in my youth. I too was revoltingly courageous and consistent."

"Well, that means I must be good enough for Zora," the guest decided.

"The question is heredity, genes," the Bishop confided. "It causes degeneration."

"Nonsense. Statistics. I already explained that. Out of a million children a certain percentage will degenerate. But the theory of probability cannot and is not meant to predict what will happen to any particular child. And yet it is this particular case that interests us. It is quite possible that free choice begins here—on the level of our cells and atoms."

"Yes," the Bishop said, "this new physics will cause still more harm than Marxism or Darwinism. By the way, what were you told about your father when you were little? What was his name? What did he do?"

"As a matter of fact, I had three fathers," the Master answered dryly. "We have already spoken about that and I am sorry I cannot satisfy your curiosity further."

From an inner door, Felix, dressed in jodphurs and leather leggings and covered with dust, entered the veranda briskly, almost at a run. Greeting them carelessly, he laid his heavy crop on the table and promptly reached for the coffee pot.

"We have been discussing heredity, probability, and evolution," the Bishop politely informed his son. "It appears that Darwin, Marx, and Newton have been shelved. They are no longer in tune with the times."

"Darwin!" Felix yelled, "Newton!" The women had already slid a bottle of slivovitz before him and he quickly downed a glass. "Abolish everything. The Emperor! The Church! Euclid. Wagner . . . even Nietzsche!" he shouted with a sob, especially bitter for some reason about the last. "Yes, even Nietzsche is now considered a prattling child."

"And the old question of whether man did or did not descend from an ape is now simply irrelevant," the Bishop continued dispassionately. "On the basis of the latest discoveries, the Professor affirms that we descend from an ape and also not from an ape and from still something else. . . . One may assume that some individuals evolved from an orangutan and that others were created in a completely different way." The Bishop carefully twirled his green cigar. "Sometimes one looks at a human being and is horrified: by God, a gorilla, a troglodyte. Yet another has an angelic appearance; one can almost see the nimbus floating above his head. Where does such variety come from, if the roots are the same?"

"By what right, Professor, do you decide who is an ape and who is an angel? Who do you think you are?" Felix shouted, pounding his fist on the marble table.

"I said nothing of the sort," Master Kassian answered calmly, and seemed about to rise from his seat.

"Just a minute. Stay!" Felix ordered. "You intend to marry my daughter?"

"Yes, if she consents."

"What do you have to offer her?"

"I don't know."

"But isn't one supposed to consider such matters when one is in love? The present determines the future. What are your expectations?"

The guest only smiled. Seriously the Bishop explained: "According to the new teaching, the cause need not condition the effect. Free choice or a sudden, spontaneous jump is always possible. At least on the microscopic level. Also, it can happen that the effect moves faster than the cause. In that case the entire sequence of events is turned upside down."

"I have no intention of philosophizing now," Felix declared, certain that, should he want to, he would be able to deal with any sophisticated problem. "There is something far too serious involved here." (To him, abstract discussions were suitable only concerning matters of secondary importance.) "After all, it is my duty to protect my daughter," he shrieked, losing all control. "I will not permit anyone to sully all that is sacred, and if I have to use this" (snatching up the heavy riding crop) "believe me, I won't hesitate. I assume you are for postatomic passive resistance, Professor!"

"Not necessarily," the guest answered, visibly brightening. "We are for heroic deeds, for affirmation, for self-sacrifice . . . against inertia, egotism, sloth. Against entropy. If you offend me and I hit you" (the Master presented a not overly large but steely fist) "it would be a vulgar act of self-defense, merely perpetuating the vicious line of causality that leads to death. If, however, you were to offend one of your women and I—with pleasure—punched you in the nose, the act would take on the character of altruism, of a spiritual deed, even of reversibility in the deepest sense of the word." He rose, and looking down on the stocky Felix in his leather leggings, continued in a different tone: "I did not want to come here and apparently I was right. I did it for Zora, knowing how important it was to her. But now I'm leaving for the village and you will be so kind as to have my things brought to the inn."

Big-headed, heavy-browed, they were both on their feet. Watching each other with almost similar angry gray eyes, they resembled two strong, hungry wolves.

"Gentlemen, please," the Bishop began, but at that moment he perceived Zora and Chako outside, on the steps leading to the portico. Through the thick pane one could see they were laughing and talking animatedly. Once inside, the girl promptly held out a cup to a woman (who appeared from nowhere) and then triumphantly announced that she was starved. Chako was still smiling. Even so, his passionate, sensitive face with the black mustache looked yet more wan in the daylight.

The Bishop, as if continuing an interrupted conversation, said: "I should also like to know how you solve the old problem of the theodicy. Classical theology relies on the concept of original sin: through the Fall, evil and death entered the world. How do you approach this riddle?"

The Master walked over to the window. From there he saw the strip of blessed lawn bordering the edge of the park. In the summer light, people were noiselessly rushing in all directions on their simple domestic chores. The Bishop was waiting for an answer.

Fortunately Zora, who had already managed to drink her cup of coffee, came to Kassian's rescue.

"We think that is a childish way of putting the question," she said. "On the subatomic and supracosmic level, the law of causality ceases. To look for a cause in everything is senseless. . . . We must give up such outdated habits once and for all. The evil that suddenly appeared in the world does not have a cause, nor is it the effect of anything."

"Is that so?" The Bishop was politely surprised.

"Yes." The girl nodded her fair head seriously. "Furthermore," she continued rapidly, "at this point the concept of complementarity enters the picture. Matter is particle and matter is wave. But these two concepts should not be applied simultaneously. So it is with God: He is all-loving and He is omnipotent. But these are two complementary images of God, unfusable and indivisible."

Chako had walked up to the window and, resolutely drawing himself up to his full height, blushing, he whispered so that only the Master could hear, "Don't worry about me. I shall not stand in your way. I would rather die first."

On the path toward the park, the deaf-mute walked with long, deliberate strides. She resembled a large bird of prey, perhaps a female condor. Suddenly she stopped, looked back in alarm, and then stared up menacingly at the castle windows. . . . She could not possibly see the Master behind the thick glass in the shadow, but he felt uneasy and quickly stepped back. It would not have surprised him in the least if the witch flew off on a broomstick.

He heard his name—as if it came from an underwater realm. Zora was calling him. Felix, standing over her with the distorted features of a betrayed father, was screaming something unintelligible.

"Did you hear, Professor?" she asked, still shining, unable to switch off that interior light.

"No, I'm sorry, I didn't. But it's probably just as well. I'm leaving for the inn." He looked at Zora and smiled happily.

6

The deaf-mute could not have gone very far. Kassian hurried after her, but the witch had disappeared in the woods.

"My mistake is that I'm following the direction logic tells me is right," the Master, out of habit, murmured to himself (early in life his stepfather had convinced him there was no better partner in a conversation than oneself). "There is nothing more difficult than renouncing old notions, and people rarely succeed in doing so before it is too late. A man only pretends to accept new findings. But in reality he is ready to produce a hundred reasons that will justify sticking to the old, straight line." He left the path abruptly and walked into an undergrowth of nut bushes and birches and of solid masses of juniper that gave off their pungent, medicinal smell.

In a clearing near a stack of freshly mown hay, the gypsy was at work with a pitchfork. His red shirt was unbuttoned and a copper cross swung on his sweat-glistening chest. Smiling with his unhuman eyes, silver-maned, tanned a deep blueberry purple, he resembled an aging, doomed, yet cheerful pagan god. Without waiting to be asked, Markali, wiping the sweat from his solid forehead, said, "She went that way. She's picking mushrooms." He pointed. And indeed, the Master soon came upon two women, of different ages and different looks, but marked by the same spirit of life and passion. The deaf-mute wore her brown shawl. Katerina the Gypsy had taken off her colorful kerchief. Her abundant hair streaming down freely, she resembled a naiad, the consort of fauns and satyrs. She carried, as it were incidentally, a large basket and, bending down from time to time, attentively picked small shiny mushrooms. The deaf-mute was gathering herbs and only one special kind of poison-colored mushroom, all of which she put into a white handkerchief.

The wood was wild and neglected; it smelled of cedar, pine, and dampness. The sun touched only the tips of the trees, which every so often bowed and swayed together in one direction. There in the treetops lived many creatures: insects droned, birds peeped faintly; but below, on the ground, as on the bottom of the ocean, reigned semideath: once in a while a bumblebee lost its way and buzzed by in the dusk, or some frightened mouselike creature, evidently belonging underground, scurried past. Another life-bringing wave of wind made the treetops rustle unevenly but did not penetrate to the very depth (the currents of air, similar to sea currents, reflected the profile of the bottom—undulating, rising, and falling with the topography).

On and off, in unexpected places, hung the pentagram of a cobweb, with a sunbeam struggling inside: as if the spider, in need of light, had woven its web to catch precisely this kind of prey.

In some areas the moss and turf and deadfall were covered by a tracework of daylight; these bright spots were round or oval: not the shadows of the leaves resembled the leaves, but the light passing between them reconstructed their image on the ground. This absurd phenomenon cheered the Master for some reason, and he promptly caught up with the slowly moving women.

Katerina was not the least surprised by his appearance. Her moist lips and her bracelets gleaming, she suggested he too get busy picking mushrooms. The deaf-mute ignored him.

"This is a saffron milk-cap and this is a Russula," the gypsy explained with a roguish smile. "But the ones with the white belly you mustn't touch. They are as poisonous as snakes."

"I'm moving to the inn. I came to say good-by," the Master announced solemnly.

"Don't be foolish, dear, we'll meet again, we'll meet more than once," the gypsy said, and made a few rapid signs with her fingers, to which the deaf-mute moved her lips in reply.

"Are there many medicinal herbs around here?" Kassian politely inquired of the matron.

"Careful, sir," Katerina said quickly, "the housekeeper doesn't like you."

"Whom does she like?"

The deaf-mute moved her scarlet lips and Katerina translated: "She says you won't get anything here. Nothing."

"Did she know my mother, Anyuta?" the guest asked.

"She knows everyone," the gypsy said after a moment's thought.

"Why did she hate her?"

"Why should any woman like another?" Katerina asked in

surprise. The deaf-mute was lowing angrily. "A toadstool, she says. Anna was a toadstool."

"What does that mean, a toadstool?" the Master asked, trying to decode their language.

"A toadstool can poison you, or you can use it to poison others, that's what it means, my dove," the gypsy explained in the tone of voice in which she probably read the cards.

The deaf-mute approached and poured her herbs, roots, and dotted mushrooms into one corner of the basket. The gypsy observed the movements of her snakelike lips and then reported: "At night, Anyuta would turn into a white wolf and suck the Bishop's blood."

"Oh, that's what it is. My mother was a werewolf," Kassian said with a serious mien. "And I thought this witch here might be a vampire who kills he-goats."

Katerina turned her face away from the housekeeper and laughed. "That happened too, of course," she whispered. "But your mother could run faster, she was younger. And the Bishop liked that—he still does."

The witch lowed again and spelled words with her cruel red lips.

"You won't get a thing here. The elbow is close to the mouth, but one can't bite it! You've come close to it, but it won't work. Look behind you. Turn around, sir. Turn around, my dove," the gypsy crooned.

Obediently he turned around and a moment later felt a sharp sting in the small of his back: his knees gave way helplessly, as if hit by an electric current. Bewildered, the Master grabbed the prickly branch of a pine tree and trustingly clung to it. A yellow lacework of light displaced itself on the ground. The wood smelled as before of evergreen and decay. Both women laughed—differently, but expressing similar feelings.

"In the same way she can also puncture the heart of Anyuta's son," Katerina giggled.

Sheepishly he rubbed his sacrum. His deadened feet were slowly coming back to life.

"From what did Anyuta die?" asked the gypsy in another tone, firing point-blank.

The deaf-mute, as if about to fly off, pulled herself up to her full height, looking in ecstasy at a piece of greenish sky that trembled in the interstice between two gothic spruce trees.

"The doctor was treating her for blood clots," Kassian answered with an effort.

Katerina nodded knowingly and said: "She died last Cassian's Day, didn't she?"

"Yes, I think so. It was at the end of February. How did you know?"

The deaf-mute began to produce hideous, indecent, dull, almost rectal sounds in her throat. Apparently she was laughing. From the distance came the pure, sad, evenly spaced call of a cuckoo, and the old witch, waving her hands, began to mumble something.

"You are like the cuckoo," Katerina translated. "She says you put your eggs in someone else's nest. But it won't work."

"Tell that viper," the guest shouted, "tell that viper . . ." He fell silent and, smiling a stubborn smile, only shook his heavy-browed head. How difficult it was to break the chain of causality in certain personal situations!

The deaf-mute suddenly came up close to Kassian, who was breathing heavily, and patted him on the shoulder.

"Exactly like Anyuta," came the crooning voice of Katerina. "She says you are just like her when you get angry." But already the old witch, without picking her path, was striding away. The juniper opened before her, and soon only her broad shoulders and her head were floating above the nut bushes and ferns: a gigantic torso wrapped in a brown shawl flying through the air.

The wood darkened abruptly. Probably a cloud had covered the sun, but that could not be seen below, and so it seemed that evening was prematurely approaching.

"Listen, Anyuta's son, don't fret," Katerina said soothingly. "Nobody can tell the future. The deaf-mute is lying. And I am lying too."

"Zora never lies," the guest answered.

"You like the wench? That is good. I have a daughter; perhaps someday a good man will cherish her too. There is a curse on our family: all the girls are abused. . . . Take my Katerina to the city! She's a beauty, you won't find any better. A cuckoo probably laid her in someone else's nest too," the gypsy finished bitterly.

The Master held out his hand: "Good-by," he said.

"Why good-by? We'll meet again, more than once. I'll still read the cards for you and I'll bring Little Katerina along."

Kassian descended straight into a gully that, according to his calculations, had to lead to the river. He did not want to get close to the castle. Crossing a swampy meadow (not without difficulties), he struggled through thorny clinging undergrowth that, on and off, made way for sandy trenches and basalt boulders. Finally he scrambled up to a stony path edging the river. Here, still compressed by the ravine, the water rushed wildly, forbiddingly. The Master climbed over a crumbling stone wall, which had probably served to enclose the castle's hunting grounds, and soon saw in the distance (like a canvas by Cézanne or Pissaro) the old wooden bridge, with the pink piazza in the background.

Now everything was familiar. At the Roman fountain, Philolai was watering the horses and donkeys. The beasts were concentrating on sucking up the cold water with their soft lips. It was easy to see they were satisfied with this occupation and that they considered it proper and quite to the point. (No questions here of Why? What for?)

For the first time that day Master Kassian heaved a sigh of relief, like a man who has escaped a great danger. With a feeling of brotherhood he stroked the satin neck of a noble Arab foal. The foal turned his round yellowish eye toward him as if to say "What's there to argue about? We are all God's creatures." Kassian even smiled approvingly at a pack of vicious dogs—a bulldog with white shirt front in the lead. And his meeting with Philolai was as between old friends.

The gypsy had already brought his valise to the inn, where one of the better rooms, with a window toward the inner court, had been assigned him. Instead of prosaic stores, Kassian could now observe clean stables and cattle sheds from which now and then a donkey, a horse, or a goat would stick out his head . . . there was even a cow. They all signaled to the guest: they shook their muzzles, moved their jaws, wiggled their ears, sneezed and snorted—warning the Master, without, however, stopping the innocent and tenacious grinding of their strong jaws.

Having hung up and folded away his few belongings, the Master went down, refused a cup of coffee, and strolled along the semicircle of stores, stopping here and there to buy some sweets or a toy, or simply to chat with the natives from the valley.

The village was getting ready for the monthly market that was to take place the next day—the first Thursday after the new moon. Only the farmers from the valley and two or three businessmen from the city came for such ordinary markets. But on the feast of Saint Cassian, held every four years on the twenty-ninth of February, people converged from the most distant places, from the borders of Austria and the shores of the Adriatic. According to the local patriots, the village then turned into a kind of Babel (or Paris on the fourteenth of July). The piazza was lit with lanterns day and night; beer and slivovitz flowed, as the saying goes, "in rivers," sweets and cakes were given away free. Lace, rugs, prunes, nuts, corn, cattle, leather, earthenware—all this left through the basalt gates of the valley, admitting in its stead carts with cotton, kerosene, salt, matches, tools and plows.

"Yes, it is gay here on Saint Cassian's," the peasants said. Everywhere there is music, gaily painted girls with naked bellies, magicians, gamblers, even a roulette wheel. And those with intellectual or spiritual inclinations can visit the church: services are conducted through the day and into the night, processions with banners and icons wind around the piazza and across the bridge, toward the castle. People are everywhere: singing the troparion, glorifying the Saint, they enter the houses, shops, and stores with lighted candles. Of course, fire, thievery, fights can't be avoided, but they are all part of the celebration. In the inn, cardsharps keep the bank. And the children take part in the entertainment and in athletic competitions. One after another they climb up a soaped mast—the winner gets a pair of boots or a dress. The women buy supplies of creams, Oriental essences, and mysterious herbs to last them for the next four years.

"Yes, it is gay," the peasants said, "and the weather is always perfect. You have to come and find out for yourself, since you were christened Kassian."

And the Master promised to return some Cassian's Day. Meanwhile, stands, booths, and awnings were rising on the piazza; farmers were unloading goods from their carts for tomorrow's market.

Near the church wall a boy of about ten was executing intricate pirouettes, as if performing a part in a ballet. His thin bare arms moved in the air like swans' necks; quickly he took a few steps and then raised himself up on his toes. The fact that the child was alone and not in a group with others was in itself strange. But his somnambulistic theatrical movements genuinely amazed the accidental witness. However, no one except Kassian paid the boy any heed.

"What makes you so happy?" he asked.

The boy gave no answer. But now the Master noticed that while he was whirling on his toes he was also singing, or reciting, a kind of poem. Kassian could distinguish some phrases:

"She's wonderful. . . . She's beautiful. . . . She took the flower . . ." the boy whispered, continuing all the while to float along the wall of the white church, moving his thin expressive little arms the way mimes do. "She's beautiful. . . . She's wonderful. . . . She took the flower. . . ." He smiled blissfully as he announced this in a whisper to the houses, the dogs, the farmers, the donkeys and to the stranger.

One could guess that the boy had presented a girl with a flower, that she had accepted his gift, and that this had thrown the suitor into a state of rapture.

"Why, you are in love!" said the Master, laughing. "How old are you?"

"Eleven."

"No, you are not yet eleven."

"Why not?" the boy asked.

"You are six weeks short of eleven."

"You are a liar." And with a sly squint, moving his head in rhythm, he continued his canticle: "She's beautiful. . . . She took the flower. . . . She's wonderful. . . ."

"Get out of here!" shouted an old man's voice interrupted by a dry cough. It was the ancient priest who, bent like a bow, hardly moving his legs under the black cassock, ran as on stilts out of the churchyard, waving his patriarchal staff. "All day long that little bastard hangs around under my windows."

"What's the matter with him, Father Nectarius?" the Master asked informally, as if addressing an old friend.

"The devil, that's what's the matter with him. The devil. Katerina, the gypsy girl, is washing my windows. And that boy, Drago, comes sniffing around. I'll get you. . . ."

The dancer retreated toward the bridge, but soon approached again, now whirling ecstatically on his toes at the very steps of the church. Suddenly, from a window in a wing, a tiny ivory-mauve face with enormous round green eyes looked out: the raven hair was so tightly plaited that the entire head seemed hardly larger than a pea. The first impression was of an animal, a small predator. But then the animal smiled and it became evident that it was a snake: a wise, good-natured, poisonous little snake. The priest was not charmed by her smile; he shook his staff at her and rushed—with his entire body, his legs lagging behind—after the lovesick mime who was gracefully and quickly moving away on his tiptoes.

Two-wheeled carts with goods and cattle, colorful booths and awnings slowly but irrepressibly flooded the gradually cooling piazza.

7

The western edge of land, with its ashy, fissured hills, had several times noticeably moved upward, and the orange luminary, which resembled a fruit or a ball, suddenly lost its heat and irritating glare. A two-wheeled cart, like a June bug crawling toward an apricot, receded into the distance on a straight line with the sun. A minute later, pierced by blunt arrows, the vehicle with donkey and peasant bravely joined the scarlet disk, covering a tiny part of it.

A cool breeze had sprung up. The cicadas began to chirp and from an orchard came the rasp of a corn crake. Quietly, soundlessly, like specters in funereal dress, bats darted above the river.

The villagers were at supper. On terraces, in covered courts, on the porches in front of stores and houses, beneath awnings and in the large front rooms, everywhere stood tables heaped with food, sagging under the weight of many dishes.

The Master had forgotten to wind his watch the night before; now he felt no need for it. A little while longer, he thought, and I won't need a calendar either. From Ascension to Assumption, from Christmas to Easter—those are the only dates needed for a happy life. But who wants a happy life?

He hoped he would be given a small table to himself, not too close to the bar. Upon entering, he would greet everyone with a general bow and that would take care of his social obligations for the time being. However, his hosts had decided otherwise: the Professor was put at the head of the main table. Around him, on heavy oak benches covered with a remarkable number of knife and saber scars, sat the Joachims and some of the local dignitaries: Philolai, Mayor Owl, and Pelikan Effendi, the comptroller and owner of the quarry.

The women ate apart, but their humming and buzzing and occasional laughter could be heard close by. The room was two stories high and, of course, windowless on the ground floor. A gallery with a white stone railing circled the second floor, and directly under the pink-tiled ceiling were numerous windows through which, miraculously, joy-bringing light still entered.

Perspiring women carrying steaming bowls and copper pans ran in and out of the kitchen. Philolai's brother Cantemir personally supervised the bar and, guided by mysterious and practical considerations, silently measured out local brew and slivovitz. Each time he uncorked another straw-covered flagon, the diners would invariably fall into the same friendly argument over the relative quality of this particular bottle and, to make quite sure, immediately down a second and third glass of it.

Kassian was feted not only as the guest of honor but also as the representative of that alien, faraway race of city dwellers and intellectuals who work little and yet manage to live well. . . . There had to be some kind of trick to it, and those around him wanted to ferret it out. They cross-examined the Master, posed complicated questions, and tried to catch him in contradictions. Most of all they were struck by the fact that there seemed to be no end to those ingenious sciences. One teaches the other—and who teaches the professor? Another professor? And does that one know everything?

The Master smiled politely and sighed to himself. Spending a few days here could be fun, but to have to stay on! God forbid. . . . (poor Anyuta!) And the simple, hearty manner of these people had little true value since it could, from one moment to the next, change into cold indifference tempered only by a sort of condescending humor. They were not afraid of dying and so they were not inclined to coddle their neighbors.

Sausages, fried fowl, and mutton laced with sarcastic remarks and with proverbs stimulated a very special kind of thirst that could be satisfied only by slivovitz or the local beer, after which, however, one was again attracted to the fried or stewed victuals. This made for a full but by no means vicious circle: having drunk, they immediately had to eat . . . and then the yellow beans with Turkish pepper sent them back to the slivovitz. But all this accommodated itself very well in their stomachs. Despite the exterior roughness of their manners, their way of eating—with numerous pauses and theatrical greetings—revealed a distinctive, ancient culture that, though the insouciant peasants were unaware of it, had been preserved by their heroes and priests through the long dark ages of history.

Around the table, beards the color of coffee grounds

swayed continuously; the peasants made their ponderous observations that seemed not altogether appropriate but later, suddenly turned out to have been shrewd and very much to the point. Some only joked, some mainly laughed and spat to the side, others even sang, accompanying themselves on the psaltery. The most active participants in the conversation were two of the Joachims (Tobacco and the Turk), Philolai and the local elite, Pelikan Effendi and Mayor Owl. Philolai generously shielded the guest, taking pains to spare him ridicule and siding with him in the unequal debate. (He knew the peasants never forgave anyone a loss of face.)

Basically the Joachims were concerned with only one thing: how to keep the harvest to themselves without giving anything to the castle or to the government, and yet survive . . . where to dig in, how to hide, so that the city and the outsiders would once and for all stop interfering with them.

This was their basic truth: that each one personally, and the entire tribe collectively, should go on resisting all natural external forces, and do it in precisely the same way as it had been done for centuries. Therein lay power and wisdom. As sometimes a shepherd, idly playing on his pipe, will come upon an intricate, sweet melody, so at times these peasants succeeded in expressing a deep truth about religion, science, or life; but just as it is impossible to master music without a knowledge of counterpoint, so it was impossible for these primitives, who had no awareness of the philosophical, social, and artistic heritage of mankind, to grasp the complicated web of life.

These people revered all kinds of etiquette, form, drama. Here weddings and christenings resembled grand opera.

God forbid the priest deviate from an ancient, probably pagan, custom! The wealth of the liturgy was complemented by the bass in the choir, the suckling pig after Lent, the procession on Saint Cassian's Day (starting at midnight, without fail).

There was a lot of talk around the table about Saint Cassian's Day, talk inspired by next day's monthly market, for which the farmers had already converged and chosen the best possible locations in the piazza. The inhabitants of the valley looked at the villagers the way the villagers looked at the city dweller: with reserve and hostility.

On the piazza, under the greenish sky, new arrivals were still unloading bales and baskets. They unharnessed the pack animals, roped off their area, and covered the goods with burlap or straw . . . then sat down beside it, pulled out some provisions, slivovitz and a pipe, ready thus to pass the night.

A few, however, stepped into the inn, ordered coffee, and exchanged greetings with the Joachims. The gendarme (Cockroach), wiping the sweat off the permanent red mark across his forehead, asked them. "Do you have a number?" and, receiving a negative reply, added self-importantly: "As soon as I'm through here, I'll take care of you big businessmen."

"It's different on Saint Cassian's," said Joachim Tobacco with a sigh and began to tell how people bribed the gendarme to get a better spot, how they argued, cheated, fought. "People come crawling from all directions like ants. They come from all over, from near and far. All those carts, horses—even automobiles. One Turk used to come on his camel, but he wasn't here the last two times. He must have died, or perhaps his camel collapsed."

"Ha, ha, ha," the Joachims laughed, as if the ruin of a camel on their roads added to their national glory.

"Rugs, lace, glazed tiles, home remedies, pots, ironware, and yarns."

"Honey, cantaloupes, prunes, nuts, sweets—in a word: Saint Cassian," the peasants decided. "He is our provider."

"Never mind, we'll harness them," stated Philolai categorically.

"And how we enjoy ourselves after the goods are sold!"

"Everybody thanks God and feasts!"

"Great merchants leap into holes in the ice and climb up a slippery pole just to win a pair of new boots. Not dignified, but fun! Here, in this room, we have a real orchestra. The big lamps are lit and we all play cards with the sharpers from the city. Plump women with naked bellies dance on this table. And each one has a precious stone in her navel—so help me God."

"No, the big city can't teach us anything," boasted the Joachims. "We'll manage all right. Without electricity. . . ."

When a generator was installed in the castle, the Bishop had offered them electric current at cost. But the peasants refused.

"What, accept a new bondage?"

"Felix, he'll give you electricity!" the Joachims laughed. "You won't even enjoy the daylight any more. Ha, ha, ha."

Exactly how the castle still abused the villagers was difficult to say. From their fragmentary and cynical remarks it was clear that the ancient *jus primae noctis* had long since ceded to additional labor and obligatory presents of homemade products. There was, for instance, "the levy of the goat," according to which the castle used to give each family a goat, in return for which the peasants had to deliver a kid to the master every spring. "Just deliver—even if you have to buy it!"

The castle no longer gave them a goat or sheep but the value of the offspring was still punctually collected. Besides, the deaf-mute gave each woman in the village a hen and for this they had to supply the castle with eggs all summer long. "Even if you have to lay them yourself!"

"The Bishop, he's a good man," the Joachims allowed. "Of course, he used to fool around with the girls, but now the doctors have gelded him."

"Never mind, we'll harness them," Philolai consoled.

Also, the pigs in the fields caused surprising offenses and arguments. Pelikan Effendi quoted verbatim an old law the natives cherished dearly. "Should a man find a pig feeding in his field at night and kill it, he shall not have to make amends for it." The castle still availed itself of this privilege, but the Joachims could no longer do so.

"That's Felix for you. He thinks up all these things," confirmed Mayor Owl.

"Beware of Felix," they warned. "He's master now."

But Joachim Tobacco turned again to pleasant reminiscences: "And how we eat on Saint Cassian's Day! Can you call this a supper?" And with one motion of his gnarled hand he swept the bowls, plates, and glasses to the floor.

"Yes, that's right. That is so," they seconded him. "You come and visit on Saint Cassian's, Professor. You'll like it!"

"The weather is always fine on February twenty-ninth," the gendarme (Cockroach, twitching his mustache) stated with authority.

"And if the weather is bad we celebrate again on July twenty-third," Cantemir added complacently. But the peasants would have none of that.

"July twenty-third is no good," Joachim Tobacco said.

"I don't like it," agreed the Turk.

"That is only as a last resort," Mayor Owl explained.

"And when is the next Saint Cassian?" the Master asked.

The people grew pensive, somber.

"Is it soon?" the guest insisted.

"No, not soon," they answered after a pause. The merchants blinked with concentration. And the gendarme, who had not wiped his forehead for some time, confirmed, "No, not so soon."

"Perhaps two more winters," they all decided.

"The priest will explain it to you. He always sees ahead," the Joachims assured the Professor.

"What do you know about Saint Cassian the Roman?" the Master asked. For a while now the full-breasted women, wrapped in shawls and nibbling nuts and *rachat lakum,* had crowded into the room along the walls; now and then gangs of children, racing across the still crimson piazza, ran through the inn where their elders sat at the table: the children's shouts mingled with the growling of the dogs, who were picking hot bones off the floor.

"What do you have in mind? Why do you want to know about Cassian?" the Joachims asked in their cautious way, pronouncing every syllable.

"Cassian was a saintly monk," Joachim the Turk said with a rush, as if taking a running jump, and immediately fell silent and arranged his unwieldy tongue more comfortably in his mouth.

"Yes, young man, go to Father Nectarius. He'll explain everything," another Joachim (possibly the Flogged) counseled the Master.

Abstract discussions obviously were alien and suspect to

the peasants. They looked down on Master Kassian, convinced that without their backbreaking labor he and the other city people would soon starve to death. And the guest was sure that without him and his likes the Joachims would have died or degenerated long ago.

"Saint Cassian," the Master began stubbornly, "is a bridge between Eastern and Western Christianity. He lived in the fifth century, when Saint Augustine and Pelagius were trading insults, accusing each other of Manichean heresy . . . just as nowadays some of us are labeled fascists or communists, enemies of the country."

The Joachims enjoyed this comparison enormously.

"Hold him, don't let him go!"

"To the police station!"

"They'll take care of him there, that's for sure!"

"The main thing, beware of Felix," the Cockroach interjected.

"Never mind, we'll harness them," Philolai said. "Don't you worry," he told the guest placatingly, "we understand everything."

"And how we understand!" said Cantemir, surprised at his own intelligence.

The Master doggedly continued: "According to Saint Augustine, man in his natural state is lost and dead."

"Well, that's for sure," the Turk immediately agreed.

"According to Pelagius, man in his natural state is sound and good."

This statement elicited the approval of the merchants and privileged members of society. Mayor Owl enthusiastically confirmed, "That's right, leave the peasant in peace and he'll do fine!"

"But our Cassian the Roman taught that man in his natural state is neither dead nor completely well. He is sick but he can be cured. It was revealed to Cassian that grace and salvation are never and in no way limited or predetermined. . . ."

The people grew listless. Philolai, in order to direct the conversation into more familiar channels, asked, "Do you remember the troparion for the twenty-ninth of February?"

"I do," readily answered the guest.

And they all, at first each to himself, harshly, but gradually more and more harmoniously and solemnly, sang the familiar prayer:

> That which is According to the Image was
> Really saved in you, O Father:
> For you accepted the Cross and Followed Christ.

The women joined in with feeling, but muddling the words:

> By so Doing you taught all to Disregard the Flesh, for it passes away,
> But to care instead for the Soul, since it is immortal.
> Therefore, O Holy Roman, your Spirit rejoices with the Angels.

And almost without pausing they repeated it from the beginning, this time in perfect harmony. (It all reminded the guest of Easter bells, sunrise, and the scent of honeysuckle.)

The choral singing ended with a round of slivovitz, after which Joachim the Turk very appropriately suggested, "Let's show the Professor how we enjoy ourselves on Saint Cassian's Day!"

They got up from the table, swaying, straightening their clothes. Then the whole crowd poured into the piazza. Lanterns and torches were lit. Dogs and women yapped excitedly. Somewhere in the darkness disturbed geese hissed. Promptly, as in a circus, a long smooth pole with a flag on top was raised and, half-naked, barefooted, the bearded Joachims attempted to climb it, slipping, sliding down, and again gripping the mast. After which they all flowed in a wave down the river bank into the dark: it seemed that a gigantic, many-limbed, many-headed monster was squeezing into the crevasse. The new moon dimly sprayed the night sky. One could not see, one could only hear the river, deep down, bursting its banks because of the antediluvian, many-voiced animal that had plunged into it.

8

The market itself turned out to be much more modest than the rehearsal the night before. The Master woke late. On the piazza, the peasants looked subdued and unkempt. Some of the valley farmers were already heading for the inn while others were still trading, sucking at their pipes, now and then taking a swig from a bottle. The animals and birds conducted themselves in their normal friendly way, all except the numerous dogs of every size that, obviously excited, snarled viciously at one another.

There are paintings in which some of the details consist of "real" objects: a plowshare, the point of a bayonet . . . if you touch it, you feel metal. The shining piazza with its Roman fountain now conveyed a similar impression, overflowing as it was with goods and fresh game, with people and livestock, and bathed in a shower of light and the fluctuating mountain air.

Women were arguing over a glazed green pot, tearing sets of colored ribbons out of one another's hands, pressing a wheel of cheese to their breasts; peasants were yelling and cursing as if with their last breath, slapping hands after a completed deal and passing the bridle of some innocent obedient foal not into the new owner's hand but, according to their custom, into the flap of his coat. The quarrelsome dogs were now keenly watching a man in a blood-covered apron who was carving up the carcass of a sheep in front of his store, and suddenly they all lunged at the discarded woolly pale-yellow head with its glassy blue-outlined eyes.

At the church, Little Katerina, thin and supple, was tugging at the end of a thick dusty rope. The ancient bell swung in time, filling the surrounding country with its tremulous glad peal. A totally bald, shriveled dwarf with red eyelids, harnessed into a multitude of musical instruments, was dancing in front of the inn, simultaneously setting in motion his kettledrum, tambourines, and cymbals.

And all around, always the same, were the receding, foggy blue mountains, the lilac blots of woods and fields, the green foam of the chained river, and floods, floods of blessed light from the sky: cold and warm, brilliant and soft, earthly and eternal.

"She's wonderful, she's shining," sang the boy Drago, floating over the piazza. Stretched on tiptoes, his small (swanlike) arms piercing the air, he twirled and twirled near the church. The girl with the eyes of a basilisk flitted out of the church. She had finished her chore and now she too began to race around the piazza, laughing, ignoring the pale, circling mime.

"She's wonderful, she's good, she's like the sun," he repeated over and over, following her, blinking and spellbound.

On the whole piazza, probably in the whole valley, nothing was more important or beautiful than these two children running in a circle, with no hope of ever catching up with each other. However, Father Nectarius was running too, waving his staff in the air; the people, the goats, and the donkeys respectfully made way for the priest.

Suddenly a gust of wind (of a completely different order) swept through the piazza. The canvas tents swelled like sails in a storm; some booths and awnings collapsed, and for a moment, in the aura of over-all frailty and instability, the entire piazza seemed to heel to the side. The music stopped instantaneously, the din of the crowd subsided, and all that could be heard were absurd exclamations from the inn. "Never mind, we'll harness them," Philolai still assured.

In a moment everything resumed its former aspect: the wind withdrew somewhere into the abyss, the piazza righted itself, the river splashed capriciously, and the people, cheered by the new avalanche of light and color, again pressed through the marketplace as one many-eyed animal.

From the direction of the castle a ladder wagon approached the bridge, where women with smaller, more delicate goods had stationed themselves. The wheels and hoofs on the planks sounded distinct, disembodied. Markali and his wife Katerina were bringing supplies of nut oil, slivovitz, and leather: some of the castle's products were known the country over.

Markali liked to sell slightly spoiled merchandise to the

simpletons—and he was good at it! That is why he showed up at the marketplace a little late in the day, when the peasants had already paid numerous visits to the inn. For his art the gypsy had been punished more than once. The Joachims (according to local custom) suspended him by the feet and flogged him in the presence of both Katerinas. Which, however, changed nothing in the economy of the valley. The following market day the gypsy would show up again, standing on his high wagon, whistling and singing, and with an enigmatic smile give the naïve Joachims short measure and short weight.

Again the distinct sound of drumming hoofs came from the bridge. At the head of a cavalcade galloped Zora and Chako on orange mares with picturesquely curved necks. They both dismounted at the inn. The Master stroked the horses' hot (orange) skin and was told they were called Flora and Fauna. And indeed, although the two thoroughbreds looked almost alike, their contrasting names suited them very well.

"She's beautiful, she's wonderful," the boy sang, floating on tiptoes across the piazza.

"Who is that?" Zora asked.

"That's Drago," the Master informed her happily.

"He's from the quarry," Chako added. "Lost his mind long ago, poor little fellow."

"He's in love," stated the Master authoritatively. "A miracle. A Florentine miracle. In the Arctic, a palm has blossomed. He's in love with Little Katerina."

"And we? Where do we go from here, Professor?" Zora asked softly, squinting (from light and happiness).

"I don't know. Nothing has changed and nothing will change. Those children have taught me a lesson."

"You are invited for dinner. Will you come?"

"If I'm properly invited, I shall come."

"You'll get an invitation—for tomorrow," Chako confirmed.

"I'm leaving Saturday or Sunday," the Master said, looking over the golden head with the soft curl on the forehead.

"Let me talk to Felix once more," the girl begged. "In any case, we'll leave together."

Meanwhile the Bishop was majestically walking around the market, lingering here and there to exchange greetings and pleasantries. He stretched out a white, ruthless hand to the Master: "The people are enjoying themselves," he remarked affably, "and also working and selling at the same time. That, I believe, is the ideal."

The young people looked at the Bishop in silence. Chako was waiting for him to continue: almost every sentence or thought appeared unfinished to Chako.

"Can you imagine, I was thinking about grace and predestination today," the Bishop announced, addressing himself exclusively to the Master. "How do you solve this puzzle nowadays? You know," he continued without waiting for a reply, "I broke my neck over Saint Augustine. Although I probably would have broken my neck without him too. But I dare say his experience contributed. Like Augustine, I came from the provinces to the capital. Like him I took a fancy to a girl and bought her. That's as far as the obvious similarities go. For he was able to escape the power of earthly temptations. Besides, there was his mother, Saint Monica, who helped him get rid of the woman and the child she bore him—to pull her out 'like a thorn from the flesh,' as he writes. While I, on the contrary, sank deeper and deeper, cherishing my thorns. And yet, so help me God, the ideal we were both seeking was the same. But the outcome was different. Was it really predetermined once and for all? That would mean that man cannot save himself alone, but that on his own he can ruin himself very well."

Despite his unquestionably serious tone, the Bishop's manner of speaking was always that of a man of the world, a courtly charmer, a sybarite who never lost his sense of proportion. While talking, he also managed to smile a greeting to a peasant, to pat a handsome woman on the cheek, to finger a piece of lace or linen at a stand. Eventually he even took hold of Master Kassian's arm, sure that the guest would be flattered, and led him through the throng.

Kassian felt obliged to answer the Bishop: "We now acknowledge only statistical, not individual, determinism. It is a fact that out of one hundred thousand elderly men, four hundred will die next winter . . . but who will go and who will survive no one can predict—that is not predetermined, not decided beforehand. On the contrary, it has been proven that on the microscopic level every particle that exists is free, since it can make spontaneous jumps. The same probably applies to grace. It is written that on the Day of Judgment a minority—one hundred and forty-four thousand—will be marked with the seal of salvation. But who specifically, of all mankind, will be condemned and who will be part of the hundred and forty-four thousand is a matter of personal choice. Statistics mean nothing to us. We are interested only in each individual case. One atom of radium will disintegrate immediately, another will radiate for ten thousand years—and nobody can predict the fate of any particular atom."

"Really? Ten thousand years?" said the Bishop, looking distractedly and yet with pleasure at the flushed faces of the women. Holding the Master firmly by the elbow, he suddenly asked very amiably: "Don't you think, Professor, that we should tell Zora?"

"Tell Zora . . . what, exactly?" Kassian felt as if he had suddenly been hit over the head.

"That you and her father are brothers."

"No, I don't think that is necessary," Kassian answered, fighting his revulsion. "Those are idle and, moreover, unnecessary guesses."

"But if you are my son—and that seems to be the truth—then Felix is your brother," the Bishop explained patiently, as if dealing with a critically sick man.

"All men are brothers," Kassian replied dryly. "Brothers and not brothers and still something else. For Zora and myself there are no irreversible processes. There is a free and spontaneous exit from every situation."

"I must admit you are consistent in your madness," said the Bishop.

"Look, Professor," called Zora, catching up with them, "here is Little Katerina, Markali's daughter."

"Not necessarily Marc Ali's," mumbled the Bishop.

For the first time the Master understood the origin of the gypsy's name—Marc Ali. (Also, the shadow of an unformed thought flicked through his mind but immediately vanished into darkness.)

The supple girl, her raven hair tightly braided and wound around her tiny head, ran close by them, drowning them in a stream of greenness from her enormous eyes. Drago, floating on tiptoes, moving his lips, followed spellbound in her wake.

"What can be done?" the Bishop lamented, for once sincere. "He has no family. And yet he is a gifted boy!"

"We have worked out a plan for social reform," Zora announced joyously. "Advance every newborn the money he'll make later in life, and he can grow up, learn a trade, and be on his way. Here the effect would become the cause."

"Yes," the Bishop said, "I have heard about it. What about politics? It must be more difficult to turn effect before cause there." He was distractedly following with his eyes a young woman nursing a wrinkled baby at her milk-white breast.

"Not difficult at all," Zora hastened to answer. "What seems to be the greatest defeat of democracy can become its victory. Because China turned communist, the Americans can now come closer to the Russians. But that is not all. Why fight the Chinese? Prove to Peking that in outer space there is a menace to all humanity and they too will join us against this common enemy. We must begin with the end. Then the missing prerequisites will appear."

Kassian was thoroughly familiar with the ideas the girl expressed, but the enraptured look in her sand-colored eyes testified to yet another triumph, still unknown to him.

"So you have perfected politics too," said the Bishop.

"Even art!" Zora continued, not noticing his sarcasm. "The new novel should not be fettered by social, logical, or psychological causality. The action should develop spontaneously, freely, undetermined by familiar associations."

"And private life, have you arranged that too?"

The Master deemed it necessary to interfere: "There the field is still open to the ambitious explorer. But some possibilities have already emerged," he continued, unperturbed. "For instance: when you love someone, you begin to understand him—and to understand, they say, is to forgive. Couldn't we turn this relationship upside down and reverse the process? That is—if we understand someone and forgive him, apparently in the end we will love him."

"Yes. Apparently," the Bishop agreed with a sigh.

Felix, in riding boots and waving his crop, was walking toward them: the people stepped aside for him, many bowed. Still from a distance, over the heads of a group of women poking some freshly killed poultry, he called to Kassian: "Zora is complaining. I hope you won't refuse to share a meal with us. At least for her sake. Kindly come to dinner tomorrow night." As the guest only bowed in acknowledgment, Felix continued, "The people are enjoying themselves."

"Well, after working hard, it's no sin to have some fun," the Bishop said.

"I know their kind of hard work! You offer them electricity and they refuse. It's only another yoke, they say. What do they want? Sleep eighteen hours a day eight months out of the year! That's what they like." Felix vigorously waved his crop and strode toward the wagon where, to judge by the din, Markali was in trouble.

"Felix is critical of you too," the Master said pensively to the Bishop. "He certainly calls a spade a spade. By the way," he continued politely, "in your personal life there were also quite a number of incomprehensible, spontaneous jumps; jumps that could not be explained and were in no way predetermined. A hussar, an officer of the guard, suddenly becomes a priest. Then the transformation into a heretic, a defrocked priest, a Casanova, a Count of Monte Cristo. And again a miraculous metamorphosis into the respected landlord, the owner of an ancient castle, the paterfamilias. . . ."

"Yes, that's what it looks like," the Bishop agreed. "You are citing Planck, Bohr, wave mechanics. And fifty years ago, so help me God, I already had a notion of all that. The principal, decisive acts in my life originated the devil only knows where. They were never the logical consequence of what happened before."

"Yes, Bishop, you are the New Man—up to a point," the guest agreed. "I understood that from the first. However, it is a pity you wasted so much of your energy on sexual exploits."

"And you, have you solved your sexual problems? I hope the doctrine of the new physics does not forbid sex."

"No, it is not forbidden," the Master answered with an effort, his eyes following Chako and Zora, who were picking out come clay statuettes at the other side of the market. "No, I don't think it is forbidden. Every cell tends to reproduce itself in a somewhat improved form. Mutation. Mutation toward a more perfect state—that is the true law of living tissue, as universal a law as the law of gravitation in the sphere of dead matter. But you, Bishop, reproduced without any intent to improve, like a crystal, a mineral. And that is a sin, a biological sin."

"And yet," the Bishop said quite earnestly, "if someone had proved to me that abstention is good and lust is evil, I could have given up the pleasures of the flesh. It seems to me I had plenty of will power. . . . But as it is, half the youngsters running around here are my children or grandchildren or great-grandchildren." He laughed. "And by God, I even like it. The general implications of it, so to say."

"Yes, I thought so. You are a demonic man."

"I was often told so in my youth," the Bishop said brightly. "Mainly by the ladies. Incidentally, I am utterly unable to recall your mother. But for some reason I recognize you. You are familiar to me, close, even if there is something hostile and dangerous about you. One should not despair prematurely. Speaking of cells and biology, perhaps you are indeed an improved version of myself." The Bishop's majestic face ruled out any suggestion of sarcasm.

Kassian suddenly felt a wild impulse to hit the old man. Instead, he continued to smile politely and said nothing. (According to his theory, that was the way to overcome the laws of thermodynamics and entropy.)

"Professor, we are expecting you tomorrow," a voice drifted across to him like a sweet scent.

Zora was mounting Fauna. Markali, his proud, passionate eyes shining, held the little silver stirrup in his blue palm.

The riders, followed by the Bishop's carriage, crossed the bridge: the distinct (filtered) sound of the hoofs came as if from another world. The two Olympian mares took off toward the park in a rapid gallop. Chako could be seen holding back his Flora to let the girl pass. The sky, the river, the greens, the mountains were like an orchestra repeating over and over again the same passage. Master Kassian, without any transition, felt inexpressibly sad. Had he made a fool of himself? Anyway, it was too late to change anything now. He groaned.

The Master, who was long familiar with these moods of his, had learned that in such cases there were only three solutions: suicide, drink, or sleep. . . . He opted for the third: to bury his head in the pillows immediately.

In his room with its north window it was cool and quiet, even solemn, as in church or in a cemetery.

He awoke in complete darkness. The smell of newly mown hay, with a tinge of sweet field flowers, drifted through the window. In the city he could never evoke this intoxicating (natural) aroma; he inhaled gratefully. From a nearby orchard came the gentle unskilled trill of a young nightingale.

The house was asleep. Unnoticed by anyone, the guest stepped out onto the terrace. The piazza was already empty. Here and there he could distinguish heaps of garbage and straw in the light of the slightly grown moon. The delicate sickle that hung directly over the river reminded the Master of Father Nectarius's beard.

Under the bridge the water seethed; a fresh mountain wind carried with it the breath of glaciers; and from the valley came the scent of the earth's fruits.

Everything alive seemed to sleep. Only the waves of light, air, water, and sound held vigil, filling the unfathomable void. Kassian crossed the bridge that the young moon illuminated directly; it was like walking on a rainbow, from one bank to the other (and beneath him the dark and evil abyss).

In the park, cedars rustled softly: so do monks in half-sleep finger their rosaries. The sacred oaks, indifferent, allowed the stranger to pass. He followed a silvery path with patches of blue shadows that fluttered like laundry on a line. The waxing moon was everywhere: above the piazza, above the bridge, above the park. (Could there be many moons in the sky?)

"She's wonderful, she's beautiful," Kassian whispered. (Was he crying?) He stopped at the high wall. The white wicket was unlatched, and with a creaking of the hinges the night visitor stepped over the threshold of stone. All was silent. Only every so often a huge moth hit the wall with all its might and, its dry wings rustling, fell, exhausted (or enraptured): it was poorly adjusted to life but still had survived eons of night. Suddenly, in this unique, blessed summer park, a distinct, solitary, almost peaceful, shot rang out.

The Master jumped back and took cover behind the stone wall. An alarmed bird whistled inappropriately, and a hare, having recalled an age-old, prophetic dream, uttered a convulsive cry. Then everything was quiet again. Intermittently the river slapped against its banks. The beams of the bridge creaked (or was it the boughs of the gigantic linden?). And unable to withstand the weight of the lunar light, silent grasses bowed down to the earth.

The Master stood for a moment and then gingerly stepped once more through the wicket. Instantaneously, a second impudent shot, somehow like Markali's laughter, rang out. That was enough. The guest turned back.

Again the shining, green, phosphorescent bridge . . . beneath it the mountain river, sobbing as if it were filled with hungry rats instead of cutting, sharp-edged waves . . . the quiet, even now pinkish piazza with its Roman fountain spouting either light or, perhaps, the essence of life. And it was incomprehensible why or for whom the moon, the mountains, the trees were making such an effort, since everything rational on earth able to delight in them lay in deep sleep.

Instinctively Kassian listened—for further shots, for machine-gun fire, artillery, the thunder of bombers lit up by bouquets of explosions. . . . The shotgun blast at night had called up sinister, long-forgotten specters.

9

It was early when he awoke. A heavy, solid body seemed to have fallen upon him: in the center of the room, like a statue, blocking out the light and air, loomed the figure of Markali. The door against which Kassian had propped a chair the night before stood wide open.

"What is it?" He started up.

"I was ordered to say the dinner is tomorrow," reported the gypsy, somewhat embarrassed.

"I thought it was tonight," the Master said, observing him attentively.

"The deaf-mute postponed it for tomorrow." After a pause Markali added: "It's a beautiful day."

"Yes, time to get up," the Master decided, and confidently inquired: "Did the sun rise today?"

In the dusk there was a flash of teeth; the cross around Markali's neck, his earring, glittered. Burly, powerful, the gypsy made the small room and the furniture seem absurd. He was like an ancient god, nearing the end of his reign but still triumphant.

"Was there anything else?" the Master asked.

"There is a quarry close by," said Markali coaxingly. "Pink marble rises straight to the sky, like Jacob's ladder in the Bible. I'll show you." Almost imploringly he added: "It's very interesting."

"All right, if it won't take too long," the Master accepted. "As a matter of fact I'm quite busy and really do not know anything about marble."

"It's very interesting," the gypsy repeated, obviously pleased.

They walked downstairs and out into the piazza, deserted except for the dogs; then they crossed the narrow bridge pierced by the rays of the morning sun. For quite a while they clambered through crevices and hollows until they finally emerged onto a steep goat path. Birds of prey hovered above the ravine: now and then one would suddenly dive down and strike the river foam with its beak . . . then the huge, unwieldy bird veered and awkwardly soared up again, maneuvering to avoid brushing the high, narrow banks with its wings.

"Full of fish, eh?" The gypsy clicked his tongue sensually.

The reeds, swaying near the water, made mysterious signals.

"What kind of fish do you have here?" the Master asked. He found it painful to look Markali full in the face; he still did not know the color of his eyes.

His head following the movements of the rangy birds, the gypsy did not answer. Apparently he was after something, and it occurred to the Master that if they were to fight, here on the narrow ledge, the burly Markali would probably win.

The path grew steeper and narrower. The Master's clumsy advance elicited thunderous laughter from the guide; however, in particularly hazardous spots he always very cleverly gave the Master a hand.

They entered a crevasse and soon found themselves on a wide, well-worn road dug directly into a flat mountain. Ahead, the pink marble shone and glistened in colorful patterns and stars. Everywhere lay mottled blocks resembling antediluvian creatures that, immobile, angular, still preserved the unconscious purity of the first day of creation.

The quarry, which extended in terraces down and away from them, had for thousands of years apparently been exploited in the same primitive, pitiless way: always only the most accessible and valuable was hacked out. Some areas, abandoned long ago, were in a state of complete neglect, as if the waters of the Deluge or polar glaciers had visited there; in other places gaped the wounds and brilliant tumors of fresh extractions and there was a track for miniature trolleys leading to the central pit. An impudent wind made the dry mule dung rustle around and around in the same spot.

Markali proudly explained that monuments from this quarry were exported to cemeteries as far away as Hungary and Turkey. For some reason angels came out best: "You tap once with your hammer, you tap again, and if you know your trade, it's done. You have an angel or an archangel," the gypsy explained cheerfully. "Devils turn out very well too. Other figures don't. But the powers of heaven almost jump out of the stone by themselves—as if they were preserved inside it, ready-made, only waiting for their turn to come alive." He roared with laughter, appreciating his many-voiced echo. "During the war, partisans held out here for a whole year," he continued, serious, almost solemn. "The enemy looked down from above and saw a battalion of demons armed with grenades and rifles. We had carved ourselves a permanent guard. It's easy to die on stone," he said softly. "Stone is the most noble thing on earth. That's why it is used for tombs and monuments."

"Do you think so?" the Master said, at a loss to understand the gypsy's inner excitement.

"When I was small and stupid I embraced the stone here as if it were a woman," Markali continued slowly and distinctly. "My semen is bluish, the marble is pink. Everything began with stone . . . inside, stone is alive. It was before us, and it will survive us all. In a word, a memorial. With stone one lays the foundation; from stone comes sand. Cement and asphalt are stone too. Many-storied cities and deserts are stone. Mountains, dunes, and the ocean floor were stone or are stone or will be stone. Whoever builds on sand actually builds on stone. Peter, the first apostle, grazed sheep or netted fish, but his name means stone. Then there is the stumbling stone for those who work unrighteousness. And the stones of the walls that will howl from iniquity. And the stone cast away by the builder that became the cornerstone."

The gypsy, standing on a rock, himself like a gigantic monument, announced inspiredly: "The altar of God is of whole stones and burnt offerings are made on it. Moses wrote the first commandments on stone. He also lifted up his hand and with his rod smote the rock twice: and the water came out abundantly and the congregation drank and their beasts also . . . and furthermore, the angel of God descended from heaven and rolled back the stone from the door of the sepulchre and sat upon it. . . . Stone is more responsive than anything else. It warms quickly under the sun and turns to ice in winter. Do you see the veins in this marble? That is our blood, from Cain down to me! After our death we turn into blocks of stone with purple bruises."

He would have continued, but at that moment the slender, supple girl with the tiny (predatory) head jumped out from behind a pile of chipped slabs and like a lizard crawled up a steep slope. At once the gypsy let out a hunting cry and took off after her, jumping from rock to rock; finally he slipped and landed on his backside. They could hear the girl's soft, venomous giggle. She turned around to look at both of them and her face seemed to flare up with a green light.

"You snake eyes, you're going to get it from me," Markali shouted with obvious admiration.

Leaping nimbly from one conical block to the other, the girl was off; soon she reached the upper edge of the quarry and, looking down at them, stuck out her pointed red tongue.

"My Katerina," Markali said. "My daughter of sorts. I have forbidden her to come here; but something draws her to the place. . . . Just you wait," he shouted ferociously, "you'll live in a cave with an ugly husband!"

"And you'll die in a cave," a sweet childish voice answered. She vanished over the ridge. As different as their voices were, both echoes held the same ominous note.

"Did you want anything else from me?" Kassian asked. "I'm rather in a hurry."

"Yes. I wanted to know why people speak."

"You mean why they exchange thoughts, impressions?"

"Why do people talk? Wouldn't it be better to keep quiet and patiently wait out one's destiny?" he asked with an urgency as if his life depended on the stranger's answer.

"Do you believe that without our participation truth will prevail, sooner or later?" the Master queried.

"You cannot change your fate. It is impossible to turn the moon around."

"It is possible," Kassian said with authority, "and we will do it someday."

"Then why try so hard, if it will come about anyway? As for everyday work, we can make do with whistles."

"When a woman is giving birth we help her," Kassian explained patiently, "and we help a goat or a camel too. In the same way we must ease the agonies of the earth and of all mankind. Besides, there is not only one truth, and we must choose the best. That's why we talk and argue. Death and falsehood are a possible reality too."

"No, one can't kick against the pricks," Markali said stubbornly. "But I have a thought of my own." He whistled, devil-may-care, and with bowed head, staring at the ground, continued with an effort: "Someday everything will be all right in the world, beautiful and understandable. Someday. Tell me, please . . . why do I know that I lived on this earth before and that I will be here again?"

"Do you really feel that?"

"And I wasn't a gypsy. So that I'm not ashamed to serve the Bishop now. . . . But to argue and debate and prove things—what good is that?" Markali insisted, scowling as if he were gnawing on a hard bone.

"You always do your work well, don't you? Now, why is that?" Since he got no reply, the Master continued. "You want to do your work on this earth as conscientiously as possible. That is as natural for a living soul as it is for the moon to attract meteorites. There are men who do other work than you do. They don't handle an ax or a saw. But they too are building new things or remodeling old ones."

"I plow. I build solid barns. Those are real things." The gypsy raised his fists to show how solid these things were. "Without them man could not survive."

"Christ neither sawed nor reaped nor built," the Master said quietly. "He only preached eternal life. The reality of it. And we, following Him in our fashion, also want to annihilate death and all other irreversible processes. From now on a gypsy does not have to be a gypsy any more if he so chooses. A thief, if he so desires, will be pardoned. We'll be able to turn around and change everything: a man's religion, name, homeland, profession, class, temperament, age. . . . From now on cause does not precede effect and effect does not need to have a cause."

"I raised Zora. I nursed her through whooping cough, measles, diphtheria, and seizures," Markali whispered in a fever. "Zora needs a lighthearted husband for everything to be all right. But you, I think, you are odd."

The Master was silent, suppressing a smile. Markali stepped from one foot to the other like a cart horse about to be on its way and said with a sigh: "Here, at this wall, they shot the partisans, and there they are buried . . . they put them in the ravine and covered them with gravel. You can't see anything but you can smell." He laughed and, shaking his lion's mane, added: "I still have a real arsenal of old weapons here."

The Master watched Markali, trying to figure out his sudden mental (and not only mental) leaps and jumps. He had bounded to a nearby sarcophagus and began to chant: "Numb and dumb, numb and dumb." Then, casually and somewhat haughtily he said: "When I was young I wanted to change my name. No, they said, send in an application, pay money, and wait twenty years. And anyway, it's useless. The peasants will still call you by your old name. You can't convince the Joachims. Can you turn back a river? I joined the Church. That didn't help. They still call me the Moslem, or the convert. No, if you are born a gypsy you die a gypsy, whatever you do. And your children and grandchildren also." He spat angrily and rubbed the spittle into the marble with his homemade boot.

"My friends and I," the Master said, trying to speak very clearly, "define culture as the sum of reversible processes. In a primitive village almost everything is unchangeable. But in the ideal society of the future even the Second Law of Thermodynamics will be reversed. Youth, health, new life and fulfillment, growth and enrichment, instead of entropy —that is our new program. Long live the culture of total reversibility," Kassian finished without affectation.

"I always keep a bottle of slivovitz here, just in case," the gypsy said, and chortled. But Kassian declined and Markali said, disappointed: "You are like a monk. But Zora, Zora was meant for another kind of happiness."

"No, I am not a monk," Kassian said, feeling it necessary to justify himself. "But today everyone strives without scruples after pleasure and personal comfort. Everyone looks out only for his own profit. Their one concern: to knock out the competitor. That is entropy, gradual self-destruction and death. But if we were to turn back this so-called natural flow of things, if we ceased living mainly for personal satisfaction, success, self-preservation, then a new order would come into being, an order of entirely reversible processes. I am trying to act toward this end."

"I know, I know." The gypsy nodded his heavy head in confirmation. "I don't completely understand, but the words are familiar. I've met you among the stones and monuments before, Professor. It was when we lived on the golden island, I remember."

"What else do you remember?" the Master asked.

"A city in the mountains. Not really mountains, but one single plateau. A four-cornered island, rising out of the ocean like a crystal. The capital is surrounded by walls, canals, sluices with drawbridges so that big-bellied ships can anchor right at the great pink piazza. The buildings are red, the earth is brown, the sun is the color of wax, and the people are blue. They wear light, colorful clothes, and their skin is lilac-colored, like mine. Now the priest approaches the rough marble altar. You are the priest: lean, heavy-browed, with a tonsured head and cruel eyes."

"I?" The Master was almost embarrassed.

"You put me on the warm altar. But before plunging the knife into me you find it necessary to make a long speech. That speech I still remember."

"What did I say?"

"You said that if the connection between the stones, creatures, and plants on the earth, in the sky, and in the water is severed, an era of disease and catastrophe will follow and the island will perish. Here you told the people the parable of the two frogs. And all those around began to whistle in a special way because they liked it." The gypsy interrupted his tale and, sucking in the air, whistled out a sentence that obviously made sense but belonged to another world. "Good, eh?" he asked, and laughed triumphantly.

"Good," Kassian agreed. "What about the frogs?"

"There were once two frogs, you told us. They both fell into a large basin with cream. One of them very sensibly folded his little paws and immediately sank to the bottom and drowned, as befits a well-behaved frog. But the other did not want to resign himself to the obvious and began to thrash about chaotically with his legs. And then a miracle happened: the floundering frog suddenly felt bottom, soft and slippery at first, but growing more and more solid, so that finally it could settle on it with a certain comfort. The miracle was that under the churning of the frog the cream had turned into butter."

The Master laughed and the gypsy, standing with his arms akimbo, laughed too.

"Then you asked: who wants to thrash about like that frog? And many volunteered. My daughter, the green-eyed Katerina, also came forward. They embarked on a large flexible raft, hoisted a brown sail . . . tell me, can one believe in such dreams?"

"It's hard to decide," the Master answered. "Generally speaking, eight percent of all madnesses turn out to correspond to reality."

"Why eight . . ."

At that moment two women, as if they had fallen from the sky, plumped down onto the marble blocks. Whistling, squealing, singing, laughing, they conveyed the impression of an invading horde; young, gay, red-cheeked, they threw themselves at Markali like hungry hawks. They began to pummel and pester, to tickle and shake him, swinging at him with their bundles and baskets.

The gypsy, smiling proudly, grabbed the young women, now from behind, now in front, enjoying their squeals enormously. "Let's have fun, Professor," he shouted. "There's enough here for everybody."

The women, noticing the stranger, stopped short, embarrassed and in somewhat compromising poses. "Katerina told us you were here," one explained, pulling provisions out of her basket. "But she didn't say anything about Zora's fiancé."

"Fiancé or not, one is always ready for sweets," the gypsy said reassuringly. "Let's have fun!"

"Fun . . ." the women said, unconvinced and yet expectantly.

"Did you bring the wine from the cellar?" Markali asked sternly.

"Two bottles only. The deaf-mute—may she lose her eyes too—is always around." They both broke into laughter as if recalling something extremely funny. They resembled each other, if not in features, then in manner and speech, like flowers and vegetables grown in the same garden.

"Sit down, friend, be my guest," the gypsy proclaimed with a bow. "Let's taste Franz Josef's Tokay."

The Master drank of the thick amber wine and broke off a hunk of freshly baked bread. The women, firm, juicy, red-cheeked (Annas both), quickly adjusted to the situation and, repulsing Markali's coarse advances, pretending to scold him, began to eat. They ate with relish and managed, while chewing energetically, to pepper the Master with questions.

"Is it true that in the city unmarried people live together?"

"Why is it the women don't have babies every year? Do they know a magic word or is there a medicine they take?"

"Are there really machines for washing laundry?"

"Is it true they don't believe in God?"

"And do you believe?" the guest asked.

"What else," answered one of them firmly. "It's the custom. On the Feast of Cassian you cross yourself, on Easter you light a candle. . . . But God is always God."

The gypsy, who had in the meantime finished off the second bottle of Tokay, turned to the women again, making peculiar, passionate, birdlike noises in his throat, a sort of warble and whistle. . . . They responded, first weakly, reluctantly, but gradually, warming to it more willingly and generously. Like artillery salvos came the echo of loud slaps on buttocks and backs. Heated from this play, they began to undress, helping each other to shed their homespun clothes. . . . Markali threw off his shirt the way a fighter of old rid himself of his outer garments before falling upon his deadly enemy.

The women no longer laughed. Pale with fear or passion, they uttered age-old muffled sighs and moans that made the gypsy lose his head completely. He threw himself blindly after them. But the women eluded him easily. Firm and elastic as birds in autumn, they jumped from one pink rock to another. Naked, their hair streaming down their milk-white bodies to their knees, their hands covering their private parts, they seemed this very moment to have sprung from the marble blocks around them.

The blue, hairy gypsy was also jumping from one slab to the next, trying to grab them and fling himself upon them. The women's sobs and moans and Markali's triumphant trilling finally reached a natural climax—all three tumbled into a crevice: their voices subsided and only the indifferent echo (knowing not what it did) belatedly repeated their awesome dark groans.

Then the ancient incantations of the women rose up again, Markali bellowed in answer, and colored gravel, like pebbles in the tide, poured down.

Master Kassian, unnoticed by anyone, crept out of the quarry (toward the sun) and without incident reached the bridge. In the shining piazza he was met by the barks of separate packs of dogs noisily asserting their independence; the aroma of black coffee wafted through the air. In this village the howling of dogs and the smell of coffee served as the prime coat, on which all other sensual perceptions of life were incrusted.

10

The dogs of the valley merited special study. Living in the company of hunters and shepherds since cave times, they, more than any other animal, are subjected to the influence of human customs, which here had remained almost unchanged for several thousand years. This conservatism apparently attracted them, for representatives of the most diverse breeds had converged in the valley.

The howling began at dawn. In clearly segregated packs the dogs crawled out of the ravines near the river to roam from one store to another, waiting for handouts, agilely avoiding sticks and stones aimed at them, rightly calculating that in the end the owner or his wife would throw them the entrails of a fowl, a sheep bone, or a mess of scraps full of pressed-out berries, apples, prunes: in the fall, the canines and livestock tottered about completely drunk. Indeed, what else could the people do with their garbage, short of organizing a sanitation crew? Without dogs the valley would have drowned in flies, ants, and rodents (which happened anyway once every quarter of a century or so, along with a flood, a conflagration, or a world-wide slaughter).

Each of the strictly divided bands had its own hetman. When civil war broke out within the pack, the leader settled it quickly and without bloodshed . . . but over the years his authority diminished and eventually, after a raucous fight, he had to cede his place to a younger and more enterprising rival. A fight between packs had the character of a test of strength, of a demonstration (as often in human society). After a lightning assault, the challenging side, still weak, immediately retreated, leaving the field to its powerful adversary. But if, since the last confrontation, that adversary had weakened, it was his turn to retreat: the whole pack would run off with bared teeth, angrily snarling at its hapless leader. . . . Every so often, in the half-dark, the dogs met at the ravine by the cemetery and mauled one another in earnest, establishing the hierarchy for the next season.

The beaten guilty leader, cast off by the gang, lived as a hermit until he could gather under his command a number of unstable, dissatisfied rebels (plus two or three young and stupid bitches); in this way new political factions emerged, often puny and short-lived but always dreaming of a thousand-year rule.

The number of sheep, goats, and deer consumed by the villagers in the course of a year was limited. Small scraps were thrown out the windows and doors; large refuse and natural wastes were carried beyond the ravine near the cemetery: there a bend in the river formed a sandy cape that was covered with water in the fall and spring. This small beach with its miniature dunes might have been an ornament to the village, but instead it had been destined as the dumping ground for carcasses, entrails, and the like. . . . The area was staked out with five tall beams that were the perch for huge, scraggly, red-beaked scavengers. Invariably, one such disgusting marauder occupied a beam, so that it seemed as if there were only five of them in the entire valley (which was not at all the case).

Migrating cranes had also chosen the river as a favorite stopover; on spring and autumn evenings their trumpeting excited the valley. There were, too, a great many storks nesting on the roofs of the farms. A violent, age-old feud existed between those exquisite feathered creatures and the vultures in their Indian war paint. Why such hatred, it was difficult to say. One could only speculate, and perhaps there was no cause at all.

Here, at this colorful dumping ground, the gangs of dogs converged (in the winter, wolves dropped by too). The scuffling and snarling never stopped: in the village it sounded like the rumble of one gigantic greedy belly. And although in the summer there was more than enough to eat, they still roamed the countryside half starved, with drawn-in stomachs and with that spark in their eyes which tells of an unsuccessful life.

Among the dogs of the valley traits of every breed could be distinguished: the clumsy St. Bernard, the powerful bulldog, the dachshund or Great Dane or terrier. They vividly demonstrated all the influences and changes of fashion the country had undergone during the last centuries. It was worthy of note that these hordes or packs were not organized according to any racial criteria: each one had representatives of many species.

The rest of Kassian's day passed uneventfully. He was happy to observe the dogs and the complicated play of shadows on the piazza. In the evening the Joachims wanted the Professor to join them again for the common meal, but he refused. He swallowed a few sausages in his room and, after washing them down with tea, promptly blew out the lights. The din and howl that woke the guest the following morning had an unusual origin. It developed that after a particularly ferocious fight, the leader of one of the packs had remained behind on the piazza with a dislocated shoulder. Whether it was from an awkward jump or from being attacked by too many at once, his foreleg dangled helplessly and an impressive swelling was forming in the region of his collarbone.

The dog, a short-haired yellowish mongrel with a white shirt front and a pushed-in nose, was obviously related to the true bulldog; battered and dirty, he had the gleam of an abused, destitute soul in his eye. The heavy jaw with its two fangs proclaimed that he depended only on himself and did not expect favors from anyone, even though he subsisted mostly on handouts. With aggressive arrogance he had dominated the piazza, relying on his power and that of his pack. On the first morning, when he was having coffee with the Joachims, the Master had already noticed this simple-minded brute that still believed in Darwin and Marx.

Now this same dog, his shoulder dislocated, hopped pitifully, in complete loneliness, across the piazza. His gang of marauders had abandoned him—they were already hunting on their own, postponing the final showdown with the hated leader until a more propitious moment.

Growling convincingly, the bulldog sidled up on three paws toward the butchershop, where he froze in front of the door in the idle hope that someone would throw him an especially juicy bone. Beneath his greasy fur the swelling was gaining by the minute.

Kassian realized that in our world of artificial, imaginary values this dog must be doomed. And yet his skill and strength and creative capacities had not been fully utilized and could still bring a great deal of joy (if not to other dogs, then at least to people). He also knew there was nothing simpler than to set a freshly dislocated joint: one had only to pull the limb toward oneself and bring it down in a semicircle. But it had to be done immediately. The captain, Kassian's stepfather and mentor, had taught him many such silly and useless tricks: how to make denatured alcohol drinkable . . . how to start a car without a key. . . .

The Master explained the maneuver to the Joachims; they understood perfectly, but they unanimously refused to take part in the operation.

"First you have to catch the devil," one of the beards declared, "then hold him, then treat him. In the meantime he'll bite your arm off."

"It doesn't make sense," Pelikan Effendi agreed. He was sorting chemicals for his quarry and was covered with a layer of brightly colored powder. "While you fix his shoulder he bites off your hand. What's the profit?"

"You can't help them," Yovan the tinsmith announced. "Animals expect only evil from man and defend themselves fiercely."

"The instinct of self-preservation!" Philolai, who had been to the city often, corroborated.

"That's what leads us to our ruin, this instinct of self-preservation," Kassian explained.

"Yes," the Joachims all agreed, "that's how it is."

"What if we tried?" the Master insisted. "We'll throw a blanket over his head and cover him up and then I'll fix it in no time."

"Of course, he is God's creature," Philolai remarked.

"That's true."

And to their own surprise the Joachims suddenly and unanimously expressed the wish to help the guest. Sure enough, someone suggested they have coffee before starting, but the Master nipped that in the bud. And in another minute he and Philolai, holding on to the ends of an old horse blanket, began to edge toward the dog, which was staring at them with eyes as big as saucers.

The Joachims, the women, and the children also advanced, driving the animal toward the ravine, cutting off his escape.

But the descendant of many valiant bulldogs, his teeth and shirt front flashing, leaped up wildly, somehow exultantly, and, somersaulting through the air, landed, against all expectations, not on the rocky bank but in the middle of the river: the waves buoyed him up and spun his muscular body, pulsating with life and anger, around in a circle. Paddling with all his strength, the dog pulled himself out of the whirlpool and swam with powerful jerks across the river. He climbed up the steep bank on the other side and fiercely shook himself. He was standing on all four paws. Apparently his violent, stubborn movements had set the dislocated joint. Before he vanished into the bushes, he looked back, once. Menacingly, contemptuously.

"You see, you can't catch those devils," the Joachims complained.

"They don't trust you."

"They run away. You can't do anything for them."

"But we cured him. So help me God, we did!" stated Philolai.

"Who cured him?" the peasants objected. "He cured himself. We didn't help any."

"We helped, and we didn't help, and still something else . . ." said Kassian with a smile, but no one had a chance to answer him.

Two deafening artillery shots thundered, one after the other, and then a hail of shrapnel fell on the bridge. Someone moaned; a woman's voice cried out; a donkey brayed, surprised, doleful—and the people, as if they had been expecting this for a long time, instantly rushed to their lairs. The piazza emptied, windows and doors were locked smoothly and noiselessly. Only an old woman, apparently grazed by a splinter, flailing one arm, hobbled silently, stubbornly across the piazza. Somehow she resembled the bulldog who just a moment before had limped away in the opposite direction.

The pastoral scene had changed; the village lay dead, petrified. Everything was silenced: people, beasts, vegetation. Even the wind had died down and the smells had lost their intensity. Only in the sky a frightened cloud, bruised by the explosion, tore off, seeking to hide as far away as possible.

Then came the sound of drums beating, the uneven knocking of motors, the grinding of caterpillars. . . . A gray-green column of soldiers was advancing through the natural entrance that led into the valley. Behind them emerged small tanks and a big armored car, several horse-drawn cannons, a few two-wheeled carts and wagons. The procession, with a rider on a white mule at the head, wound solemnly through the narrow pass and smoothly descended into the village. In the piazza the column made a half-circle around the fountain and at a sharp command froze to attention.

The soldiers wore patched, dusty German uniforms; most of them had Iron Crosses pinned to their chests. More crosses and swastikas were painted on their vehicles. Without dismounting from his mule, an obese officer in cloudy (brick-colored) glasses peremptorily raised his hand, at which the drums began to beat again. Then, in a falsetto voice that he injected with a mixture of sternness and benevolence, he screamed "Heil Hitler!"

A younger officer, who was holding his gunners at attention in front of the village hall, also raised his arm in the air and called back "Heil Hitler!"

Bewildered, Master Kassian still stood in the same spot he had been when the dog made his escape. Realizing at last that he was attracting attention, which in this case was hardly desirable, the Master walked slowly to the nearest garden fence: to judge by the quivering sunflowers, people had just run by with their bundles. He climbed over and disappeared behind the currant bushes.

Meanwhile the two officers had been stretching their legs (each in his own way) on the piazza and now walked up the steps to the village hall, escorted by a sergeant and a clerk. Again there was a roll of drums, the soldiers fell out, and, in groups of two or three, systematically went through the houses, chasing out the inhabitants and herding them toward the village hall. There the sergeant and the clerk were carefully tacking a square cardboard poster to the wall.

The Joachims and several Annas were forced to file by the poster, which bore a huge swastika, and in this way acknowledge the German text. After that they were all lined up at the bottom of the steps.

"Peaceful inhabitants," the colonel screamed in his high-pitched voice, his brick-colored glasses shining bloodthirstily. "Most peaceful citizens," he said again in German, convinced that history had taught the natives of this country a multitude of foreign languages. "Hard-working plowmen, you have read the proclamation of our Führer and now you know that nothing will happen to you if you are sensible and obey the orders of the military command. But if you are not sensible and do not obey the orders of the military command. . . ." His voice quavered with the paternal severity and false good will of a wise administrator. "Good men and women, go back to your hearths and wait calmly for our brave soldiers. You will voluntarily hand over all food, materials, books, machines, instruments, everything necessary for the victory of the Third Reich. Heil Hitler!" he finished wearily, but his reddish glasses never lost their untiring, greedy expression.

While he was talking, the artillery crews near the fountain took care of the cannons: having chosen a suitable place, they arranged the platforms and set up hitching posts for the horses. The infantry stacked their rifles and then they all busied themselves making fires. A few began to build huts out of branches, vines, and old corn straw.

The machine gunners, starting out in opposite directions, skillfully, methodically moved from house to house, not leaving out a single one, occupied or empty. Anything of value—rugs, woollen materials and leather goods, and, of course, provisions such as pork, salami, cheese, sugar, coffee—they collected in neat piles and then strictly supervised the peasants who carried the goods to the vehicles. Old magazines and prayer books and the skeleton of a rudimentary radio transmitter were thrown in a heap, destined for an immediate auto-da-fé. The provisions and winter clothes were put into the armored car with the black swastika.

Heated from their creative efforts, the graying Germans intently watched the loading with their red-rimmed, lashless eyes and generously gave out receipts in return for the goods; their entire behavior expressed the special joy of people who imagine they are most cleverly cheating their neighbors. Bluish smoke, and with it the cheerful smell of burning wood, rose from different corners of the piazza and drifted toward the river. Meanwhile the horizon had several times jerked upward, closer to the sun—apparently again turning toward night.

"Krauts," said Philolai, climbing up to the gallery where the Joachims had assembled (next to the Master's room) to watch their age-old enemies from the window. "Krauts! Books they burn, lard they carry off."

"Never mind, we'll harness them," remarked—for once—Joachim the Turk.

"And how we'll harness them!" Philolai rallied himself. "We'll harness them all right," and they all spat.

"Before you harness them, they'll swallow you head and foot," said a sullen peasant, apparently from the valley.

"We've had the Krauts before," Joachim the Turk said. "They'll take the sausage and hang a dozen people. So what?"

As a sign of approval, the Joachims spat once more.

"What, the Germans again?" asked the Annas, looking out of their quarters with babies in their arms.

"You would prefer a Turk!" one of the Joachims cynically cut them short.

"Oh Lord, it's sickening," the women complained, as was their wont, and vanished behind their screens.

Kassian listened to the peasants, trying to understand what was hidden behind their trite remarks; but he failed—probably because there was no special meaning in their flow of words. He felt, however, that the Joachims were preparing (as so often before) for a long, passive resistance.

"They are out of their minds," the Master finally blurted. "Literally and absolutely."

The Joachims reacted to this announcement with indifference. They sucked on their pipes, scratched their beards, and said ponderously: "The Germans are always mad."

"They may be mad, but they'll show you what's what!" stated the sullen farmer, as if this fact gave him pleasure.

"Never mind, we'll harness them," said Philolai.

"It makes no difference," they all agreed, "we'll get them!"

"That's right!"

"That's for sure."

Silence set in. From the window of the gallery one could see soldiers without jackets, some even in their underwear, chasing after hens, ducks, and geese. They cut the birds' throats on the spot with their bayonets, or simply choked them with their hands. The soldiers' jokes were probably extremely funny, for they were all bursting with high-pitched (womanish) laughter.

The smell of fried meat rose in the air. An enormous, handsome ram that Markali had driven from the castle was speedily knocked down by a blow on the head. The cook, with a soft smile, felt for the heart beating beneath the layers of fat and carefully (furtively) pushed a long blade into it.

Water was boiling in the cauldrons: the soldiers scrubbed their feet with the Oriental oils that the local coquettes used in place of soap. The women were already busy with the soldiers' wash.

A pack of dogs approached too close and was greeted with a round of machine-gun fire. From the river came the squeals and shrill laughter of flaccid, freckled men trying to bathe in the torrential stream.

A patrol, led by the Kommandant astride the bay mare he had taken from Philolai, was crossing the bridge. Markali ran ahead of them; whenever he stumbled, the mounted officer whipped him on with his crop. The giant silvery-blue gypsy, bloodstained and hatless, was impressive, terrifying. But the Germans did not notice.

"Now the Bishop will get his due," the Joachims said.

"And Felix too!"

"That's one good thing at least."

"The gypsy isn't one of us, let him get it," they all decided.

Unobtrusively the women had brought up coffee, hiding the kettle in their skirts like a chamber pot. The pervasive smell of the Oriental potion rose again.

"Now everything will vanish: sugar, tobacco, candles," someone said.

"Don't worry, the women will take care of that," the others assured him. "The Krauts!" the Joachims repeated meaningfully and laughed, drinking the scalding, tar-black liquid.

Indeed, the Annas had for some time been hurrying about in all three dimensions. Oddly puffed out and angry, they hid anything of value in different cracks and corners of their attics and cellars. Each family also had its own hiding place in the garden or at the river—deep pits in which for centuries they had secreted new clothing, furs, silver, money, grain. . . . The children and dogs roamed orphaned in the back yards, avoiding strangers and kin alike.

Inside the inn a second, more thorough search was under way: the soldiers carried dusty bottles and decanters from the cellar into the open. Cantemir, his face bashed in, lay in bed on the second floor, spitting blood. Now only Philolai, his pipe in his mouth, escorted the sergeant.

The Master's suitcase attracted special attention. The Germans, with laconic observations, expertly searched it. They took his shirts and books. The officer with the stripes of a lieutenant and a skull and crossbones on his sleeve handed Kassian a receipt for the confiscated objects, adding with great authority that later, in due time, he would be reimbursed for everything by the Third Reich. "Heil Hitler!"

"When later?" Kassian asked. He spoke the language fluently but he made it a point to pronounce the words with a Swiss accent.

"What do you mean, when?" The lieutenant seemed astonished. He was a fair but almost bald, middle-aged man, rather tall and thin, with a long, pock-marked face and a skull that ended in a sharp point. His eyes were inflamed, bloodshot. His sickly appearance and shabby uniform aroused pity rather than fear. "It's quite clear when—after our victory," he said, with the same mixture of threat and kindliness affected by his superior.

Hearing him raise his voice, several soldiers looked into the room. Beyond the door, on the gallery, the bearded Joachims stood watch, smoking their pipes—imperturbable.

"After which victory?" Kassian inquired.

"You are obviously an intellectual," the lieutenant said with a malicious smile. "And yet if you showed some wisdom and tact," he continued almost amiably, "you would all be safe. We have only come for a few days. For repairs and supplies. . . ." He nodded his pointed head, as if to guarantee the truthfulness of this statement. Armed, supported by a myth and a column of soldiers, he was still the one who seemed to need help.

"Would you be able to tell me the date?" the Master asked. "What day and year it is?"

"Today is the twenty-second of June," the officer answered thoughtfully. "This date I cannot forget."

"But today is not Sunday."

"No? What day is it then?" the officer asked distractedly. "Anyway, it's of no importance. Our Kommandant has absolutely no sense of humor; he'll strangle you with his bare hands at the first opportunity. That, by the way, is his favorite pastime."

The lieutenant formally clicked his heels and walked out; the soldiers' boots thundered down the staircase. Unhurriedly, the Joachims gathered around the Professor; assuming that he had, out of pride or vanity, exposed himself to danger, they patronizingly began to explain the facts to him:

"It doesn't pay to argue."

"The Germans are always the same."

"That's true."

"Only if you break their necks—that they understand."

"That's it. A German understands only that!"

"That and sausages!"

"He'll trade his woman for a sausage," they joked through their beards. "And his wife would exchange him for a ham."

"Very simple."

"Never mind, we'll harness them."

From below came the shrieks of women defending themselves or their belongings. Donkeys and noble little horses were led out of the stables. The soldiers selected the liveliest and hardiest for the needs of the thousand-year Reich. . . . And without interruption—on the move—the Germans chewed and swallowed, whatever else they were doing.

Behind a nailed oak door in the attic of the village hall they found a heap of old newspapers, which prompted the lieutenant to summon several Joachims to the steps and again read them the order of the Kommandant, forbidding the peaceful population to store arms and provocative literature . . . and to announce that at sundown there would be a curfew and they must remain in their houses. The Joachims listened to the German speech without comment. They seemed almost to approve of the rational measures taken by the authorities, even though they were doubtful of the results.

Two soldiers and a sergeant carried the newspapers dating from the Balkan wars to the piazza and threw them into a huge fire, the same fire above which the magnificent ram had been turning for some time. The cooks began to argue with the sergeant, refusing this kind of fuel, until the lieutenant shouted at them. Flakes of paper and cinders floated over the pink piazza. The pigeons vanished.

The gendarme, already deprived of his leather straps and sword, and Mayor Owl were carrying an ancient radio with Tesla bobbins down the steps from the village hall. The Germans carefully deposited this junk on a truck. They had also unearthed some rusty steel parts and mangled coils: the Joachims looked at these pieces extracted from oblivion as if they were their resurrected ancestors.

11

Part of the garrison left for the farms farther down in the valley. The rest, harried by the corporals (and constantly throwing glances at the slowly browning ram floating on the spit), reluctantly occupied themselves with the repair of motors, harnesses, vehicles, and clothing. They had mobilized a crowd of Annas and Joachims, but the natives, indistinguishable from one another, kept disappearing. Besides, their slow and apparently haphazard way of working incensed the Germans. Drunk already, their bellies almost full, the invaders still seemed rushed and jittery. The piazza rang with a continuous clamor above which one could distinguish crude cursing and, from time to time, unmistakably, the vile sound of a slap.

A current of cool air streamed from the mountains. The sun hung completely unattached in the crystal sky, like a golden-orange glob of thick, vital juice (or honey). The decisive hour was approaching when day is almost over but evening has not yet arrived, the hour when one can, for the last time, look back and try to catch up, redeem . . . that feeling of "sunset" that inspires children and poets to praise and regret the so-called past, that feeling out of which evolved our science and religion, philosophy, and literature whose intent is to reverse and repeat the life disappearing beyond the horizon.

The cook announced the meat was ready, and the men (though already full) bolted to the charred carcass with mess kits, pots, and pails.

At a neighboring, smaller fire, birds were cooking and stewing. The Germans ran from one kettle to the other, afraid of being cheated out of their share. Gravy, potatoes, mutton fat were a source of arguments and even fist fights. Illuminated by the fires, the cooks, in chef's hats, with smiling eunuch faces, resembled Oriental Buddhas with a multitude of arms. In the background, at their carts, the horses and mules peacefully chewed oats, fastidiously brushing off the drunken outcries and curses.

Big ladles and double-edged knives . . . wings, necks, and bones . . . straw-covered bottles gurgling repulsively as they were raised higher and higher. The soldiers too made peculiar noises with their lips, which aroused general hilarity. Many of the Germans, particularly those with stripes, the corporals and sergeants, were frying and stewing additional portions at individual fires. This also made for fights, since the men would often distractedly reach out for someone else's pot. But rifles were not used and the sergeants had no trouble keeping their men in check.

Having boiled one load of wash, the women were carrying it to the river to rinse, driven on by soldiers brandishing a cooked turkey or a fried duck instead of a rifle. The Joachims poured fresh water into the vats, calmly (almost haughtily) eying their insignificant-looking enemy. They were especially impressed and reassured by the miserable condition of the Germans' underwear: completely rotted away in places, it was held together only by patches. It was impossible to wash out the accumulated grime of many years in one session: the steam somehow rather set it. The men struggled into "requisitioned" skirts and blouses and, smiling bashfully, handed their only, damp, lice-infested underwear to the Annas.

The Joachims who still remembered occupations by the Austrians, Turks, Russians, and, of course, Germans, thoughtfully shook their beards as they scrutinized the uniforms and pants and the half-naked soldiers themselves, who were covered with boils, ulcers, and rashes.

Oddly enough, washed and shaved, the Germans looked more wretched and unsightly than before.

"They look like corpses, not soldiers," decided Philolai.

The same thought, in different variations, was expressed by the others:

"Ripe for the hospital, not for battle!"

"Dead on their feet and still heroes."

There were moments when the crates of artillery were left unguarded, a circumstance that irked the peasants and aroused in them a feeling of undefinable uneasiness about the enemy. . . . The ill-fitting, faded uniforms seemed sewn together from odds and ends. The women who were mending the tunics of the noncommissioned officers noticed that the buttons were of assorted kinds and that the stripes did not always match. They could see this even more clearly after the repairs.

The detachment looked like a band of deserters picked up here, there, and everywhere by the authorities and thrown back to the collapsing front. But their glee as they reached for the pots or a shining necklace of sausages, their skillful farts and vulgar jokes were genuine—German. There could be no mistake: only Germans howled with such triumphant laughter when slabs of pork were served them.

Stuffed and heavy, they still remained faithful to their peculiar sense of humor, which, if they happened to throw a bone to the dogs, made them follow this up directly with a burst of machine-gun fire. They began to grab for the women—in an awkward, pathetic way, chasing two or three at the same time without regard to age or looks. (As it was, the younger women had run away anyhow and were hiding in ravines and rocky caves.)

From the start the Germans had singled out the Master. The soldiers addressed him stubbornly as *Herr Doktor*. He knew this attention was dangerous, but there was nothing he could do. A stranger to the peasants too, he was naturally an outsider, isolated, exposed. Philolai reported to him confidentially that the lieutenant had inquired whether the Herr Doktor wasn't by any chance a Jew. . . . "Never mind, we'll harness them!"

"Krauts, that's what they are!" chuckled the Joachims on the gallery.

"Very simple."

The lieutenant ate by himself in the empty inn. A number of tables had been moved out and some soldiers had brought in an enormous screen and were setting up a movie projector, apparently getting ready for a performance.

Several paintings in heavy, hand-carved frames had been hung on the walls. The lieutenant, who, eating and drinking, was in a good mood, admired the French impressionist landscapes.

From the gallery the Joachims imperturbably watched the officer. Although the golden shafts of the passed day's sun still poured down on the piazza, Cantemir, his cheek bandaged, was already lighting the big kerosene lamp. The lieutenant continued to eat, sometimes making an approving remark to his orderly. It was hard to decide whether he was admiring the stew in front of him or the grainy yellow landscape on the wall. Suddenly bored (or mellowing under the influence of the slivovitz), he sent for the Professor. Kassian, followed by the whispered warnings of the Joachims, went down into the big room.

"Sit down. Would you like coffee? Brandy?"

"You are probably tired of the company of the military," Kassian said, taking a seat. He felt sorry for this balding simpleton who had left for the war as a youth and still had not returned home.

"A German soldier always does his duty," the officer stated

pompously and not quite to the point. "You speak our language very well."

"I studied at a Swiss university."

"German is the greatest of all languages," said the lieutenant. "Long live the German language!" He raised his glass.

"I cannot agree with you," the Master said softly. "All the miseries of Germany stem from its language. Change the language and your entire history will evolve in a new, normal way."

"I have never heard that before." The lieutenant was sincerely surprised. "That, I beg your pardon, is absurd."

"Take your literature," the Master continued. "There are no great German writers. And that is no coincidence."

"Come, come. What about . . ." and he mentioned several old and famous names.

"In such disputes the poets of the eighteenth or nineteenth century are always brought up," Kassian said with a smile. "That too is typical. . . . But where are your Tolstois, your Prousts, Dickenses, Melvilles? You have Bach and Mozart and Goethe and Kant, but where are your great prose writers?"

"Well, there is Kafka, for instance."

"He's Austrian, or Czech, or a Jew. I thought you had renounced the Jews?"

"What are you trying to prove?" The officer's voice rose. At the door, the orderly stiffened professionally.

"Prose reflects the soul of a human being and of a nation," the Master said succinctly. "Prose cannot exist without consciousness and reason. Poetry can be mad, music irrational, painting sensual, philosophy abstract. Prose has all these qualities, plus the light of reason. It embraces everything that makes up man's nature. The novel appeared in the

Christian era, where the concept of time occupies a special place. Christ died and rose again; but it is equally important that this happened under Pontius Pilate. In poetry, music, painting, time is not the foundation of everything. There are variations and repetitions in music, but that is not a true development in time. A poem often becomes a novel or a story—that is, prose; but real poetry jumps out of the story and out of time. The theme of the novel, its basic axis, its last reality, is always and above everything else time. The sanctified, concrete time that was born in the Christian era and for which we bear responsibility. No," the Master concluded amiably, "to this day the Germans have not created a great novel."

"We like music," the lieutenant declared angrily.

"Of course you do, but that is not the same thing. . . . You and I value Wagner or *The Merry Widow*. Many hangmen have liked them too. We are all attracted by Cézanne. Any fat, castrated thief can like Gauguin and steal his pictures from a museum. Marauders and murderers, false witnesses and corrupters of minors can admire Schiller, Goethe, Baudelaire. But Tolstoi is the demarcation line. He separates us from hangmen, scoundrels, liars, and lunatics. A Göring or Goebbels could not possibly appreciate *War and Peace*. Glory to the Word, to the story, to the novel, which embraces life and man in all their breadth and scope, with all their gifts. Long live prose! Now I'll drink with you." Kassian solemnly raised his glass.

"Just as I thought. You are crazy!" the lieutenant said, and they both broke into relieved laughter. "By the way, how do you like that Van Gogh there? Do you see how the fat wheat ripples?"

"You stole it?"

"After the war I'll give everything to a museum."

They sipped their coffee, admiring Van Gogh's pink-yellow (enchanted) straw. Profiting by the general mellowing in the mood, the Joachims began to steal up and down the staircase to settle their urgent domestic affairs. The merchants locked up their stores and, with boxes and bundles under their arms, scrambled over fences. The blacksmith and the saddler, whom the Germans had swamped with work, suddenly let down the shutters on the doors and windows to their workshops. No lights could be seen in the houses. The village seemed to have been deserted long ago. Around the main fire the soldiers were engaged in a game of cards. Bands of children and dogs, estranged from everyone, had gone into hiding near the river.

"You are a born victim," the lieutenant said. "Why don't you run! Leave for a day or two."

"But this is madness," said the Master. "The war ended with the defeat of the Germans. Are you completely out of your minds?"

"Yes," the lieutenant confirmed sadly, "you are a victim, a typical victim. Don't you know that the world is full of madmen? To a certain degree you and I are both mad. The difference is that we have the machine guns. That's why you have to think in our terms, not we in yours. Do you play dominoes?" he asked suddenly.

"I believe so, a little."

The German reached into a saddlebag hanging over a chair and extracted a delicate box resembling a miniature coffin. "I hope the Kommandant won't come in," he said meekly to the orderly who, still chewing on something, condescendingly shook his head.

"Our Kommandant does not approve of familiarities. Distance, the proper distance, that is his ideal. Those former artillery men!" the lieutenant complained, mixing the ivory pieces.

"Why former?" the Master asked quickly.

But the officer dreamily continued: "I am always struck by the simplicity of those people who are convinced that the longer they shuffle, the better shuffled the cards are. What nonsense! Only afterward, when you have looked at your hand, can you decide whether they have been sufficiently shuffled. And it is always possible to invent a game where the particular combination of suits you hold would be especially advantageous—that is, the deck would be stacked."

The Master smiled. "It is astonishing to what extent we all, strangers to one another, are becoming preoccupied with the problem of entropy and reversibility. Of different countries, friend and foe, ignorant and educated, good and bad, we are all bombarded by the radiations of one and the same powerful, contemporary comet or newly flared-up star."

The German had no time to react. The astute orderly reported that the Kommandant was returning from the castle. The officer rose, buttoned up the collar of his tunic, and took a careless, unsmiling leave of Kassian. The colonel apparently was feared.

Several Joachims and Annas still lingered on the gallery. At the Master's appearance the women instantly melted into the walls. The peasants winked at the guest in sympathy and continued to keep the darkening piazza under surveillance.

From the window the colonel could be seen crossing the bridge at a slow trot (the sounds of hoofs were not audible inside the house). He was followed by a long wagon and by a dozen or so two-wheeled carts piled high with all kinds of goods. On one of the carts, incongruously, sat the two Katerinas, the gypsies, in colorful hats. The soldiers followed on foot, gingerly leading Flora and Fauna, who glowed like the sunset. The machine gunners, looking as belligerent as if they had just conquered Stalingrad, brought up the rear.

Somehow (possibly through the children) it became known on the gallery that the Germans had killed Markali. They had thrown his body into the quarry, where, incidentally, they discovered an entire arsenal of weapons.

Dismounting from his bay mare at the village hall, the Kommandant passed the bridle to the orderly and went into his office. The Mayor and the Comptroller must have been summoned earlier, for there they were, Owl and Pelikan Effendi, one close after the other, stepping across the threshold of their own familiar village hall. However, they did not remain there long: describing a trajectory as if shot from a cannon, they landed at the foot of the steps—which brought the Joachims a degree of satisfaction. The Katerinas, under arrest, were led to a building behind the village hall. Drago, who, sobbing bitterly, tried to speak to Little Katerina, caught it too: he was kicked into the air as if he were a soccer ball.

The colonel, having exchanged his heavy jacket for a light tunic and gaily whistling a tune from *The Merry Widow*, walked over to the inn where the noncommissioned officers, the orderly, and the lieutenant were waiting for him. He was immediately handed a thick cigar and a glass of transparent slivovitz.

Meanwhile the clerk was posting a new proclamation at the village hall, making known to the "peaceful populace" that the gypsy had been shot for resisting the authorities, that his wife and daughter were taken hostage, and that, in the event of acts of sabotage, they, as well as more hostages, would be executed. This literary creation, written in typical German style, was a single sentence, consisting of words soldered together from three or four nouns. The main verb, which was the key to the entire text (*verboten, erschossen*), naturally appeared at the very end, so that Kassian, to grasp the meaning of the proclamation as fast as possible, first searched for that last verb and then, as it were, read the odd document backward. The Joachims waited patiently for him to decipher the German prose. Having done so, he conscientiously summarized the contents for the peasants, who interjected elaborate sounds meant to express unquestioning approval.

"Well, after all, they are Germans," one said.

"Very true," another added.

"Certainly, if you rebel . . ."

"Was Markali a rebel?"

"He was a gypsy."

"He liked to drink."

"And, of course, he appreciated women too."

"That he did."

"Never mind, we'll harness them," said Philolai.

And the Joachims walked with inscrutable faces past the gray-haired guards, who looked at them out of the corner of their eyes.

From the inn came laughter and the brisk thunder of mechanical music. Orderlies were running to and fro with bottles, tools, batteries, and metal cassettes. Soon the lights were extinguished and the characteristic crackling of a movie projector could be heard. Their eyes pressed against fissures and openings in the wall, the Annas and Joachims watched the dim screen suspiciously: the Master too, with the tacit approval of the guards, got a chance to admire the performance for a minute or two. The film showed the execution of some famous criminals, all in shining German uniforms of high rank, with rows of decorations. The peculiar feature of the scene was that the hangman strangled them with his bare hands, obviously not an easy chore. One half-naked general died in such agonies and convulsions that the Kommandant almost choked with laughter. In a shrill voice he ordered the scene run again; to see it better he took off his brick-colored glasses.

12

The boy Drago, no longer on tiptoes and far from dancing, scratched and tear-stained, slunk up to the Master and, cautiously looking around, informed him he was expected at the castle.

Slowly, lazily, the summer evening was spreading across the earth; in the distance, in the west, icy pinkish bars of light still trembled. Kassian decided he had enough time to cross the bridge without running into trouble. Sure enough, the soldiers merely frisked some of the passers-by in the places where one might expect them to have pockets and let them through.

On the other side, in the grove, the Master was welcomed by the love-stricken nightingale, already emitting short, preparatory trills, like a tennis player practicing his serve before a decisive match.

The oily spots of fireflies sparked dimly in the grass. Bats, like thieves in rented tail coats, darted by. A belated swallow soared up the precipitous bank, searching for its nest in the dusk. The brooding park opened its aging arms to him; the yellow path (Zora) beckoned, leading into the depths. High above, the thick crowns of the trees flapped like sails: up there a perpetual capricious breeze blew in from the mountains.

A patrol was posted in the courtyard. The sergeant was berating a private who, long-legged, with heavy buttocks and an inordinately short waist, had drawn himself up and, sighing impatiently, was listening to the monotonous sermon. A fire crackled vengefully, steam was rising from a kettle filled to the brim with plucked fowl. The guest was met with surprised glances but he was not prevented from entering the house.

Several women dozed in the vestibule; when they saw the visitor they started up and fled. Kassian walked into the big hall that now looked utterly deserted and bare. All the metal decorations, the brass and the bronze, had vanished from the walls. Weapons, armor, candelabra had been removed, even the funereal grandfather clock: in its place yawned a damp, rectangular spot.

Dozens of candles had been lit in the hall. From the farthest corner came the muted sounds of a violin. Zora, standing next to the piano and keeping time with the sole of her foot, was playing a very difficult, very famous sonata.

She nodded, austere and inaccessible as usual during her musical exercises. Though she was musically gifted and had fully mastered the technique, Zora played the violin in a strained, rather uninspired way. The piano answered to the touch of her fingers easily and blissfully with a wave of keys. But only when she sang was her seraphic nature entirely expressed: effortlessly, as freely as breathing, sounds issued from her throat (or from her soul) like a continuous hosanna, alleluia. Zora, however, considered the violin her vocation and concentrated her energies on it, particularly in times of stress and painful setbacks.

In the huge, also denuded dining room, women were as usual setting the table. Felix, chewing on something near the sideboard where the bottles and hors d'oeuvres were laid out, was yelling: "Can you imagine? Those bastards forbade me the use of my own horses!" Noticing the Master, he nodded to him as to an old acquaintance and repeated, "Those goddam bastards. . . ."

"What happened to Markali?" the guest asked.

"The fool did not want to part with Flora and Fauna." It was the Bishop who answered.

Chako, quite coherent for once, recounted how the Germans had at first wanted to take the gypsy alive, and how he, with his bare hands, had flung them away, injuring several of them. It was then that the colonel ordered his men to fire; riddled with bullets, Markali still continued to fight them off.

"What a man! A real hero," Chako murmured. But he could not explain how the Germans had uncovered the arsenal in the quarry.

"The deaf-mute gave it away," the Bishop said at long last, "and a good thing she did. To the gypsy it's all the same now, and it was an excellent opportunity to get rid of those old arms."

"Guns always come in handy," Chako said heatedly.

The Master felt a growing sympathy for the young man. Zora continued to keep time with her foot.

"And what did they do to the Katerinas?" the Bishop asked.

"They locked them up. It would appear that you have an

honest-to-goodness jail in the old caravansary. But why take the Katerinas? What kind of hostages are they?" the Master asked, casting a quick glance at the Bishop.

"Well, the family of a rebel," he explained. "Gypsies. Half-Jews perhaps, or some such thing."

"Jews?"

They all were silent. Only the violin, synchronized with the beating of Zora's foot, variated the basic theme. There was something alarming, cataleptic, in the rhythm of it. A seizure, Kassian decided—she's going to have a seizure. And he took a step in her direction.

"I thought it would improve the situation," confessed the Bishop. "In fact, it was the deaf-mute's idea. It was probably a mistake. Marc Ali is not even her father, so why punish the girl?" The deaf-mute at the fireplace began to emit noises resembling the hissing of a goose.

"Go to hell!" the Bishop shouted.

"What are we going to do?" yelled Felix, who in the meantime had downed several glasses. In the course of one day he had grown thin and somehow more human, more approachable. "They are looting, killing, deporting our people. So far it's only the servants, but don't worry, they'll get to us too. What shall we do about those madmen? Where have they come from?"

"In any case, they have guns," the Bishop noted, sipping from his glass.

"But they are mad," Felix insisted.

"Do you think they were sane in nineteen thirty-nine?" asked the Bishop.

"Of course not! But this is a complete phantasmagoria. An hallucination."

"What is fantasy, what is hallucination? The tanks? The

machine guns?" The Bishop's eyes had turned green, like Little Katerina's.

"It's intolerable, and you know it perfectly well!"

The Master, who the previous day had been ready to tear Felix limb from limb, suddenly saw an ally in him.

The violin stopped on a pitiful note; Zora entered the dining room and approached the table, wiping the corner of her eye with a handkerchief. The women lit more candles; the smell of stearin filled the room.

"The Colonel has shut down our generator and intends to carry it off," the Bishop said with a smile. "In a thousand-year economy, any rag is useful."

"How can you joke? The war is long over. Hitler's been burned to death!" Felix screamed: there was something in the situation that seemed to revolt him especially—more than the rest of them.

After a silence the Bishop said in his usual (condescending) way: "Yes, you are right. The Germans are mad. The war is a lie, the Third Reich a fairy tale. And yet Marc Ali's death, which came about as a result of those fabrications, would seem to be true enough. What do you say about all this, Professor?"

"Bishop," Zora interjected quickly, her sand-colored eyes happy, "you have false teeth, but if you bite someone the wound will be real, with every possible complication."

"I understand," the Bishop drawled. "You want to say that a fantasy can produce truth. But is the reality produced by a lie a genuine reality?"

"For God's sake, stop philosophizing," Felix interrupted. "It's sickening enough without that. Let's decide what to do. That is the question."

"How are the Joachims?" the Bishop asked.

"Philolai claims they'll harness them."

The Bishop and Zora smiled an almost identical smile. Felix shrugged disgustedly. Chako alone did not betray his mood: only his dark velvety eyes with the soft long lashes glittered.

"I guess for the time being it's best not to do anything," the Bishop said, studying his well-kept fingernails. "In a couple of days the Germans will withdraw to the mountains, or the authorities will notice that there's trouble in the valley and send a detachment."

"And in the meantime they'll hang the two Katerinas, kill several Joachims, and perhaps get us too," Felix screamed. "Do you expect us to wait around like sheep?"

"It ought to be easy to slip away at night and reach the city," the Master either asked or stated. They were already sitting around the table; the guest had been given a fresh, starched napkin.

"Yes, someone familiar with the road could get through," Zora confirmed. The deaf-mute looked at the company with the melancholy eyes of a suffering beast and lowed dolefully. No one touched the cold meat, but the wine they drank freely.

"The Joachims could do it, of course, but they won't," Felix said, bitterness in his voice.

"Why should the Joachims risk their necks, since they'll harness all of us anyway?" the Bishop remarked good-humoredly.

"I think," Kassian began suddenly, "that in this case it makes no difference whether the Germans are stark raving mad or absolutely sane. They are aggressors and we must defend ourselves as one does in times of war and occupation. There is no other reality."

"Then a lie multiplied by another lie becomes a truth?" the Bishop asked.

"Yes. A lie too is a reality, or part of it, just as death is a segment of life."

"But is not the end of Marc Ali, which resulted from so many illusory premises, perhaps also an invention, a mirage? Such an absurd end cannot be final," the Bishop persisted. In the light of the candles, his long yellow face strikingly resembled a famous portrait by El Greco.

"I refuse to philosophize now," Felix cried. Like all people who loathe abstract deliberations, Felix truly believed that at another time, under different circumstances, he would with pleasure keep up his side of a nebulous, general discussion. But not now, not today. . . . He jumped up, rushed to the sideboard, and, bending over, reached for a heavy, amber-colored bottle. Downing a glass, he offered the brandy around. In the course of the day the house had undergone a noticeable change: the host himself poured the drinks.

"What can we do?" Felix asked again, with more assurance.

"I'll get out at night," the Master said. "The Germans are only watching the main exit from the valley."

"Someone familiar with our ravines should do that. When I was a girl I used to climb all over those crevices. Of course, in the dark it's more difficult." Zora smiled, radiant, like a child, like an angel, or like a young woman delivered of her first-born.

"And *I* think that nothing should be done for the moment," stated the Bishop.

Chako rose brusquely and began to fasten the gold buttons of his tightly cut jacket.

"Sit down," Felix ordered with rare gentleness.

Chako obeyed. "I know the way," he mumbled.

"Just keep still," Felix repeated.

"They have hostages," the Bishop said. "They are bound to find out that someone escaped to the city, and they'll execute the hostages. That's the reason they were taken, isn't it?" They all watched him in silence as he sipped with relish from his glass. He continued in an altogether different tone. "Professor, do you remember Plato's cave? Where the people lie chained and can see only shadows of the real world that fall onto the wall as onto a screen? Do you remember? What do you think of that parable?"

Kassian did not answer immediately. The Bishop's long, yellow, lemonlike face dominated the dimly lit table.

"We know about the cave," Zora declared. (The Master blinked.) "But we also know that the Egyptian priests calculated the height of the pyramids from the relationship of the shadows cast by different objects. Shadows are specters, but their relationship is an absolute reality . . . at times the only reality."

(What makes her so jubilant, why does she always laugh with her eyes or with her skin or with her soul? Kassian asked himself for the thousandth time. She probably knows that all was well in the cosmos once, and will be well again. "God saw that it was good." Hence this joy of hers.)

"That means," the Bishop took up, "that by manipulating mirages we can discover the truth. What does such a truth prove? And is it really true?"

"Have some of the paprika cabbage," Felix offered.

"I'm afraid it's time for me to go back to the inn," said Kassian.

"It's late," the Bishop said. "It's after dark, and to the Germans, crazy or not, an order is an order."

"The Master will sleep here," Zora said. "He sleeps here," she repeated, turning her shining face toward the deaf-mute, who heaved a deep sigh, like a large wounded animal.

"I don't completely understand the spirit of the order and whether one can spend the night with friends," the guest remarked. "In the forties, some friends of mine went to a concentration camp because they were found at their neighbor's apartment, playing bridge."

"What apartment? What are you talking about? This is a village and you are our guest. Everyone knows that," the Bishop replied. "Tomorrow the Germans will return for the wine, so tonight we can drain an extra bottle of Imperial vintage. Perhaps the last. Only think, Professor, how many times during this century they have robbed my cellar. . . . Scientists talk about geopolitics; they don't realize that the problem is much less complex: the Germans, as in the time of the Huns, are always ready to start a war for the simple purpose of stuffing themselves with someone else's sausage."

The women, uncombed and gloomy, brought in several dusty bottles. The thick wine gurgled as though it were emerging from another world. In high spirits, the company clinked glasses (it was not the first time an enemy occupation had drawn together people who were actually alien to one another).

Chako, pale, his jacket tightly buttoned, looked more romantic than ever. Zora shone unaccountably with her eyes. She overflowed with a joy of which she herself was perhaps unaware, and Kassian found it painful to watch how easily and generously she dispersed her inner riches.

He drank the precious wine without noticing its quality. For a long time now he had known that love wipes away pain and suffering and boredom and sin as with a sponge. Perhaps under those ardent rays death too would be transfigured. Another moment, and his body would defy the earth's gravity and he would, at long last, fly, soar (or walk on the water as on firm ground). But here he remembered Markali lying hard on hard marble, full of bruises, and his own body again filled with lead.

13

At the fireplace the deaf-mute had fallen to her knees with a thump—at least that was the impression. But immediately after came the smell of smoke and, sighing mournfully, the fire behind the screen flared up. The Bishop politely complimented the housekeeper.

Fire, despite its predatory ways, has something of a good, close companion about it. When, along with the cozy smoke, the eyes of the first live coals begin to glimmer, it seems that a capricious and wise friend has entered the room.

Fruit was served: unsightly and rather colorless, it smelled intoxicating, exactly as real fruit ought to smell. The taste was familiar, too, and had been since the creation of the world. Slivovitz and coffee contributed to the general animation, so that toward the end of the meal the table had a truly festive air.

The Bishop presided—a courtier in disgrace or on leave, combining in his appearance modesty with majesty. Felix sat next to him, in leather leggings but without his crop, a coarse though well-meaning fellow. The Master and Zora sat opposite each other, a pulsating unstable rainbow stretching across the table, visibly or invisibly uniting them. Chako for one surely noticed the purple arc sparking directly above their heads. But he was silent, only rarely batting his long dark lashes (like a butterfly its wings).

The Bishop wiped an apricot with his napkin and bit into it (his lips grew fresh and scarlet). Then he said, self-possessed and as if continuing an interrupted conversation: "Yes, I always admired Abraham, who could raise a knife against his only son. But I couldn't possibly send Felix out through the German patrols." Nobody spoke, only Chako gave a loud laugh. "And yet," continued the Bishop, "is it not precisely such sacrifices that God expects of us?"

Kassian felt called to answer. "Yes and no. All this has been somewhat distorted by the commentators. In Abraham's childhood, everyone in his immediate surroundings knew about such sacrifices—his uncle or cousin, if not his father, may have made such a sacrifice. So that when God demanded his son, it sounded altogether different to Abraham from the way it sounds to us today."

"I don't understand and I don't care to understand," Chako announced suddenly.

The Bishop too was about to say something, but at that moment, from outside where unquestionable night already reigned, came loud noises, the stamping of boots, and the abrupt cries of military commands. A minute later four Germans, the lanky lieutenant and three machine gunners, burst with a menacing racket into the room. The officer saluted and said politely: "A meeting is taking place here. We know all about it."

The soldiers blinked against the light. Their round eunuch faces exuded satisfaction.

"We are having dinner. This, I believe, is still permitted," Felix shouted, taking a step toward the intruders.

The Bishop rose also and, interrupting his son, said: "May we offer you a cup of coffee?"

"Under the guise of a supper one can plan acts of sabotage," the lieutenant remarked dryly, and turning toward Chako he asked: "Are you a member of the family?"

"I . . . I . . ."

"That is our young friend and relative," the Bishop said, nodding his large head as if he considered the question very much to the point and his own answer fully exhaustive.

"And you? It seems to me I met you at the inn?"

"The Professor too is our guest. For his convenience we reserved a room at the inn for him—"

"I am very sorry," interrupted the lieutenant, "the order is for the inhabitants to be in their legal residence by nightfall. I am obliged to arrest you."

The dining hall was now filled with people and shadows. The barely breathing fire and the flickering candles multiplied the darkness, picking out here and there in the gloom a pale face, the shining clip of a submachine gun, or the independent (severed) sweep of the deaf-mute's arm.

Master Kassian got up. "Listen to me, Lieutenant," he said. "I am a prophet, I can give you valuable information. Tell your superiors that the war will end with your defeat in May, nineteen forty-five."

And Zora said in her clear, ringing voice: "Are you completely mad?"

"Pardon me," the officer interrupted her, "I would not like to take extreme measures."

"It seems to me you are only pretending," Zora continued, firmly believing every man could be reasoned with and brought to his senses. "Why? After all, life goes on, you could take part in it in a new way. The Bishop has connections. We'll help you!"

In her attempt to transfigure an absurd reality she was serious to the point of saintliness. The Master, however, noticed that her face was losing its luster, as if it were suddenly covered with a layer of dust or ashes. A seizure, he thought, and decisively stepped to the door, taking the enemy with him.

"Quick, march, march," the lieutenant ordered, somewhat belatedly but in the prescribed tone. The soldiers shook themselves and, submachine guns swinging, followed their prisoner out the door.

It was dark in the court. A fire smoldered near the stone wall. The birds in the park had long since quieted down and only a few huge (probably colorless) moths danced spellbound above the fire. Driven by the guards, the Master still inhaled with delight the scents of the earth: it smelled of hay and honey. (Only yesterday Markali had mowed this meadow skillfully, painstakingly.) They reached the bridge by way of the stony path: the wooden planks felt warm and alive. Below flowed the river, but one could not see it. One could only hear the resilient waves, compressed by the banks, squealing like rats. There was the piazza of Saint Cassian, lit by bivouac fires, as on canvases of old battle scenes. The horses were audibly grinding their dry oats. Near the village hall the guards roughly called out to one another.

The prisoner was thrown into a kind of storehouse adjacent to the village hall; it was old, two stories high, with a domed ceiling. He was left in the darkness. From somewhere close by came the sound of breathing or of sighs; probably the Katerinas, the Master guessed, and smiled wryly (the thought that on the macroscopic level causal relationships still helped to make the right deductions was no consolation).

He groped his way to the wall and squatted against it: his back defended, a man feels at home. The situation seemed so absurd that it was difficult to take it seriously, and this weakened, lulled the will to resist, even though elements of Greek tragedy were already discernible . . . (the Germans, mad, half-mad, or ultrasane, could execute their hostages at any moment).

The Master was aware that a man close to death often refuses to believe the end is near, that an inescapable metamorphosis is upon him. This is absurd, the sick man repeats. (Even if it happens to others.) It's not fair. It's unnatural. There is no logic to it! So he comforts himself, not suspecting the existence of another, phantasmagoric logic.

"And yet it was you who advocated that," said or thought the Master. "You preached freedom from causal dependence, at least on the microscopic level. Now you have it, so digest it! Finally you are about to realize a completely spontaneous, unpredetermined jump into the unknown."

"Alas, even when you refute causality, you reason causally."

"What do you mean?"

"You say: now you have it—so accept it. That is cause-and-effect reasoning. In your place a philosopher would say: I have it, though I did not seek it; and I have what I did not seek . . . and that is right, for on the atomic level everything happens spontaneously, unexpectedly."

"By the way, whom are you lecturing?"

"This way it's easier for me to think."

"One must think in jumps, not in a straight line. By zigzagging, you will—suddenly, gratuitously—hit the bull's eye."

"But if that is the case, how can anyone on this earth succeed in defending himself? How can he defeat the macroscopic enemies?"

"Ha-ha. He dedicated his whole life to self-defense and died. He died because all his life he defended himself."

"But I cannot do otherwise. We all do nothing but defend ourselves. Perhaps it is our language that has distorted us. Human speech is built haphazardly, any which way. No one today would consent to live in a Kaffir hut, but our language is still at the cannibal stage. Our auxiliary verbs, 'to be,' 'to have,' are those of the caveman. They are the ball bearings on which our world, our thoughts, our acts still turn. Everything rests on them. And yet these verbs lost their original meaning long ago."

"We must create a new language. We must find new auxiliary verbs to correspond to our reality."

"Which ones? That is the question."

"The opposites of the old 'to be' and 'to have,' which lead directly to entropy and death. In place of 'to have' perhaps 'to give'. . . ."

"If the Bishop sends Chako out tonight, they'll shoot or hang the hostages," the Master whispered, apparently having all along followed yet another, innermost line of thought. "And the Bishop is sure to send him," he decided.

It was drafty on the stone floor; in the dark, Kassian brushed together some straw on the floor and tucked it under him; it smelled of cats. Immediately beneath the ceiling were deep windows, reinforced with strong bars of white stone. Outside, a moon, by now of quite considerable dimensions, must have risen and set about its usual business; it lit up first one embrasure, then the next. A shadow pattern resembling a tarantula crawled along the opposite wall. "Zora," the Master murmured, "Zora" (autonomously), like an incantation.

Zora had indeed had a seizure. The women carried her upstairs while the men remained at the table waiting for the deaf-mute to bring them news about the girl's condition. Soon the splendid, gray-haired witch returned (cheerful, animated, rejuvenated) and informed them that everything was all right—there was no cause for alarm. She seemed to enjoy the customary complications with which she knew how to cope.

"Now the question is," the Bishop said to Chako with his most charming smile, "whether we should wait for our arch-enemy to show mercy or whether we should act like men."

The Bishop sat, his white hands folded as if in prayer; the deaf-mute was moving restlessly about the room. Suddenly, and very sweetly, he said to her: "Why don't you go and take a rest? And you should also look in on Zora."

The housekeeper angrily shook her monumental body and froze defiantly where she stood.

"Well," Chako announced, "it's very simple. It would be easy to get through."

"Shut up," Felix yelled. "If the Germans find out—and they're bound to—they'll execute the hostages, the Professor first of all. Especially the Professor."

"Perhaps they won't find out," the Bishop argued. "Chako is clever, he'll get across. Even Zora used to do it."

"To get through is easy, to keep it a secret is impossible," Felix insisted.

"In that case the Germans will round up everybody. They have their etiquette too and they'll stick to it. But in the meantime Chako will have reached the authorities and they will send airplanes, maybe even paratroopers. The Krauts will run! They won't have time to deal with the hostages."

"They always have time for executions," Felix said.

"The risk is great, of course," the Bishop agreed (stealing a glance at the deaf-mute). "But there is no other way. Chako always had heroic inclinations. Now it is time for him to prove himself."

Chako again buttoned up his jacket. Felix no longer held him back.

But the household was to be disturbed once more that night. They had hardly reached their rooms when again there was a thundering knock at the door. Two Joachims from the valley had persuaded the German guards to let them through: the soldiers stood next to them with lit torches, listening to the conversation. . . . Illuminated by the torches, the boy Drago, no longer dancing, was walking up and down in the courtyard. The peasants explained that the boy had been hanging around the quarry all evening and that a dog, in all probability a mad one, had bitten him. This kind of accident was not uncommon in the valley. Usually the victim was driven to the city . . . but now?

About this the peasants were conferring in a low voice with the lords of the castle. Drago meanwhile was apathetically circling the courtyard. Finally the sergeant, having grasped the essence of their deliberations, declared authoritatively: "Take him to the Colonel. The Colonel has all the necessary injections and medications."

At the mention of the colonel the gray-haired farmers exchanged glances and the boy began to whimper. But the Bishop agreed: "They have the medicine. Of course he must go."

"Maybe the dog wasn't mad after all," the bearded elders now declared. "Who can ever know?"

But the Germans considered it their duty to report the incident to the Kommandant. And one gallant soldier, after having pulled on an additional shirt (as if there were frost in the village), helmet and rifle shining, led Drago off toward the bridge, singing something inoffensive about Mädchen or Gretchen. The peasants hurried off in the opposite direction, relieved to get away.

A solemn moon had appeared in the sky: the rocks and crags cast thick (three-dimensional) shadows. The old men ran, white in the moonlight, one close on the heels of the other. Although they kept stubbornly silent, they obviously communicated mentally; they both veered left or right at the same moment, slowed down, or, still running in place, halted altogether and then, in unison, turned back to retrace part of the way.

They knew the terrain well and despite the crevices and overhangs did not consider it particularly difficult. But they were frightened by the historical, traditional, and mythological obstacles disseminated everywhere.

Here, for instance, in this ravine, one Joachim, still under the Austrians, had contracted to dig a well for a rich civil servant. He dug and he dug, poor wretch, wasting all his money and some he had borrowed besides, and never struck water. In the end he decided to save at least his and his family's honor. According to a reliable ancient belief, water will spring up on the spot where a man dies a violent, wicked death. The well-digger hanged himself. And at dawn the well was filled with crystal water. Alas, even in the daytime the people would not drive their goats there to water;

soon the hole caved in and the spring disappeared underground.

To pass near such a place, especially at night, was clearly the height of foolhardiness. Without exchanging a word, the two companions turned toward the cliffs and the hills. But danger awaited good people there too. Ahead glittered a massive, stony lump that, even in the darkness, resembled two lovers shamelessly embracing. There, centuries ago, a brother and sister had made love to each other. Their irate father pursued them with a knife, and God, in order to save the father from such a sin, changed the couple into a statue. The peasants never ventured near this monument to forbidden passion; they even avoided looking in its direction (particularly at night). But the companions stopped for a moment to study the shining path that led around it and directly to the main road. There, to their horror, they suddenly noticed a small figure, unnaturally thin, as if of glass, agilely jumping from rock to rock, up to the statue's very foot. It was Chako, but they did not recognize him. They piously crossed themselves.

Now only one road remained to the old men: the stony grade along the edge of the ravine, a narrow, slippery path notorious for werewolves. This was the place where, high up, as if on a hanging bridge, they liked to show themselves to the inhabitants. The peasants considered under the circumstances werewolves and vampires the lesser evil, and so two hunched, bearded shadows turned toward this fearful isthmus.

They had barely taken a dozen steps along the slippery path when the image of a wolf did in fact appear before them. Not the usual, small, gray kind the Joachims hunted in the winter, but a large, smooth-haired and, what was most important, pure white one.

"The deaf-mute," the old men mumbled in one breath.

There are different kinds of werewolves, and this must be understood. Good ones and bad, well fed and hungry, commoners and aristocrats. With some it is easy to come to terms (if you know the trick) but others are beyond human relations and emotions.

Judging by the serene, innocent, powerful appearance of the animal, with his huge, jutting, batlike ears, it was not the deaf-mute. But then again, werewolves (and other fiends) often assume a character completely foreign to their own nature. Otherwise why would they undertake such a dangerous masquerade at all?

Now one had to be as cunning as the serpent and as meek as the dove. Above all, one must not lose one's head; then there was still a chance to save oneself. One had, of course, to get away as fast and as far as possible, without, however, creating the impression of cowardly retreat and without ever, God forbid, turning one's back on the fiend, who fears only the image of God (and of man).

The problem was to create a kind of unstable equilibrium between retreat and sham attack. (So does a fountain eternally send its spray of water upward, despite the fact that it continuously falls to the earth.)

"It might be Markali," said one of them. In the moonlight the wolf did rather resemble Markali, although overly white, clean, and silky. And he did bare his teeth impertinently, condescendingly, as if about to break into laughter.

From the quarry came the cowardly, ugly warning howl of dogs. The white wolf chastely twitched his large flapping ears, as though the wild yapping of those fallen animals made him suffer.

The elders, their entire bodies bent forward in pretended advance, gingerly backed away. As a matter of fact, the one guarding the rear could have turned around and run. But he did not.

The dogs howled again: a vile, bloodthirsty howl. There was something about it that repelled the white wolf. Awkwardly he began to shift his massive, muscular body in order to turn around on the narrow grade. But the stone was damp and slippery and the edge crumbled. . . .

The beautiful animal somehow all at once (and as if not quite in earnest, as if all of this could later be repaired, brought back, re-established) slid down. For a moment he scraped the rock with his forepaws (not very convincingly—embarrassed) and then a pitiful, almost relieved sigh escaped his huge mouth and he fell into the abyss.

The peasants stood in silence on the steep pass and listened. Then they nodded their thick beards approvingly and sedately advanced in single file, taking care not to step on the spot that, a moment ago, the werewolf had scraped with his sweaty paws.

Soon the familiar road shone ahead of them. From there one could usually see the lights of the farms that dotted the valley. But tonight all the farmers, to a man, had put their lights out early, although the Germans had not mentioned this point in their proclamation.

14

Kassian woke up rubbing his cheek: the sharp end of a straw was scratching him. It was growing light. From the windows above, a mixture of cold air and the scent of herbs poured in, together with the birds' racket; from the river came the honking of storks.

"So you are awake." He heard the plaintive, deep voice of Katerina. She was sitting close by, her hair in disarray and her face streaked with tears. At a distance, almost in the center of the barnlike building, Little Katerina was asleep atop their bundles.

The Master was glad to see the gypsy—she seemed like an old friend. He had slept only a few hours but now he felt refreshed and full of energy.

"They took you too," she whispered, creeping still closer.

"Yes," he said with a laugh, "although I am not guilty of anything."

"Guilty?" Katerina shrugged angrily. "It's fate, not guilt."

"Never mind, the authorities will be informed very soon," Kassian consoled her.

"The authorities will be informed," she drawled sarcastically. "You are a fool, Professor. Don't you know it was the Bishop's doing that you are here?"

"But Markali? Why him?" the Master asked with curiosity in quite a different tone.

"Markali. That was the deaf-mute. He's on her conscience. But you will perish through the Bishop."

"Is that so? And yet he considers me his son."

"His son! So what!" She spat in disgust. "He has a stable

full of sons like you. And daughters too. You are not the first, or the last."

"Apparently he is doing it for Zora's sake," said the Master, his eyes fixed on the gypsy. "If I'm her uncle . . ."

"Uncle," Katerina repeated. "You make me laugh. Who says that Zora is Felix's daughter?"

This shook the Master, even though he had expected something of the kind all along.

"For God's sake, don't talk like that," he said. And influenced by her way of speaking, he repeated, "Don't talk like that, woman."

"Zora is Chako's sister," the gypsy crooned. "Felix's wife was their mother. But Felix has no children. Can a man beget a child by a man?"

"So that's it," the Master said with great relief. "I thought so. . . . But isn't it disgusting how people behave in bed around here?"

"That's true enough. Still, thirty years from now it won't make any difference. All gone with the wind. Death will even it out. And no one will be the worse for it. . . ." She stopped, and in another tone, childish, straightforward, finished: "Your Anna should not have made trouble over nothing."

"You mean Anyuta?"

"Yes. She was called Anna here."

"Tell me about her."

"Oh, my love," the gypsy began promptly in her usual singsong. "Your mother, my dove, was a lady, and yet they say she threw bombs in Russia. The Bishop, of course, singled her out immediately. He had all of us sent downstairs and her brought up. She thought it was love. A queen! A queen, but not for long. The deaf-mute knows when to wait outside the door and when to slip in another girl. Anna began to howl like a wolf. She was already carrying you. Much later, when I was pregnant with Katerina, I felt bitter too. And I am just a gypsy. But your Anna, she was proud. She could bite with her eyes. I look at you, my dove, and you are very different—good and strong and educated. But when you have that glint in your gray eye it makes one shiver: it's Anna all over again. The same roots. Tell me, please, why are some people wolves, others cats or snakes or lizards, and some even skunks? Why would a skunk choose to be a skunk? To live like a skunk? Surely God did not order it to be a skunk, nothing but a skunk—forever? I can't believe that."

"Tell me more about Anyuta," the Master reminded her.

"After that Anyuta began to turn into a wolf," Katerina continued readily.

"A werewolf?"

"That's right: a werewolf. The deaf-mute caught her many times. What do you think of the deaf-mute?"

"I?"

"Do you know that she can talk and hear perfectly well if she wants to?"

"Tell me more about Anyuta," said the Master.

"Your mother had the evil eye. After a quarrel she would give you a sidelong glance and smile, and for a week you would hemorrhage from your bowels. That's the truth. Believe me. And yet we liked Anna. But of course, one's own child is closer to one's heart. Only afterward you see that this isn't right. But it's too late."

The Master lay stretched out on the straw, listening to the deep, crooning voice of the ripe, handsome, repentant gypsy. Her husband was resting (with marble bruises) there in the cold quarry, and her daughter would probably fall prey, first to the Kommandant with the brick-red glasses, and then to the other lice-infested Germans. Absurd! And the suffering of the wronged Anyuta, who had escaped from St. Petersburg, that was a farce too. But as a result of violence and lies multiplied by nonsense and ignorance, he, Kassian, had emerged, a reality, a world . . . and he could not consider his own presence in life a coincidence or a mistake.

Little Katerina was tossing about, mumbling something in her sleep. Beneath the domed, tiled ceiling the windows suddenly quivered and turned pinkish. Several dogs began to bark in chorus, but not in tune, and a shot was fired. German voices could be heard and the even stamping of boots. Soon a rider galloped heavily through the piazza and halted in front of the village hall. Importantly, conscientiously, the third rooster crowed, instantly supported by his comrades on the outlying farms.

"I am glad Zora is not Felix's daughter," the Master said.

"It makes no difference. You won't live with her anyway, my treasure," came the gypsy's hot whisper. "Shall I tell you your fortune before we part?"

It was growing light, solemnly, with pauses and sudden jumps: as in church when the priest intermittently says a silent prayer. Suddenly, like the ringing of the bell, a sheaf of orange arrows struck the window: part of them reflected and dispersed, the other part lay in rainbow-hued symbols (like musical notes) on the opposite wall. Since his arrival in the village, the Master had been a faithful witness to the miracle of sunrise; up to then he had had occasion only to admire the sunset.

The soldiers in the vicinity were already about their

chores—arguing in raucous voices, knocking, clanging pails and kettles. One could hear the horses neighing for attention, the drivers yelling in high falsetto voices.

Soon an unkempt German with enormous ears brought coffee and bread. The coffee cooled immediately. Another guard told the prisoners with a stupid smile that the Kommandant had shot a boy who had been bitten by a rabid dog . . . and that a machine-gun detachment would be sent to deal with the packs around the quarry. "Now everything is under control," he concluded.

The Master could hardly get his coffee down; he ate nothing. Katerina, in a very businesslike manner, asked the soldiers several questions, flirting and making eyes at them.

A bemedaled sergeant showed up. He reprimanded the guards and chased both Katerinas off into the farthest corner. He then ordered sawhorses put up to separate the men's prison from the women's, as is customary in civilized countries! An officer had apparently just given him a dressing down and now he was anxious to show his zeal.

From Katerina's conversation with the guard and from the sergeant's fragmented remarks, Kassian gathered that someone had left the village during the night and that, though shots had been fired at him, the body had not been recovered. The sergeant kicked Little Katerina, who was again lying on the bundles, and declared that if she was lazy she would end up like the boy Drago—or even worse. . . .

"We strangle little girls. Like that!"

This cheered the soldiers and in an almost friendly manner they informed the Master that a gallows was being raised for the hostages. Indeed, from outside came the screeching of a saw and the solid bark of an ax. The Germans observed the prisoners with indecent curiosity, as if looking at pornographic pictures, and then left, locking the door behind them.

The girl, that same little green-eyed serpent who, the day before, had enchanted poor Drago, Little Katerina with the mauve face and glossy dark hair (which would make a good fishing line) explained to Kassian that, if he helped her, she could climb up to the window and look out. She got onto the Professor's shoulders, from where she easily grasped the stone rail. "They're building a platform. The Germans and the Joachims are working on it. The officer is going to the village hall. A buggy is coming from the castle," she reported excitedly.

The Master felt a familiar nagging pain in his chest—a pain so easily transformed into rapture. Zora. Zora was coming. He was about to put Katerina down, but she would not let go: she dug her bare feet into his side like spurs, and began to whip him with her small hands. He galloped around the blank walls, looking for a safe place to throw off his wild rider. "There is Drago," he cried. "Can't you hear him? He's singing on the piazza: she's wonderful, she's beautiful. . . ." The girl's knees relaxed and she slid down.

"Don't be angry with Katerina," her mother pleaded. "She's a good girl. But in her heart she knows her fate and she revolts."

The sergeant stormed in again, and the Master, between two guards, was led to the village hall, which the Germans called the Kommandatur! Rather than going through the regular front entrance, they entered through the back door that, on the inside, had been disfigured by iron bolts and a gigantic lock (as if the criminals within were protecting themselves from the outside world). They emerged into a corridor with a narrow staircase at the farther end. On either side of the corridor were offices with many cabinets, files, and shelves. In the largest room, the colonel, clean-shaven, swollen, with bloodthirsty eyes, sat at a round table. A portrait of a young, handsome Hitler hung on the wall. A clerk with a long pen in his hand sat waiting behind an up-turned barrel in a corner: perhaps he had been sitting thus since the days of the Thirty Years' War. Behind the colonel, his face turned toward the window, stood the lieutenant in a clean, mended uniform. The pink piazza shone in the sun; the axes knocked busily, the saws screeched. . . . From the fountain, donkeys trotted earnestly back to the stables . . . and an edge of clearly defined sky was already flooded with a wave of amber colors.

If time is reversible, must it mean that this day is bound to repeat itself, completely and entirely, in every detail? Or only in its essential traits? The Master seemed absorbed in only these thoughts. Since he had not been invited to sit down, he remained standing, sucking in his stomach, thrusting out his chest in the way of a captured but still unsubdued warrior. There is much more good and light and music in life than we generally assume, he continued calmly to himself. But we are always complaining and taking offense.

Meanwhile the colonel was saying something in his high-pitched voice, speaking in the careless manner of a military leader who arbitrarily governs an entire region. Dissipated and a coward, Kassian noted, and turned his face away. The only pleasant sight in the room was the medieval clerk.

The Kommandant cleared his throat and continued, his glasses shining bloodthirstily: "Last night someone left the village. We have decided to execute one hostage as a punishment. But it would be a mistake to hang a friend of the Third Reich. Can you prove your loyalty?"

Kassian politely kept silent.

"What can you say in your defense?"

"I don't know of what I am accused."

"Yes. I thought so. You are our enemy," the colonel said with a shade of regret. "It's strange, in every country we meet such stubborn individuals."

"I would like to say good-by to my fiancée," said the Master.

"That I cannot promise. There is little time left."

"Why is there so little time?" the Master asked curiously.

"I am a German officer. I am doing my duty. At this moment, believe me, I would prefer to be in your place," said the Kommandant, half-convinced himself.

"So why don't we change places?"

"Yes. You are a madman!"

"If the hostage is mad, how can you send him to the gallows?" The lieutenant, his face still turned toward the window, entered the conversation for the first time.

"Have you forgotten the situation we are in?" the Kommandant shouted.

"With your permission I can sketch the situation for you," the Master said. The officers, the clerk, and the sergeant froze, waiting with morbid curiosity. "When the war ended, you were in the mountains—cut off from friend and foe alike, with huge untouched supplies of matériel. You decided to hide. Ever since, you have been sitting in your caves, crawling out into the daylight only to procure a fresh supply of sausages. After all those years you have probably completely degenerated—psychologically and maybe even anatomically. . . ."

The colonel slammed his fist on the table. The clerk, bending picturesquely forward, handed him a folder. Two guards burst into the office.

The Master was led back, along the corridor and through the barricaded back door, to the stone barn with the red dome. There they had had time to make order: water had been splashed about, several heaps of fresh straw were on the floor, and a makeshift screen (a wire net nailed to a wooden frame) had been put up.

Presently, in the doorway spilling over with blinding sunlight, the Bishop appeared. He was followed by an orderly who carried a stool.

"I asked to see Zora, not you," the Master said firmly.

"Zora is here," the Bishop said, nodding his long, lemon-colored face.

"The young lady will come too. She'll come," the guard confirmed with a smile.

"I am sorry," said the Bishop, trying to arrange himself as comfortably as possible on the stool. "All this is very annoying. But," he added, speaking quickly, "Chako got through. Tomorrow our detachment will arrive. One more day—only one kilometer in the vastness of space. But for you it is a question of life and death. Absurd. Truly absurd."

Kassian saw no need to dispute this statement.

"Incidentally," the Bishop said, "I told Zora that you are my son."

"Did you also tell her Chako is her brother?"

"No, that did not come up. You cannot do everything at once. . . . Anyway, truth too has its priorities and must be screened, else life would become chaos. According to the Uncertainty Principle, one cannot simultaneously establish the velocity of a particle and its situation in space. If one is correct, the other is distorted, and vice versa. This we must accept. But you go on seeking the absolute and final truth. Here is a contradiction, my friend. A contradiction."

"Immortality has value only if it is the truth. Therefore any quest for the absolute truth is also a quest for immortality."

"You believe in immortality?" the Bishop asked casually.

"Yes, and no—and still something else," Kassian answered distinctly.

"And do you believe in God?"

"Yes, and no—and still something else."

"Is such faith a consolation?"

"It is much more than you suppose. In any case, we can no longer be satisfied with a simple yes or no."

"God bless you," the Bishop said with dignity and rose from the uncomfortable stool. "If ever it should happen that, under new stars, we meet once more, and do not meet, and still something else, I hope you will be charitable." Majestically he walked through the wide-open door that lay drenched in a continuous shower of sun.

The Master was staring so intently at the golden rectangle that when Zora appeared there he did not immediately recognize her. He only noticed a dim shadow that, enveloped in yellow rays, floated through the air.

Her eyes were smiling but tears streamed down her luminous face: fine tears, quick, as if alive. Her shining hair fell freely, yet in perfect order, down to her neck. With her she brought a breath of peace, of paradisial fields where antelopes graze beside tigers, of orchards in bloom where the fruits of life ripen in abundance all year round.

"Master," she said, "dear Master. What shall we talk about in these few minutes? Surely not about death?"

"No," he answered hurriedly, "quite the opposite. I never

believed more in the permanence of my life than today. My heart is filled to overflowing with you, with eternity and light. I pity poor Socrates, who lacked my experience and who therefore had to prove the same theorem so boringly from a different angle. Everything I know about God and light and love I know from you; you have explained it to me involuntarily, in passing. I am readying myself for a spontaneous leap into another orbit, like an inspired electron, or like the ape who suddenly decided to become a man."

Several soldiers and even the sergeant had come in to take a look at the pretty girl; they stared with protruding lobster eyes, smiling woodenly, like old photographs or the paintings of Rousseau, Bombois. The condemned forced himself not to notice them and continued in an even voice: "The evil of the world loses its sting by the very mention of That which stands behind you. I want to die now, because today I am strong and good. I see the light that passes through you; you absorb it and reflect it, freely and generously, inexplicably and fully."

"But without you no one will recognize it," Zora cried. "Only you see it. I want to die too."

"No, no, Fräulein," came the trebles and falsettos of those soldiers who had managed to follow the conversation. Garbling languages and words, they insisted, "The Fräulein mustn't think of that. That would be a great mistake. *Das Fräulein* must live long. . . ." "And bear many children," the sergeant added. They all laughed—in German.

"The apostles," the Master went on, "initiated everyone they chanced to meet into the mystery of salvation. And the ancient scientists risked their necks to tell anyone and everyone of the earth's miraculous rotation. I am driven by that same sacred power to tell over and over of our love, of our happiness, of our immortality. Glory to life, glory to its Creator, and to the last, the decisive reversibility."

"If you remained alive," asked or stated Zora, "we would have the right to ordinary human happiness. . . ." There was an unfamiliar note in her voice; but her eyes, wet with tears, shone.

"I don't know," Kassian answered. "We are tracing a new path. A thoroughfare to new forms of life and thought. We must renounce worn-out calculations, habits, symbols. We are the modern order of troubadours. As they did, so we have to throw out a lot of personal, superfluous baggage. I don't know . . . I believe we must walk an unknown road, explain ourselves in an unfamiliar tongue or by strange signs. Sometimes it is enough merely to change the sequence of our reasoning to bring the unexplored essence of life to the surface. In any case, we should no longer participate in the traditional fight for existence, in the pursuit of personal comfort. We have come to the point at which, if someone were to shout 'Enough!' many—if not all—would stop and change direction."

Tall, delicate, strong, Zora listened, keeping her luminous face stubbornly turned to the stone floor: an enormous bug was heavily, worriedly crawling there in the thick straw.

The dapper figure of the Bishop, in gloves and gray spats, reappeared in the wide-open, sun-drenched doorway. Behind him came the lieutenant, smiling.

"It seems I cannot part with you," the Bishop laughed. "Senile sentimentality!" And in another tone: "I have been trying to convince the Kommandant to deport you with the Katerinas. After all, you certainly would be as useful to the Reich as those stupid females." The last sentence he said in German; the lieutenant giggled.

The Master said nothing, and the Bishop, pushing Zora aside, away from the wire partition, continued in a brisk, distinct whisper: "I am eighty-four years old. I can say without hesitation that I have led a happy life, though I have never taken the end for the beginning or the cause for the effect. . . . Out of human weakness I abused women and sometimes offended the peasants. But despite this I was always content, and my conscience never troubled me, even though I was completely unaware of the notorious freedom on the microscopic level. For more than eighty years I lived precisely as I wanted and I did evil. And now I still do not repent. How do you explain this, Professor? In fact, I came back specifically to ask you this question. I am terribly curious to hear your answer." The word "terribly" he drawled out capriciously, coquettishly.

"Yes, that is interesting," the Master answered reluctantly. "Probably you are a monster. It happens."

Zora, her face distorted, looked up at Kassian and then stared again at the rough, uneven stone floor where the bug she had just crushed shimmered like a wet star.

The Master, averting his eyes from the spot on the floor, continued with an effort: "There is much talk now about universes where antimatter exists in antitime. Well, Bishop, you resemble such a distorted world. Your entire life was one uninterrupted process of devouring and digesting valuable material. You destroyed untold tons of complex solar light and produced only crude garbage."

"That's it! That's it!" The Bishop appeared delighted. "Antimatter, antienergy, antichrist . . . but those are conventional labels. Perhaps, in reality, you are 'anti' and I am the true, positive system. It is not only I who devour you,

you too are destroying everything that is close and dear to me."

"No," Kassian decided after a moment's thought. "We know the direction more or less. We do not know the exact nature of God—perhaps He is a Mother, not a Father . . . perhaps His right hand is not opposite His left. But that It is love and truth and light, that It is directed toward these things, this we know as surely as the mariners of old knew there existed an immense continent to the west of the Pillars of Hercules." He took a deep breath and added, "Everything in you, Bishop, is wrong, turned inside out."

"Am I the devil, then?" asked the Bishop, savoring the name, and laughed; the guards in their green uniforms good-humoredly echoed his laughter.

"No, not the devil," the prisoner replied seriously. "You were something flat and useless from the beginning. The devil was once a great archangel, one of the Lord's closest servants. But you, you are an empty hole in a vacuum. One has to turn oneself inside out in order to understand at least partially what makes you tick. When that hole in the vacuum is filled, you will, at long last, become zero. That is the extent of your career."

The Bishop laughed in high good humor. "I am happy to see that you preserve a Socratic state of mind in your last minutes. To tell the truth, I was afraid that before dying you would turn sour and begin to repent. Apparently some noble blood really does flow in your veins."

The shower of light splashed golden drops onto the wall opposite the door. The officer and a sergeant were playing dominoes at a folding table.

"Bishop, you have disturbed us," Zora said with a frown.

She wanted to go on but restrained herself. (Her face had suddenly turned a silvery ashen color.)

"No kisses," the Master said, backing away from the Bishop. The Bishop shrugged and with a fastidious grimace went out through the screen of sunlight at the open door.

From the piazza came summer voices. An impatient bird whistled, the axes thumped, and the dogs howled happily, realizing the Germans were getting ready to leave. The soldiers were already harnessing the horses and backing the trucks around.

"How must I live now?" Zora asked.

"They killed Drago," said Kassian. "Above all, don't humiliate yourself before the enemy."

"And who is our ultimate enemy? I mean later, when there are no more Germans?" she asked.

But he was not permitted to answer. The uniformed clerk, dripping with sweat, blissfully smiling, ran into the barn. The lieutenant, the sergeant, and the soldiers began to bustle about guiltily.

Zora held out her hands to the Master. She was ordered to leave.

15

The uniformed barber advised the prisoner to change his shirt. Kassian walked to a mirror in the farthest corner of the barn where both Katerinas had settled down. In colorful dresses, festively beribboned, they twittered excitedly, like tropical birds. . . . They were in a happy mood. The lieutenant had informed them they would be taken to the mountains: the Germans needed housekeepers.

Out on the piazza the church bell rang; a drum rumbled hoarsely, orders were cried out. Little Katerina slithered snakelike up the wall and clung to the window rail.

"They're rounding up the people," she announced, twisting to all sides. "The Germans are filling up their gas tanks at Owl's store. Joachim is fastening a rope to the gallows. The platform is lopsided," she reported conscientiously. Suddenly she slid down and hid behind the bundles.

In the bright rectangle of the doorway stood Father Nectarius. A guard was gently nudging him on: tall, withered, stooped like a bow, in his long black cassock, his narrow, soft, silvery beard resembling the young moon in the sky, he swayed forward on his feeble legs, breathing laboriously. It was torture to him to pronounce the words of a prayer loudly and distinctly, and so he concentratedly mumbled something as he blessed the prisoners.

The guard led him to the folding table where he immediately began to busy himself: he covered it with a white cloth, placed his paraphernalia and a Bible and a cross on it. Taking several deep breaths for future use, he asked severely: "Do you believe in God?"

"If I had known, I would have prepared myself better for a confession," said Kassian.

"Do you believe in God, heretic?" the priest repeated.

Kassian thought for a moment and then, carefully choosing his words, explained: "When I answer yes, there is a God, I am immediately overcome with doubts. All the dark, puzzling spots of existence float up to the surface. Then I decide to say, there is no God—and immediately I see that it is not true. So this answer is also unsatisfactory. To your question, Father, I am therefore forced to reply: yes, and no, and still something else."

The priest seemed to concentrate fully on the difficult task of breathing. But the look in his eyes was sharp and clear. "Numb and dumb, numb and dumb," he mumbled—words with which the Master was already familiar. Then he asked, "Do you believe in the holy sacraments?" and without waiting for a response peremptorily shoved the spoon deep into Kassian's open mouth. Dismissing him without delay, he called both Katerinas.

The Germans, like people covertly eying their naked neighbors in a public bath, followed the assured and beautiful movements of the priest and exchanged whispered remarks. The Master squinted blissfully. He was always struck by the impossibility, the inadmissibility of a mistake in the ritual. A physician can misinterpret or overlook a symptom, he can do harm; an engineer can forget a screw or put a decimal point in the wrong place. It is important that these people be intelligent, educated, sober. But a priest's service is always perfect, intrinsically a success. To him personal merit may even be a handicap, since the performance of his duties depends in no way on talent, technique, or perceptiveness.

Here is an affirmation of real freedom, spontaneous freedom, Kassian thought, smiling rapturously.

He settled down on the straw in the same place he had spent the night, already considering it his home; behind a beam he noticed a dirty pack of cards, forgotten by someone (perhaps a prisoner of a previous war). The Master distractedly flipped over the pictures of ladies and knights that, though battered, still shone with unearthly attraction. It was a tarot deck. He had often seen those elongated cards in the bloodless hands of the slowly dying Anyuta. Now he idly laid out the entire deck, like a child playing with old photographs of relatives he cannot identify.

The sky-blue lady, though, definitely resembled Zora astride Fauna. Moved, the Master fingered the card. Big Katerina unceremoniously sat down next to him on the straw and, taking the deck, began in her gypsy voice: "Wands, cups, swords, pentacles. . . . The knight and the traveler. The Arcanes, the twenty-two Arcanes. Through them is revealed what comes to be and what does not come to be." The gypsy crooned on smoothly: "The emperor is the Bishop, the eternal husband to whom the wife answered 'yes' but still remained a virgin. For he is also attracted to another world. . . .

"The star is Zora. Unclothed, she pours the water of life and beauty on the earth. Freely she offers everyone the gifts of existence and of the spirit. Through her come hope and immortality and inner light. She is truth, without a veil. And that is why the emperor cannot see her. The great mother who remembers and forgives all.

"The last Arcane is the image of the fool: thou, my dove," Katerina whispered, melancholy and cloying. "The fool, a prince from another kingdom, traveling unrecognized through our valley. The sun is behind your back: it alone knows from where you come and where you go and by which road you will return again. The spirit of inquiry, you stand at the edge of the abyss with a flower in your hand, prepared for a fall, but the angel from the island of Patmos will hold you up, my treasure.

"And here is my Katerina, the empress," the gypsy continued, embarrassed and proud. "Behold . . . the daughter of earth and sky. She is the fruit-bearing orchard, the Eden, the mother of the human family. Through her you enter this earth. Others will lead you farther, higher, but the beginning is in her, in my child. . . . The Germans are taking us with them. They are taking us away, but where—who knows?" she finished in a different tone and apparently expecting an answer.

"Well," the Master said evasively, "our soldiers will soon be here and free everyone." He did not want to say more.

"Yes, free everyone. They'll begin by throwing bombs. Then we'll be free. . . . And you will be hanged, ha?" she asked soberly.

"So it seems."

"If you want, I'll read your fortune," the gypsy offered magnanimously. (Thus would a famous violinist agree to play an elaborate sonata for a condemned man, or a prostitute consent to share his cot the last night.)

"No, thank you," he said. And in order not to belittle her well-meant offer, he added: "I know my fate."

"Nonsense, my falcon," she crooned. "No one can see behind himself. The Bishop is a wise gentleman and still he used to come to me for his future." She shuffled the grimy but eternally young cards. "Cut, Prince," she commanded. "Not like that. From your heart. With your left hand."

It was the end of June and the sun in this region, though it baked down, still had a springlike freshness about it. On and off a current of icy mountain air broke through the hot shower of light. (And so one was, simultaneously, exposed to the different temptations of all four seasons.)

An age-old smell of orchards, human habitation, flowers, horses, and smoke hovered above the piazza. Sundry objects, put out on the roofs to dry, shone and gleamed in the colors of the rainbow. Melons and pumpkins in the gardens pushed furiously. From the looted stores came the scent of leather and vanilla. The entire valley beyond the bridge looked like a single park, evenly divided into lilac, lemon, and pink squares. Under the heat of the sun, berries, fruits, flowers, herbs gave off sensuous optical-olfactory waves and from the woods came a mist of vinegar and turpentine. The birds filled the acoustic dimension of the world with their racket. The mountains made their contribution in the form of silvery pale reflections. And the sky, its blue wings outspread, contained all this earthly splendor, welding it together, preserving it from ruin and disintegration.

Meanwhile the Germans had herded the people around the scaffold. (The soldiers were already helmeted, ready for the march.) The Joachims silently lined up around the platform, which smelled of fresh pine shavings, and behind them, holding back, stood flocks of shawled women with their children.

It was evident that the people were there only because they had been ordered to come. From time to time one of the Joachims would say weightily: "The Germans, they know!" With which his thickly bearded neighbor would concur, "They know!"

"What a day, what a day," sighed the women.

"A day to bring in the hay," one whispered back from the first row.

"In such weather it hurts to die," Joachim the Turk said.

"Do you think it's better when there is a frost?"

"The day they hanged the Austrian, that was a frost!" Philolai recalled, and spat under the platform.

"God forbid you have a frost for a hanging," several voices said.

"The Austrian was naked. It was shameful."

"Yes, that it was."

"And now the sun is shining. It's warm," decided Philolai, once more spitting angrily.

"A good day to bring in the hay," they said again in the first row. The women only sighed.

The villagers stepped aside to let the notables pass: the mayor, the comptroller, Cantemir, with his bandaged jaw, and a few merchants and artisans. They all walked forward without resistance: the Germans had ordered them to stand in front of the peasants. The sight of the rich ones on the piazza pleased the Joachims.

"Here, come over here," they said.

"In the shade, it's cooler in the shade."

"It's no good in the sun."

"Make yourselves comfortable."

Squeezed back, the women began to curse audibly: the most elaborate maledictions relating to obstructions of the bowels and perforations of the eyes . . . but without any particular bitterness and with their ever-present humor. Their faces remained impenetrable.

The sun hung above the people's heads; the light poured noiselessly, vertically down on them. A great silence had set in. On the other side of the river the trees were bowing, all in the same direction; but on the piazza there was no wind. Inexplicably the animals, the birds, even the insects had vanished. Only on the second plane, harnessed donkeys and small horses could be seen: silent, undaunted, they switched their tails, impatient to get going.

In this tense emptiness the drum began to roll, nauseatingly, like African tom-toms, and Master Kassian was led into the pink piazza. . . . His arms tied behind his back, wearing a white shirt, he seemed to bend under the weight of the light and colors that came rushing down at him. Several times he raised his young pale face, squinting (or smiling) with surprise (or rapture), to look at the serene sky and the jubilant sun in the zenith. Above the river, farther down in the valley, a short thick rainbow played in all colors: atomized water above a mountain river, miraculously reflecting the sun. (Zora! Zora! . . . The Master remembered another radiance.)

"Hangman, stop, stop!" suddenly came the breaking cry of an old man.

It was Father Nectarius, silvery, bent like a bow, who, swaying on his withered legs and waving his staff, ran toward the convict, legs lagging behind, unable to keep up with his long torso. The lieutenant barred his way, but he explained fearlessly that he had not accomplished a very important part of the rite and must correct his omission.

The officer looked at the Kommandant for a sign, but the latter was engrossed in curbing Flora, whom he had mounted for the first time. And the soldiers in their squashed helmets (the same that had disfigured Europe for several decades) let the old man through. Father Nectarius stumbled, as on stilts, toward the platform. (He had omitted to give the Master absolution after hearing his confession. So must a surgeon feel when he realizes he has dressed a wound without first disinfecting and washing it.) With a bewildered smile, Kassian waited for the priest, who was approaching unevenly, in jerks.

In the bushes near the river the Master glimpsed a pack of dogs led by the familiar reckless bulldog. The fierce animal was baring his fangs good-naturedly, seeming to suggest "Run! Follow my example and that of the frog in the cream.

Or at least sink your teeth into the throat of one of your enemies."

"It's not only a question of myself," Kassian answered him. "Our life is more complicated. . . ." But the dog, having lost interest in the city dweller, had turned away. Again the Master raised his face toward the sun; squinting, he sought to impress upon himself forever the earthly beauty of the sky.

At last Father Nectarius had pulled himself up to the wooden planks of the platform. The Kommandant, now safely astride the stolen Flora, was shaking his crop and yelling something. But at that moment an unforeseen circumstance completely altered the course of events. An ever-increasing noise like the whine of a dentist's drill could be heard, and above the gallows, the hangman, and the condemned, above the Joachims and the Germans, above the women and children, an old-fashioned military plane shrilly buzzed by. It made an uneven circle and, with a friendly dip of its wing, veered around, triumphantly swooped down nose first, and diagonally blanketed the piazza with a healing, restoring, salvation-bringing round of machine-gun fire. Again a sharp turn of the wing and, almost brushing their heads, it released another stream of lead.

Almost with a feeling of relief, as if they had expected this development all along, the Germans, to a man, dashed to their trucks, wagons and horses. Engines roared, whips cracked, and in another minute, without speeches or fanfare, the entire column was speeding toward the stony gates that led out of the valley. Both Katerinas, like a bouquet of flowers, rocked back and forth on a two-wheeled cart with a red cross pasted on it.

On the empty pink piazza stood the abandoned wooden platform. On it lay Kassian and Father Nectarius, almost side by side: Kassian face up, still admiring the earthly sky; the priest, with his soft, sickle-shaped beard pressed against the pine planks. The plane, its ammunition exhausted, turned south and melted into a pale cloud. The noise of the column also stopped the moment the Germans were sucked into the ravine: the rear guard gave one last salvo before all were swallowed up by the earth or the rocks.

The Joachims and Annas cautiously stuck their heads out of their century-old hiding places. In the empty inn, the flies were buzzing peacefully again. A bottle, still half full, clinked joyfully.

"Our soldiers will be here soon," Philolai said, sipping the slivovitz the Germans had not quite finished.

"Well, we are liberated," Joachim the Turk decided.

"Now we must bury them," whispered the women, and sighed.

The Joachims made no answer. Only after a second round of slivovitz and a cup of coffee, aromatic and scalding as always, only thus fortified, puffing on their pipes, did they grimly begin the debate.

"How do we bury them if the priest is dead?"

"Will you perhaps bury them?" they challenged one another, ignoring the women's plaintive sighs.

"The priest does the burying. But who buries the priest?"

"That's right."

"The gypsy we can bury ourselves," said the gendarme (Cockroach), not quite convinced.

"The gypsy—yes. We can bury the gypsy," the Joachims seemed to agree. "And the Professor is not one of us either."

"But what does the law say?" Joachim the Turk asked angrily. "It's forbidden to touch a corpse. He is a professor, an important man."

"We must wait for the authorities," Mayor Owl decided. "The authorities. Absolutely."

"Perhaps they'll even bring a priest along."

"There are no more priests," Philolai asserted. "The new government promises land, not incense."

"They'll give you land and then they'll take away your harvest," Pelikan, the Comptroller, observed with a laugh. "For us it's always the same. Break your back!"

"Never mind, we'll harness them," Philolai reiterated.

The peasants sat around the wooden table in front of the inn; the women served them scalding, aromatic coffee in small cups.

A slow, desultory breeze blew through the piazza: it lifted the dust, garbage, and straw and whirled them about. The dogs crawled out of the ravines; in the gardens, birds began to twitter and a stork affectedly alighted near the fountain. The children, still subdued, circled the piazza, casting frightened glances at the empty gallows.

On the deserted bridge appeared the graceful figure of a young woman: she walked lightly, noiselessly toward the sun, squinting (or smiling). The peasants squirmed uneasily; some precipitously vanished into the inn.

The girl climbed onto the platform and with her back to the Joachims stood there, fair and graceful.

"What a misfortune, what a terrible misfortune," the women whispered in their habitual way, watching Zora avidly.

After a moment she kneeled and touched her fiancé with her hand. Then the miracle happened: Master Kassian raised his head and sat up. He rubbed his eyes and looked around in amazement, as if trying to remember something. His shirt was stained with pale-red blood.

"He's alive," called the Cockroach.

A general hum broke out: "Well, really, that's something."

"Why should he be dead?"

"A clever man!" Philolai decided.

"A professor—no doubt."

"But the priest is done for," Joachim the Turk remarked angrily.

"He was old, the priest."

"He was old, but he gave absolution," the Turk insisted.

"That's how we are liberated!" complained the women. And politely, to the approaching Zora: "Would you like some coffee? To fortify yourself?" The peasants rose, smiling uneasily. Zora declined the coffee.

"I want the Master carried into the inn. He must be transferred to the city, to a hospital." She spoke distinctly, as if speaking to children.

"Of course," they said, "that's natural."

"That's easy. Take him into Cantemir's, and later to the city."

"A horse can do it easily."

"We'll carry him ourselves. Such a man should be helped."

"No question about it. Lift him up and take him directly to Cantemir."

Zora stood, listening to them with trustful attention, until Philolai finally interfered. "Enough," he shouted. "Let's do it. It won't take more than a minute." The Joachims trudged heavily to the platform and without further speeches carefully lifted the Master. (He was watery pale and groaned pitifully.)

Cantemir gave him his best bed, in a spacious downstairs room. Zora watched silently as the women undressed Kassian and bandaged the wound in his shoulder.

"Now we have to hide everything again, that's what we have to do," said Philolai suddenly.

"They'll pick us clean, our militia!" confirmed Joachim the Turk.

"What a life, what a life," cried the women, running to the larders.

As if to justify their age-old wail, an explosion thundered somewhere deep in the mountains. The noise was softened by many obstructions, but it seemed nevertheless as if an angry volcanic element had erupted and, as suddenly, worn itself out. After that there were a few more rumbles, like a spring avalanche.

The peasants sucked concentratedly on their pipes, now and then sipping their coffee (the women had hidden the slivovitz).

The piazza was again completely deserted: children, animals, and birds, even the insects, it seemed, had instantly vanished. It was as if this side of the river had been abandoned.

Meanwhile the earth had had time to turn three quarters away from the sun, and lengthening shadows began to crawl up the base of the gallows. The shower of light weakened perceptibly; only the fountain was still bathed in radiance. From beyond the stony gates a valiant, cheerful song could be heard . . . the singing grew and spread, the voices gathered, were supported (as a stream shored up by a dam) by the military step of marching soldiers.

"Holy Mother of God, Saint Cassian help us," the women screamed. They recognized the familiar song and, with flushed cheeks, began to straighten their shawls and skirts.

A column of soldiers marched briskly into the piazza. Smiling, showing rows of white teeth, the young militiamen proudly stepped past the Joachims and halted in front of the village hall.

"Our boys, by God, our boys!" the women whispered, delighted, fussing with their hair and shawls.

"Did you expect the Turks?" the Joachims scolded, always dignified. "Stupid. Now you are happy, but soon you'll be crying! Just wait!"

"The way they hold their rifles! As if they were carrying a stick on their shoulder," Joachim the Turk remarked with bitterness. He had served under the Austrian emperor and found fault with any innovation.

The mayor, the comptroller, and the gendarme met the detachment at the steps of the village hall. A dust-covered, downy-faced little lieutenant reported excitedly:

"We'll catch up with the Germans, don't worry. Three units are after them, cavalry and artillery. Kaput! They won't get away." His visage mirrored the Joachims', only he was beardless and still lacked their Sarmatian prudence. "The Germans blew up the pass, but we'll dig them out and finish them, for sure. Don't worry. Meanwhile you have to offer hospice to the militia."

"Hospice. That's all right. It's simple to offer hospice," the Joachims began to hum in their usual way.

"Yes, hospice."

"For the militia, that's the first thing."

"Absolutely."

"Hospice," the bearded men repeated glumly. "Hey, women, get a wiggle on. You heard: hospice for the militia."

They seemed to have taken a liking to this word and invested it with many shades of meaning: approval, sarcasm, threat, and even some metaphysical nuance. But Philolai did not miss the opportunity to seal all their empty exclamations with his eternal: "Never mind, we'll harness them."

Epilogue (and Prologue)

The Bishop died of cancer, in excruciating pain. Felix migrated to Zagreb where he became administrator of a forestry school; the deaf-mute managed his small household.

Chako perished on the outskirts of Budapest during the uprising when his cavalry detachment charged a Soviet tank.

In the old village with the pink piazza there is now electricity and a narrow-gauge railway. A technical school and a maternity ward are under construction. The Joachims tried to burn down the castle, but the authorities saved the white manor and severely punished the rebels. Over the years the quality of the local slivovitz has deteriorated; the valley's agricultural production has also declined. But the yield of prized marble is increasing, and the Joachims work the quarry untiringly to fulfill the government quota. The piazza is still drowned in light, and toward late afternoon the rays of the sun are freely reflected in the high windows.

Philolai has aged noticeably. But he still drives his horse to the county seat and, in congenial company, over a mug of local brew, faithfully declares: "Never mind, we'll harness them."

Little Katerina alone survived in the mountains by some miracle, and returned to her native village where, at the feast of Saint Cassian, a rich merchant saw her and carried her off to Rhodes.

Thanks to Zora's care, Master Kassian soon recuperated. His wound healed completely, but he had to give up smoking (which, in the beginning, was torture). The newlyweds made their home in Geneva, where they worked with the Congress for World Peace. Zora's seizures, however, became more frequent and she was threatened with complete paralysis. Kassian accepted a lucrative offer from an American scientific institution and the couple moved to New York where, according to the physicians, diseases such as hers were cured with lasers and the latest medications. But that proved to be a lie.

After Zora's death, Kassianov returned to Europe. It is known that his New York bank made several transfers to an account in Greece, on the island of Patmos. There all trace of him vanishes.

A suitcase with manuscripts Kassianov had left with a neighbor (a dark, dry, birdlike young woman) was never claimed. On the basis of these notes, fragments, and diaries, it was possible to retrieve Kassianov's life.

The long stretch of time between the two parts he devoted mainly to sociological, statistical, and mathematical studies. Though it might puzzle the average reader, an example of Kassianov's contribution to a new system of coordinates is added here to make his story complete.

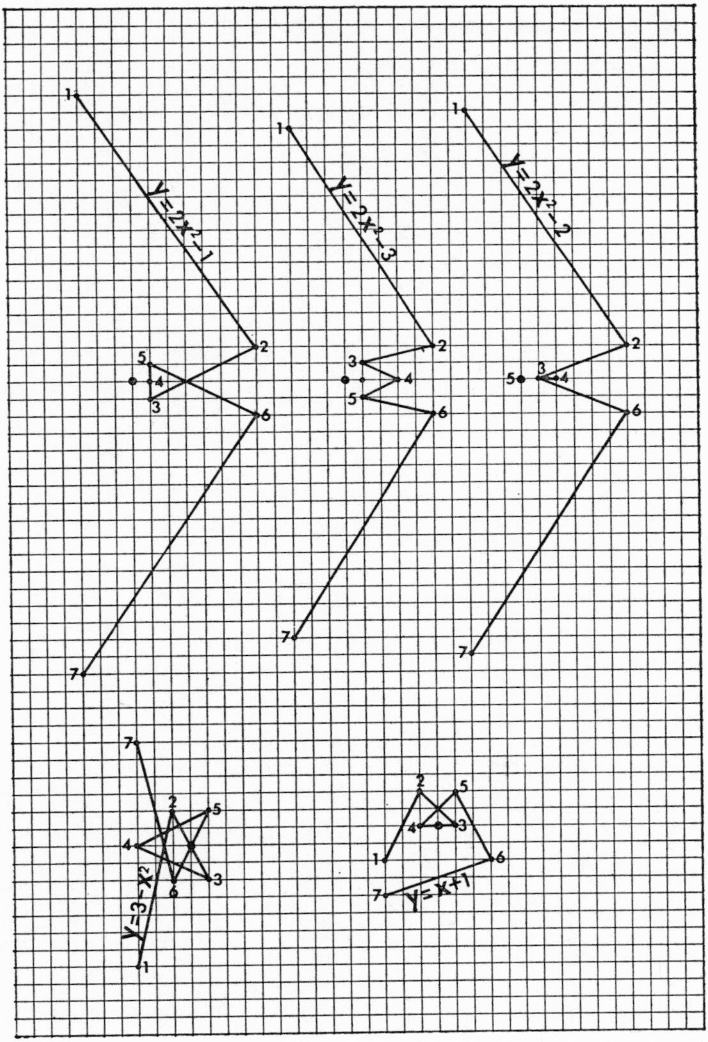
Y=2X²−1
Y=2X²−3
Y=2X²−2
Y=3−X²
Y=X+1